# THE ADVENTURES OF DANIEL BOOM AKA LOUD BOY

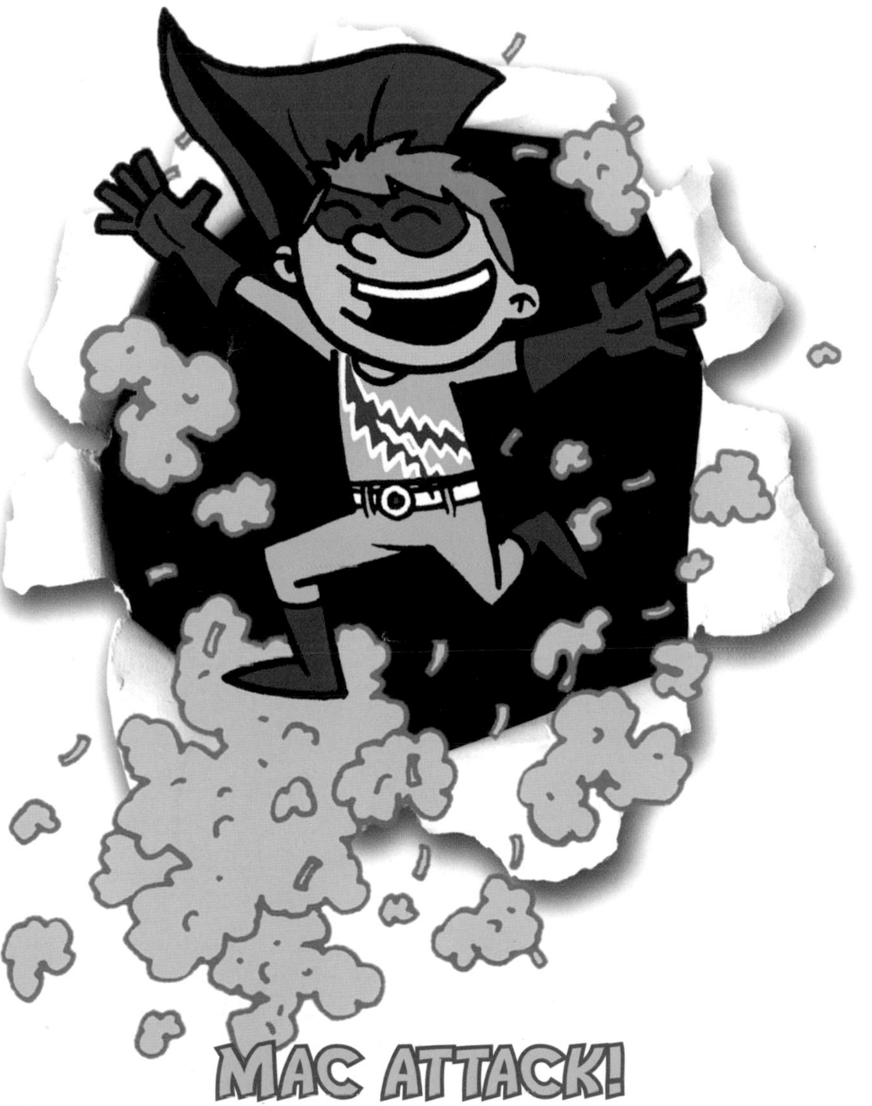

## MAC ATTACK!

WRITTEN BY D. J. STEINBERG

ILLUSTRATED BY BRIAN SMITH

GROSSET & DUNLAP

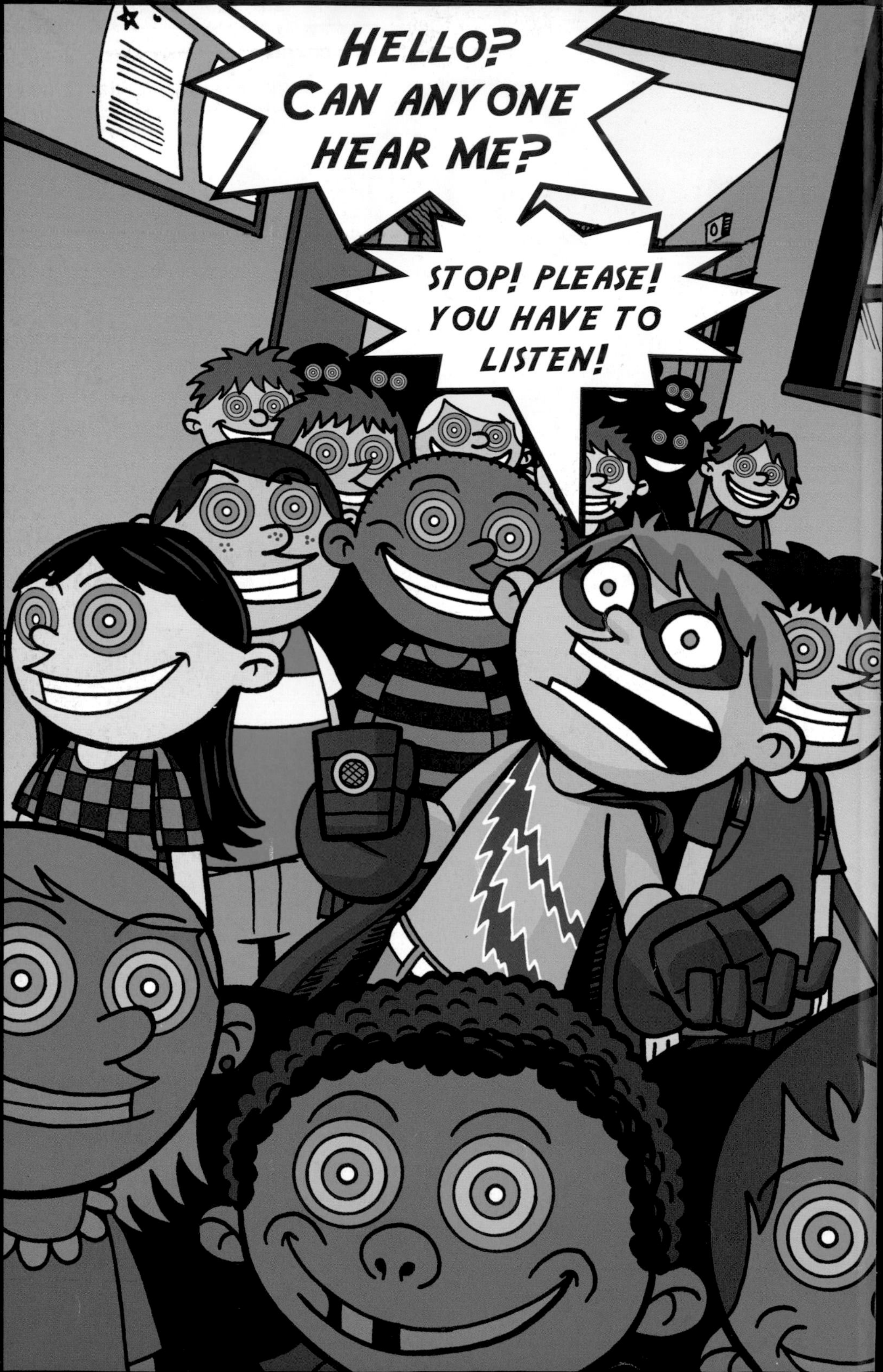
HELLO? CAN ANYONE HEAR ME?
STOP! PLEASE! YOU HAVE TO LISTEN!

Will LOUD BOY be able to

stop the invasion of the

# ZOMBIE KIDS?

Can he save kids everywhere before it

is too late? And what is that horrible

**SMELL** coming from the lunchroom?

But wait—we are getting ahead of ourselves . . .

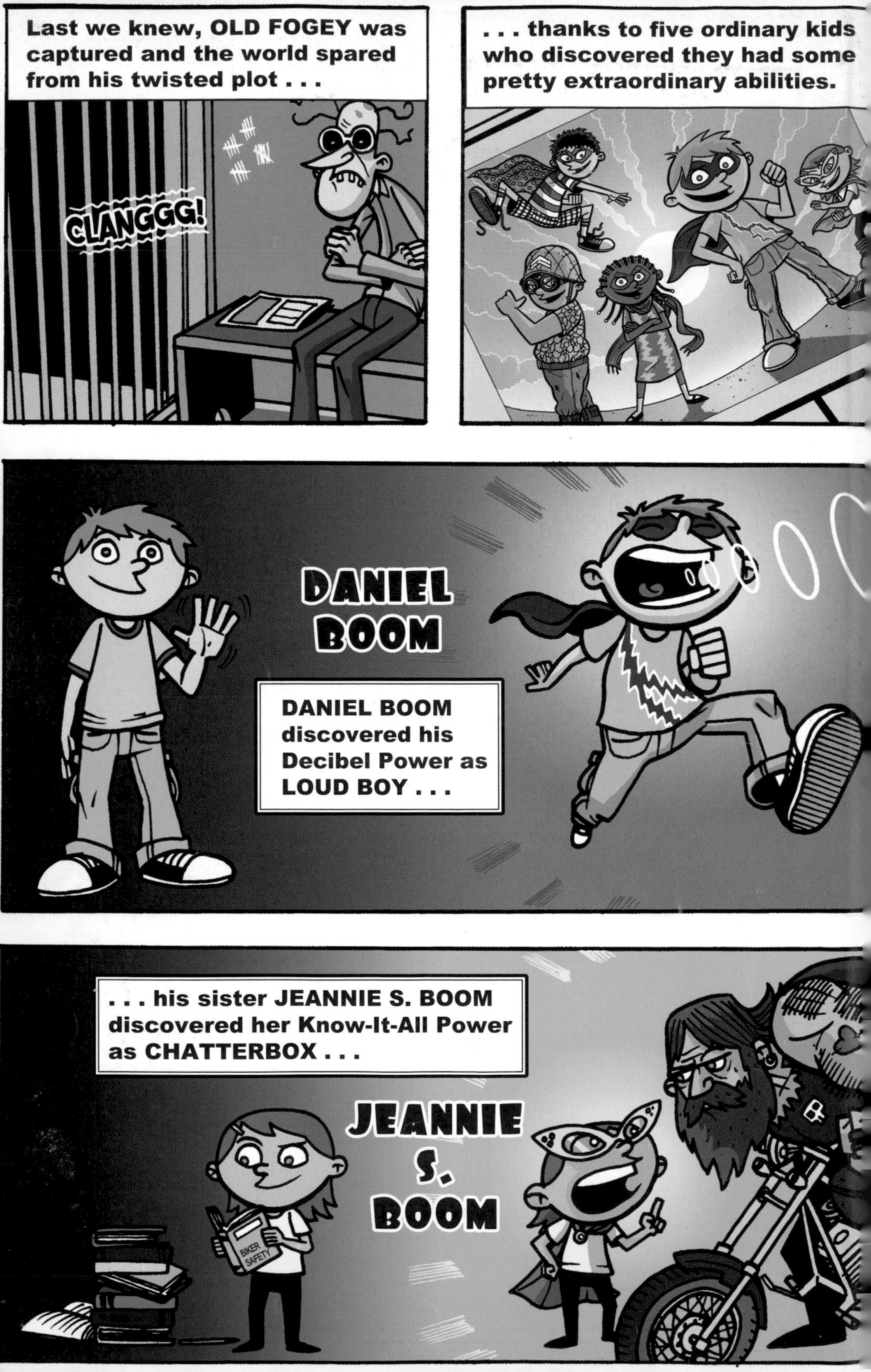
Last we knew, OLD FOGEY was captured and the world spared from his twisted plot . . .
CLANGGG!
. . . thanks to five ordinary kids who discovered they had some pretty extraordinary abilities.
DANIEL BOOM
DANIEL BOOM discovered his Decibel Power as LOUD BOY . . .
. . . his sister JEANNIE S. BOOM discovered her Know-It-All Power as CHATTERBOX . . .
JEANNIE S. BOOM
BIKER SAFETY

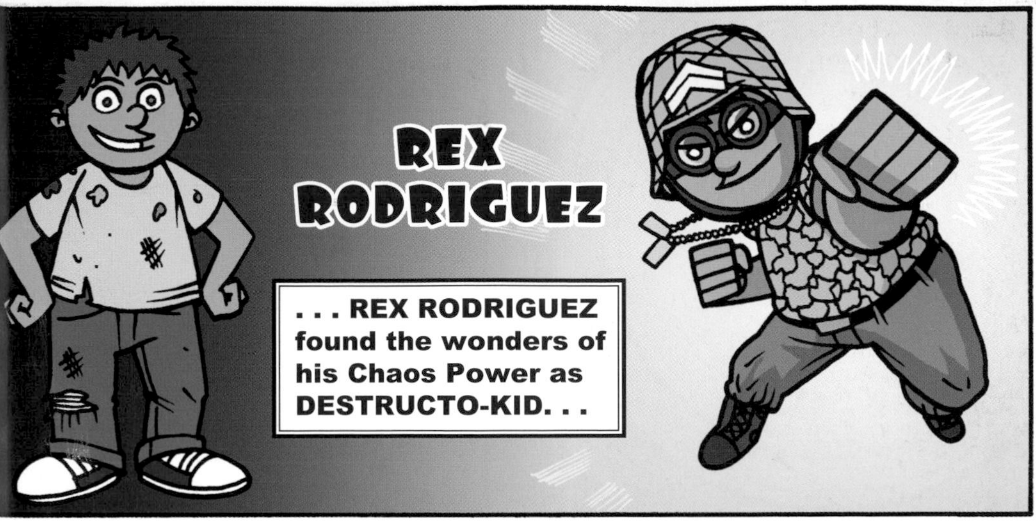
REX RODRIGUEZ
. . . REX RODRIGUEZ found the wonders of his Chaos Power as DESTRUCTO-KID. . .

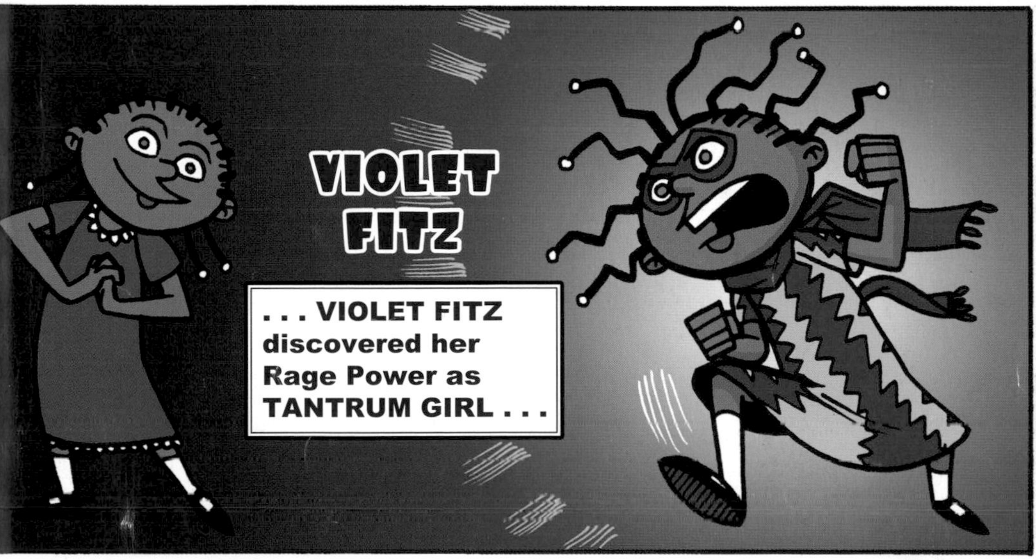
VIOLET FITZ
. . . VIOLET FITZ discovered her Rage Power as TANTRUM GIRL . . .

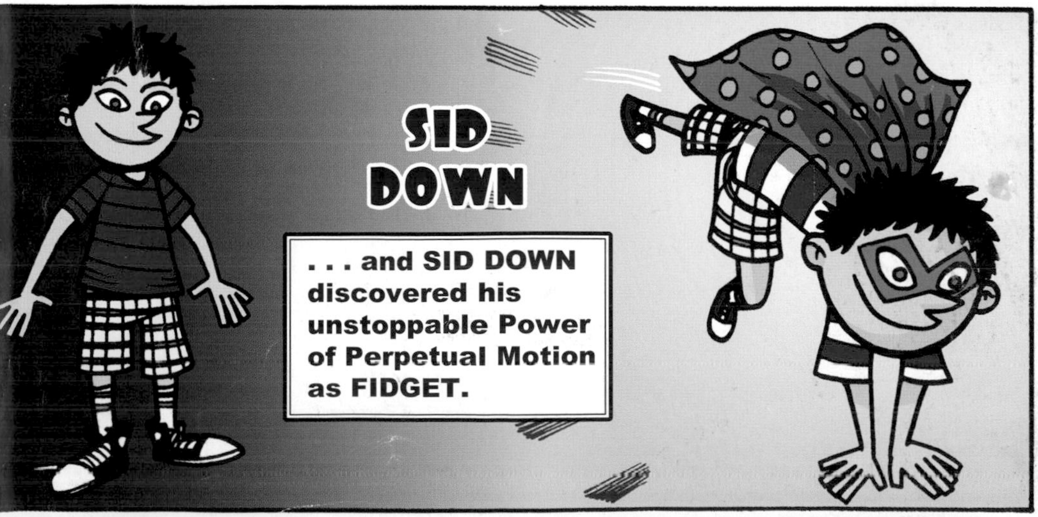
SID DOWN
. . . and SID DOWN discovered his unstoppable Power of Perpetual Motion as FIDGET.

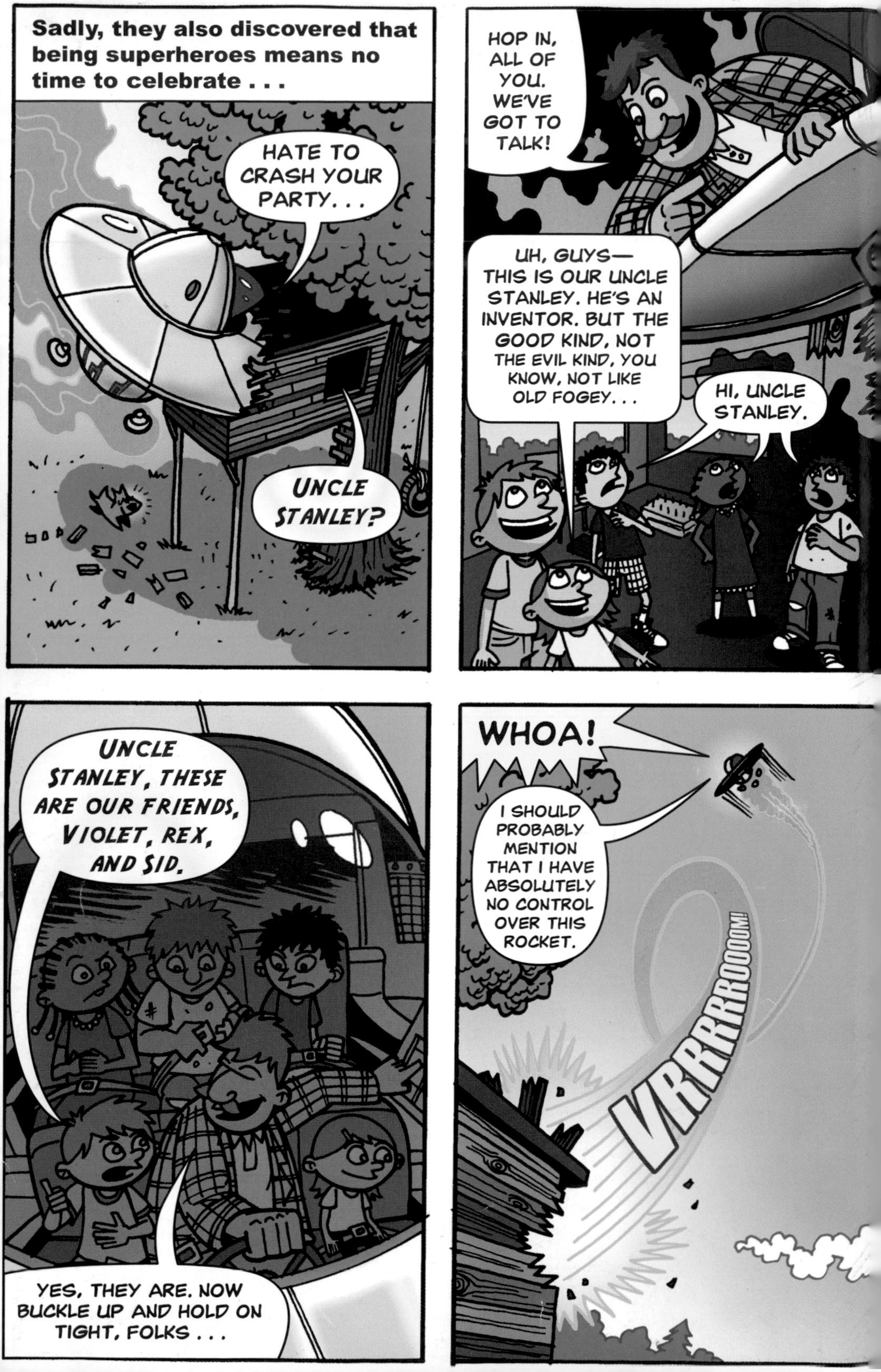
Sadly, they also discovered that being superheroes means no time to celebrate . . .
HATE TO CRASH YOUR PARTY. . .
UNCLE STANLEY?
HOP IN, ALL OF YOU. WE'VE GOT TO TALK!
UH, GUYS— THIS IS OUR UNCLE STANLEY. HE'S AN INVENTOR. BUT THE GOOD KIND, NOT THE EVIL KIND, YOU KNOW, NOT LIKE OLD FOGEY. . .
HI, UNCLE STANLEY.
UNCLE STANLEY, THESE ARE OUR FRIENDS, VIOLET, REX, AND SID.
YES, THEY ARE. NOW BUCKLE UP AND HOLD ON TIGHT, FOLKS . . .
WHOA!
I SHOULD PROBABLY MENTION THAT I HAVE ABSOLUTELY NO CONTROL OVER THIS ROCKET.
VRRRRROOOOM!

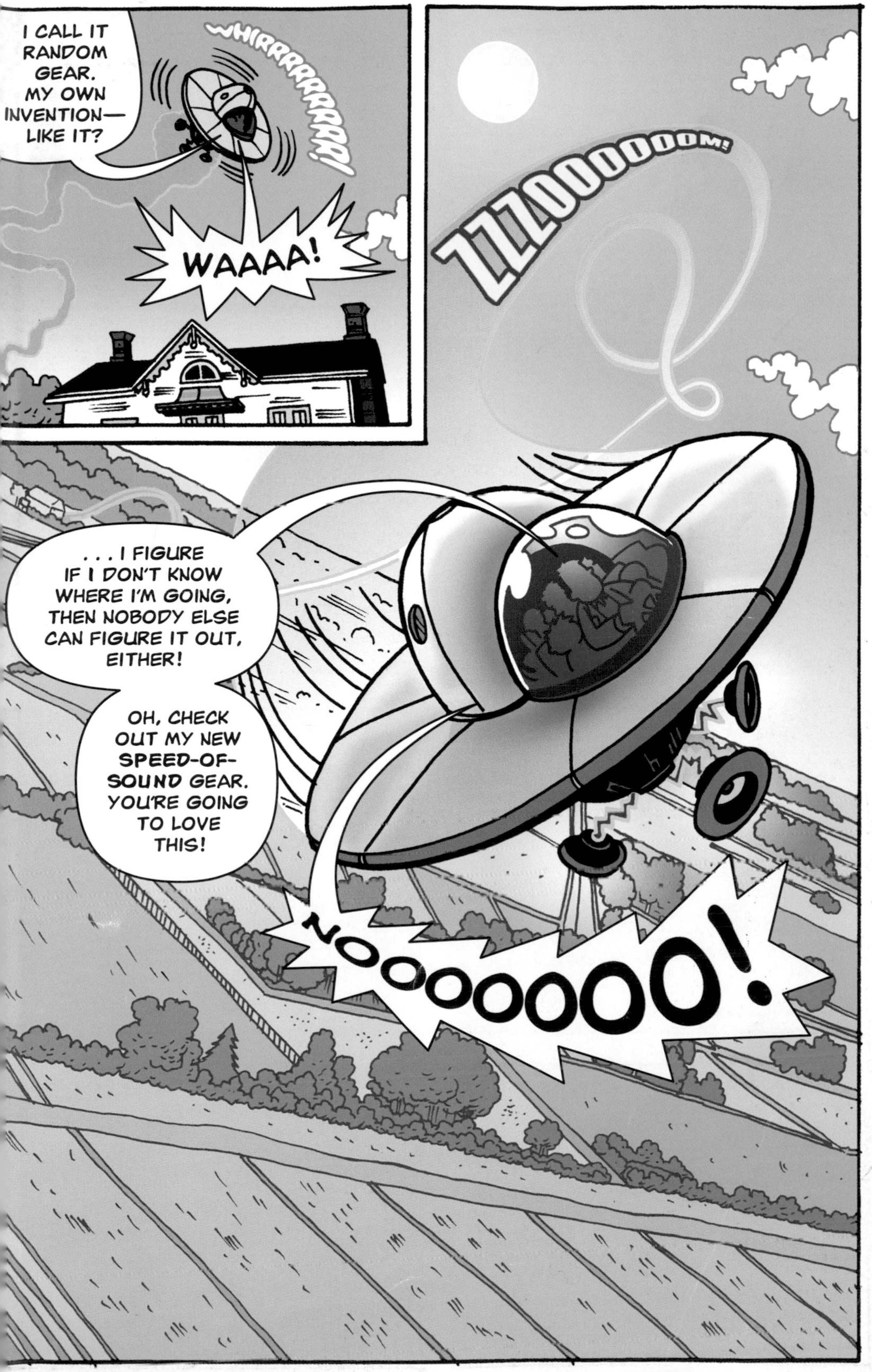
I CALL IT RANDOM GEAR. MY OWN INVENTION—LIKE IT?
WHIRRRRRRRR!
WAAAA!
ZZZOOOOOOOOM!
. . . I FIGURE IF I DON'T KNOW WHERE I'M GOING, THEN NOBODY ELSE CAN FIGURE IT OUT, EITHER!
OH, CHECK OUT MY NEW SPEED-OF-SOUND GEAR. YOU'RE GOING TO LOVE THIS!
NOOOOOOOO!

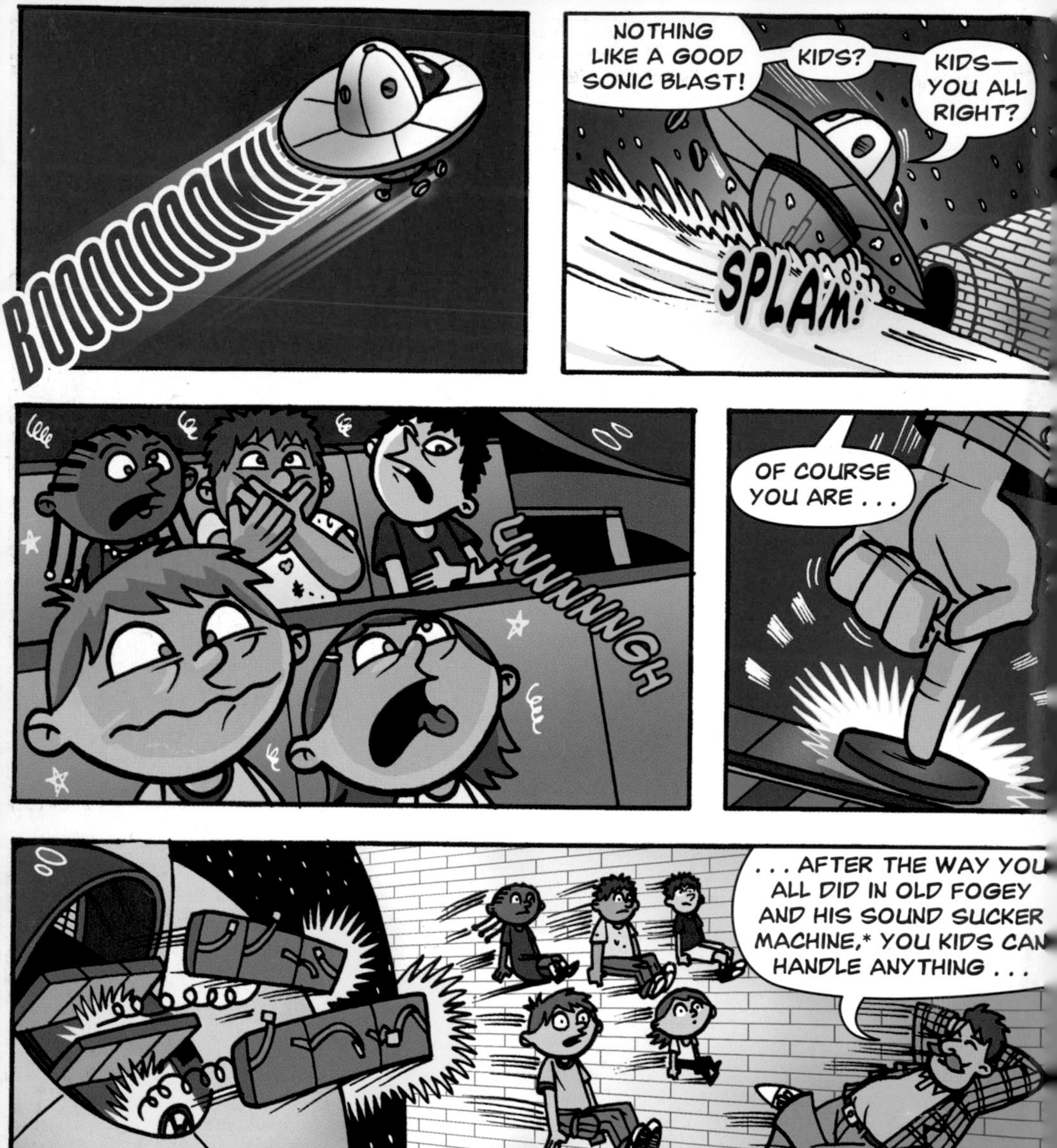
BOOOOOOOM
NOTHING LIKE A GOOD SONIC BLAST!
KIDS?
KIDS— YOU ALL RIGHT?
SPLAM!
UNNNNNGH
OF COURSE YOU ARE . . .
. . . AFTER THE WAY YOU ALL DID IN OLD FOGEY AND HIS SOUND SUCKER MACHINE,* YOU KIDS CAN HANDLE ANYTHING . . .

******Loud Boy #1*. **Didn't read it? Get it!**

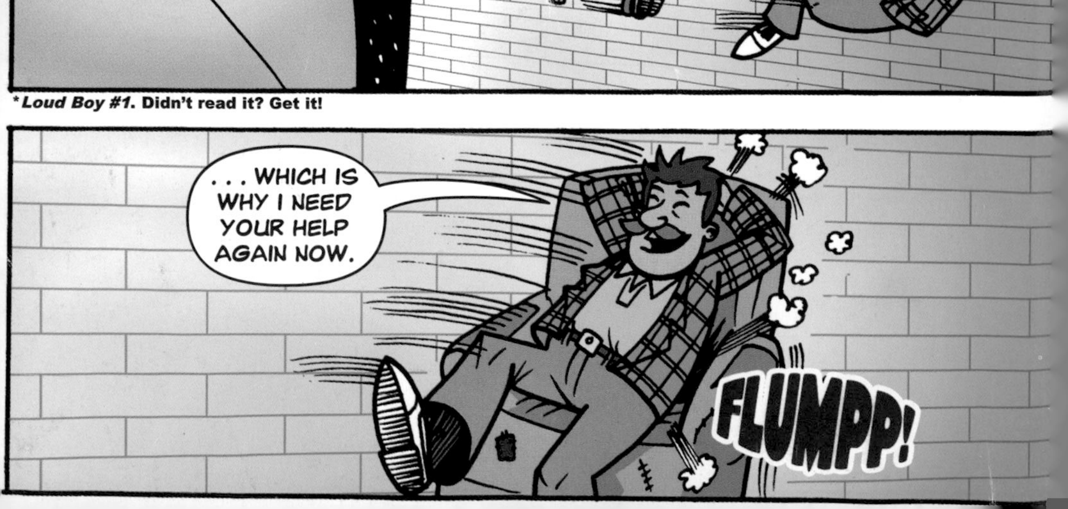
. . . WHICH IS WHY I NEED YOUR HELP AGAIN NOW.
FLUMPP!

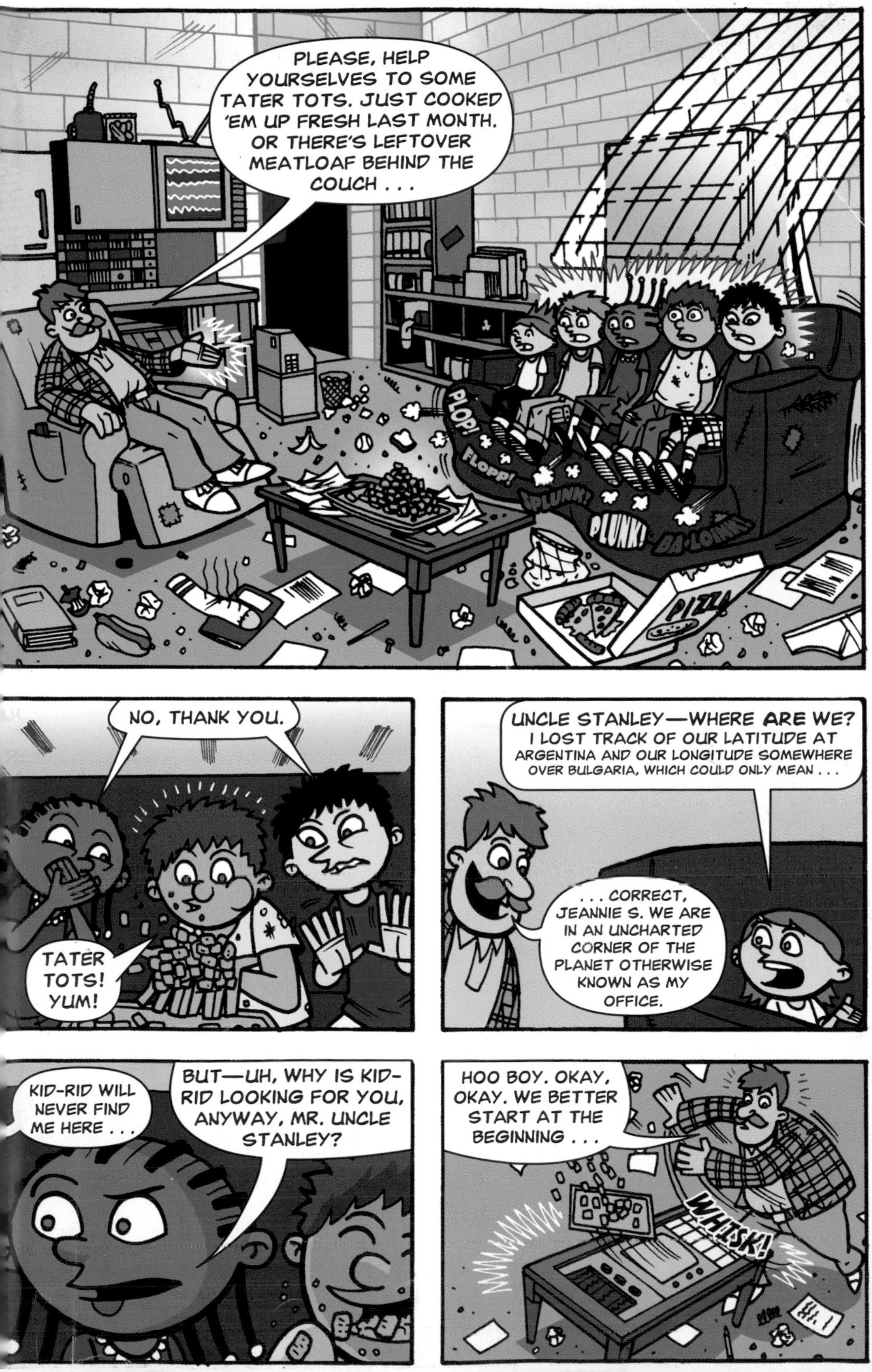
PLEASE, HELP YOURSELVES TO SOME TATER TOTS. JUST COOKED 'EM UP FRESH LAST MONTH. OR THERE'S LEFTOVER MEATLOAF BEHIND THE COUCH . . .
PLOP!
FLOPP!
SPLUNK!
PLUNK!
BA-LOINK!
PIZZA
NO, THANK YOU.
TATER TOTS! YUM!
UNCLE STANLEY—WHERE ARE WE? I LOST TRACK OF OUR LATITUDE AT ARGENTINA AND OUR LONGITUDE SOMEWHERE OVER BULGARIA, WHICH COULD ONLY MEAN . . .
. . . CORRECT, JEANNIE S. WE ARE IN AN UNCHARTED CORNER OF THE PLANET OTHERWISE KNOWN AS MY OFFICE.
KID-RID WILL NEVER FIND ME HERE . . .
BUT—UH, WHY IS KID-RID LOOKING FOR YOU, ANYWAY, MR. UNCLE STANLEY?
HOO BOY. OKAY, OKAY. WE BETTER START AT THE BEGINNING . . .
WHISK!

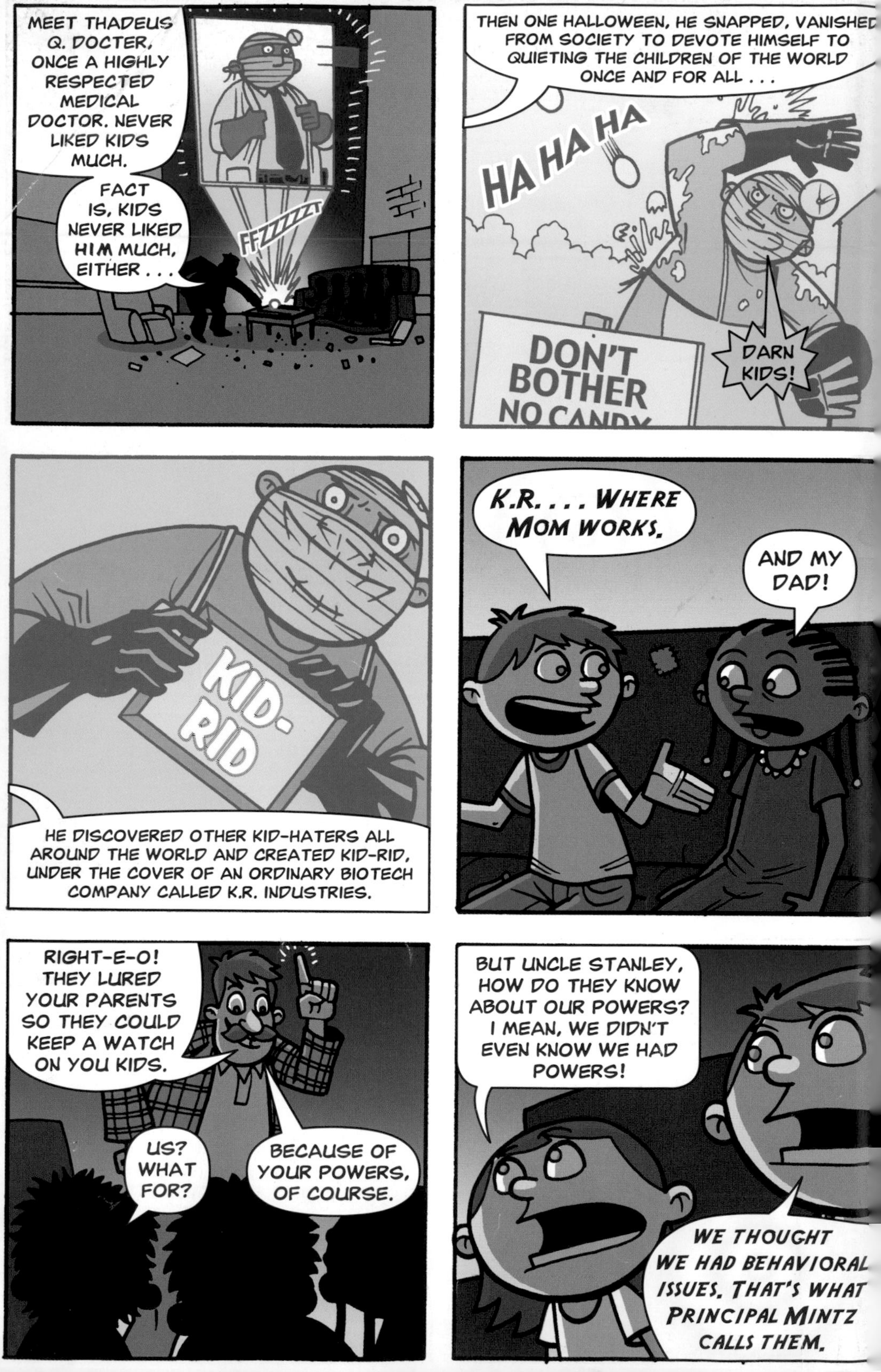
MEET THADEUS Q. DOCTER, ONCE A HIGHLY RESPECTED MEDICAL DOCTOR. NEVER LIKED KIDS MUCH.
FACT IS, KIDS NEVER LIKED HIM MUCH, EITHER . . .
FFZZZZZZT
THEN ONE HALLOWEEN, HE SNAPPED, VANISHED FROM SOCIETY TO DEVOTE HIMSELF TO QUIETING THE CHILDREN OF THE WORLD ONCE AND FOR ALL . . .
HA HA HA HA
DON'T BOTHER NO CANDY
DARN KIDS!
KID-RID
HE DISCOVERED OTHER KID-HATERS ALL AROUND THE WORLD AND CREATED KID-RID, UNDER THE COVER OF AN ORDINARY BIOTECH COMPANY CALLED K.R. INDUSTRIES.
K.R. . . . WHERE MOM WORKS.
AND MY DAD!
RIGHT-E-O! THEY LURED YOUR PARENTS SO THEY COULD KEEP A WATCH ON YOU KIDS.
US? WHAT FOR?
BECAUSE OF YOUR POWERS, OF COURSE.
BUT UNCLE STANLEY, HOW DO THEY KNOW ABOUT OUR POWERS? I MEAN, WE DIDN'T EVEN KNOW WE HAD POWERS!
WE THOUGHT WE HAD BEHAVIORAL ISSUES. THAT'S WHAT PRINCIPAL MINTZ CALLS THEM.

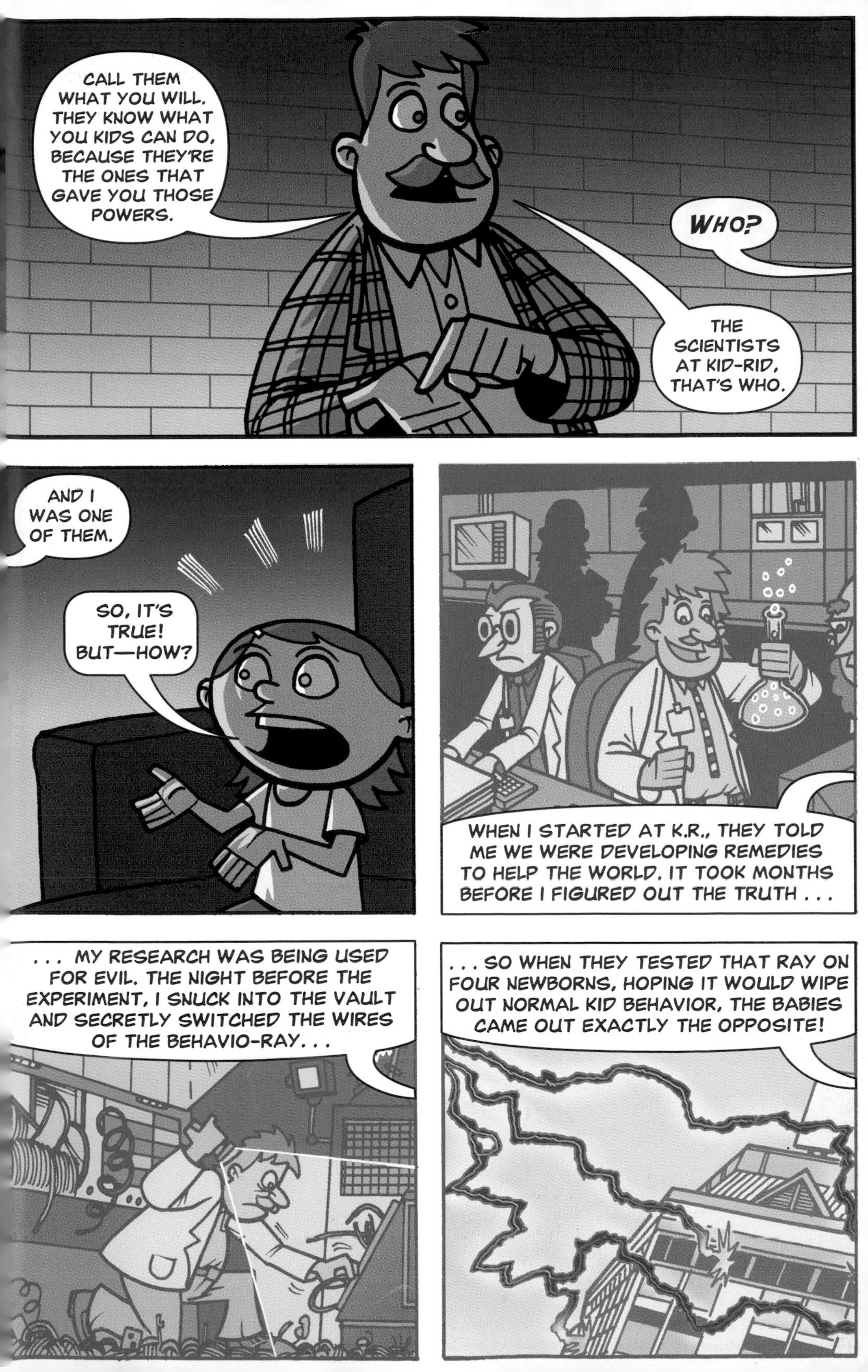
CALL THEM WHAT YOU WILL. THEY KNOW WHAT YOU KIDS CAN DO, BECAUSE THEY'RE THE ONES THAT GAVE YOU THOSE POWERS.
WHO?
THE SCIENTISTS AT KID-RID, THAT'S WHO.
AND I WAS ONE OF THEM.
SO, IT'S TRUE! BUT—HOW?
WHEN I STARTED AT K.R., THEY TOLD ME WE WERE DEVELOPING REMEDIES TO HELP THE WORLD. IT TOOK MONTHS BEFORE I FIGURED OUT THE TRUTH . . .
. . . MY RESEARCH WAS BEING USED FOR EVIL. THE NIGHT BEFORE THE EXPERIMENT, I SNUCK INTO THE VAULT AND SECRETLY SWITCHED THE WIRES OF THE BEHAVIO-RAY. . .
. . . SO WHEN THEY TESTED THAT RAY ON FOUR NEWBORNS, HOPING IT WOULD WIPE OUT NORMAL KID BEHAVIOR, THE BABIES CAME OUT EXACTLY THE OPPOSITE!

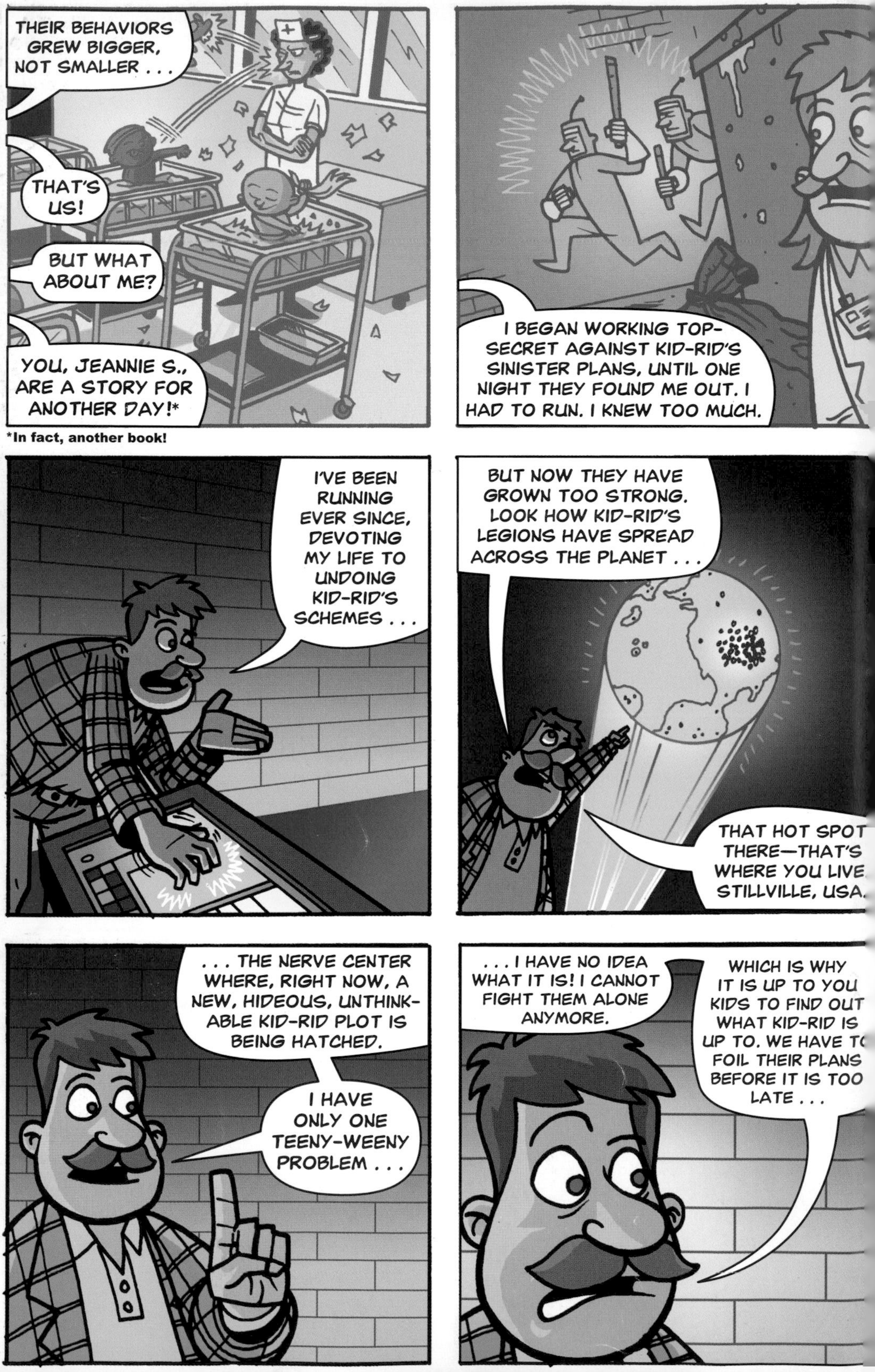
THEIR BEHAVIORS GREW BIGGER, NOT SMALLER . . .
THAT'S US!
BUT WHAT ABOUT ME?
YOU, JEANNIE S., ARE A STORY FOR ANOTHER DAY!*
I BEGAN WORKING TOP-SECRET AGAINST KID-RID'S SINISTER PLANS, UNTIL ONE NIGHT THEY FOUND ME OUT. I HAD TO RUN. I KNEW TOO MUCH.
I'VE BEEN RUNNING EVER SINCE, DEVOTING MY LIFE TO UNDOING KID-RID'S SCHEMES . . .
BUT NOW THEY HAVE GROWN TOO STRONG. LOOK HOW KID-RID'S LEGIONS HAVE SPREAD ACROSS THE PLANET . . .
THAT HOT SPOT THERE—THAT'S WHERE YOU LIVE STILLVILLE, USA.
. . . THE NERVE CENTER WHERE, RIGHT NOW, A NEW, HIDEOUS, UNTHINK-ABLE KID-RID PLOT IS BEING HATCHED.
I HAVE ONLY ONE TEENY-WEENY PROBLEM . . .
. . . I HAVE NO IDEA WHAT IT IS! I CANNOT FIGHT THEM ALONE ANYMORE.
WHICH IS WHY IT IS UP TO YOU KIDS TO FIND OUT WHAT KID-RID IS UP TO. WE HAVE T FOIL THEIR PLANS BEFORE IT IS TOO LATE . . .

*In fact, another book!

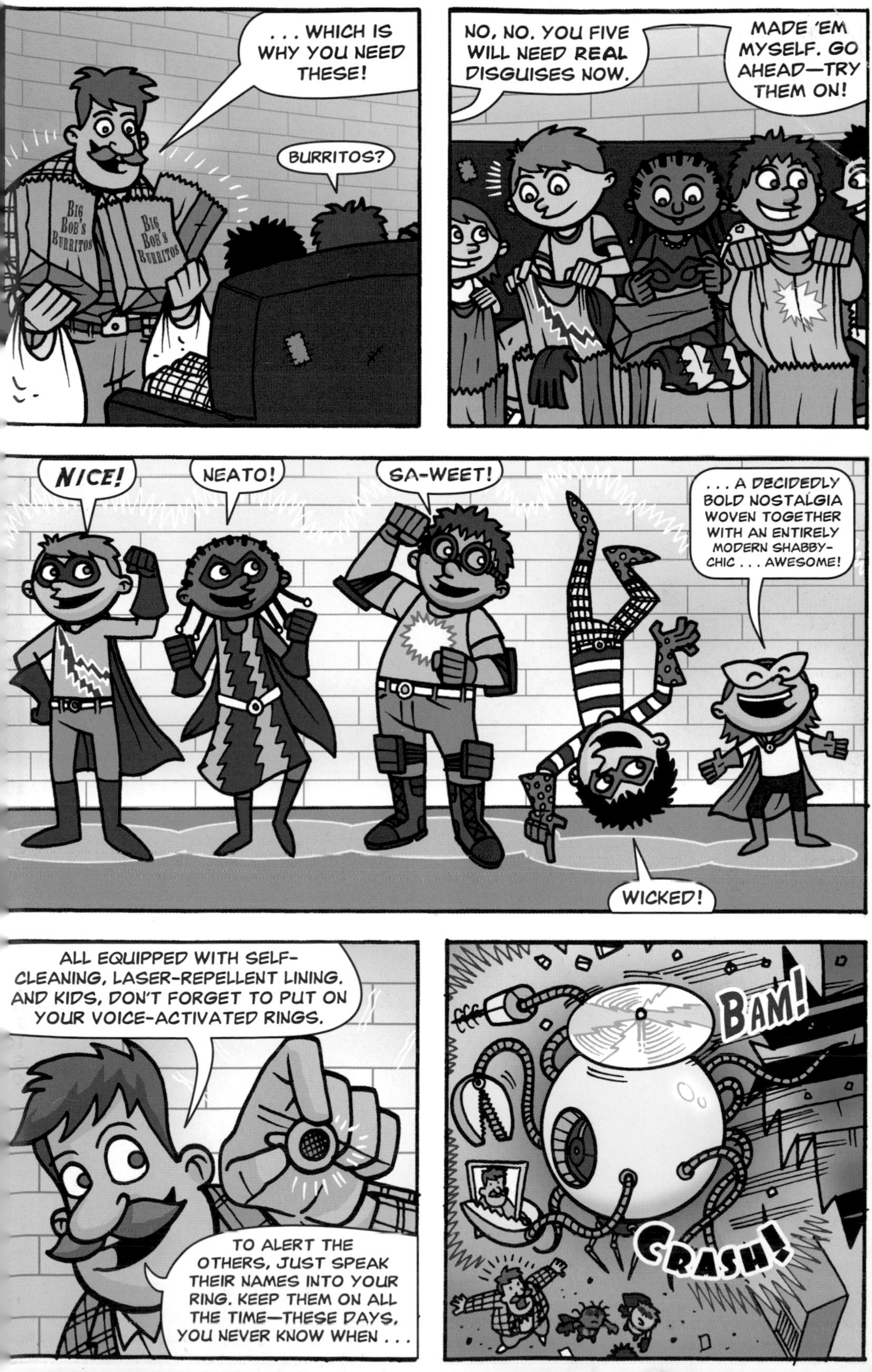

. . . WHICH IS WHY YOU NEED THESE!
BIG BOB'S BURRITOS
BIG BOB'S BURRITOS
BURRITOS?
NO, NO. YOU FIVE WILL NEED REAL DISGUISES NOW.
MADE 'EM MYSELF. GO AHEAD—TRY THEM ON!
NICE!
NEATO!
SA-WEET!
. . . A DECIDEDLY BOLD NOSTALGIA WOVEN TOGETHER WITH AN ENTIRELY MODERN SHABBY-CHIC . . . AWESOME!
WICKED!
ALL EQUIPPED WITH SELF-CLEANING, LASER-REPELLENT LINING. AND KIDS, DON'T FORGET TO PUT ON YOUR VOICE-ACTIVATED RINGS.
TO ALERT THE OTHERS, JUST SPEAK THEIR NAMES INTO YOUR RING. KEEP THEM ON ALL THE TIME—THESE DAYS, YOU NEVER KNOW WHEN . . .
BAM!
CRASH!

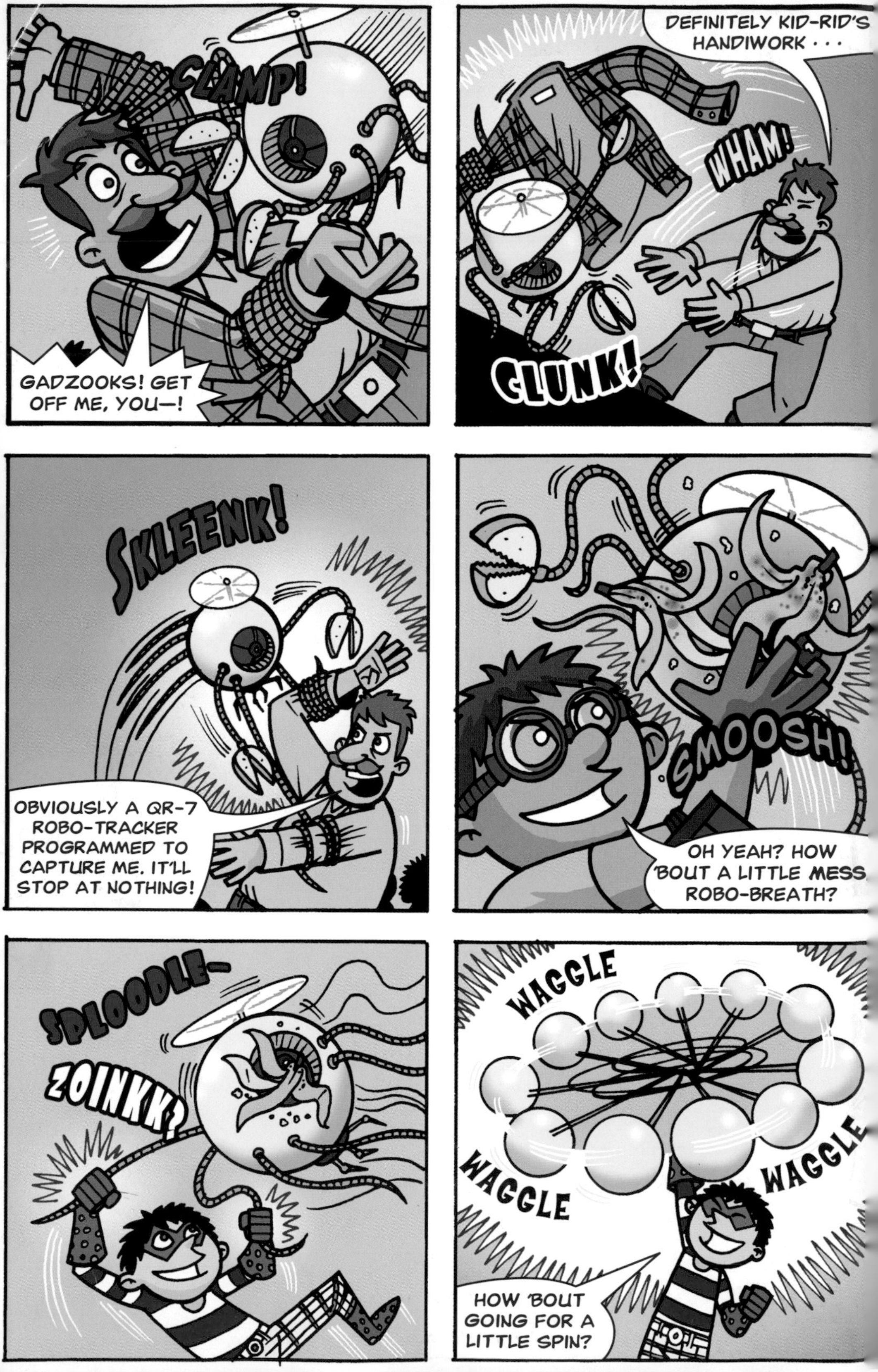
CLAMP!
GADZOOKS! GET OFF ME, YOU—!
DEFINITELY KID-RID'S HANDIWORK . . .
WHAM!
CLUNK!
SKLEENK!
OBVIOUSLY A QR-7 ROBO-TRACKER PROGRAMMED TO CAPTURE ME. IT'LL STOP AT NOTHING!
SMOOSH!
OH YEAH? HOW 'BOUT A LITTLE MESS ROBO-BREATH?
SPLOODLE-
ZOINKK?
WAGGLE
WAGGLE
WAGGLE
HOW 'BOUT GOING FOR A LITTLE SPIN?

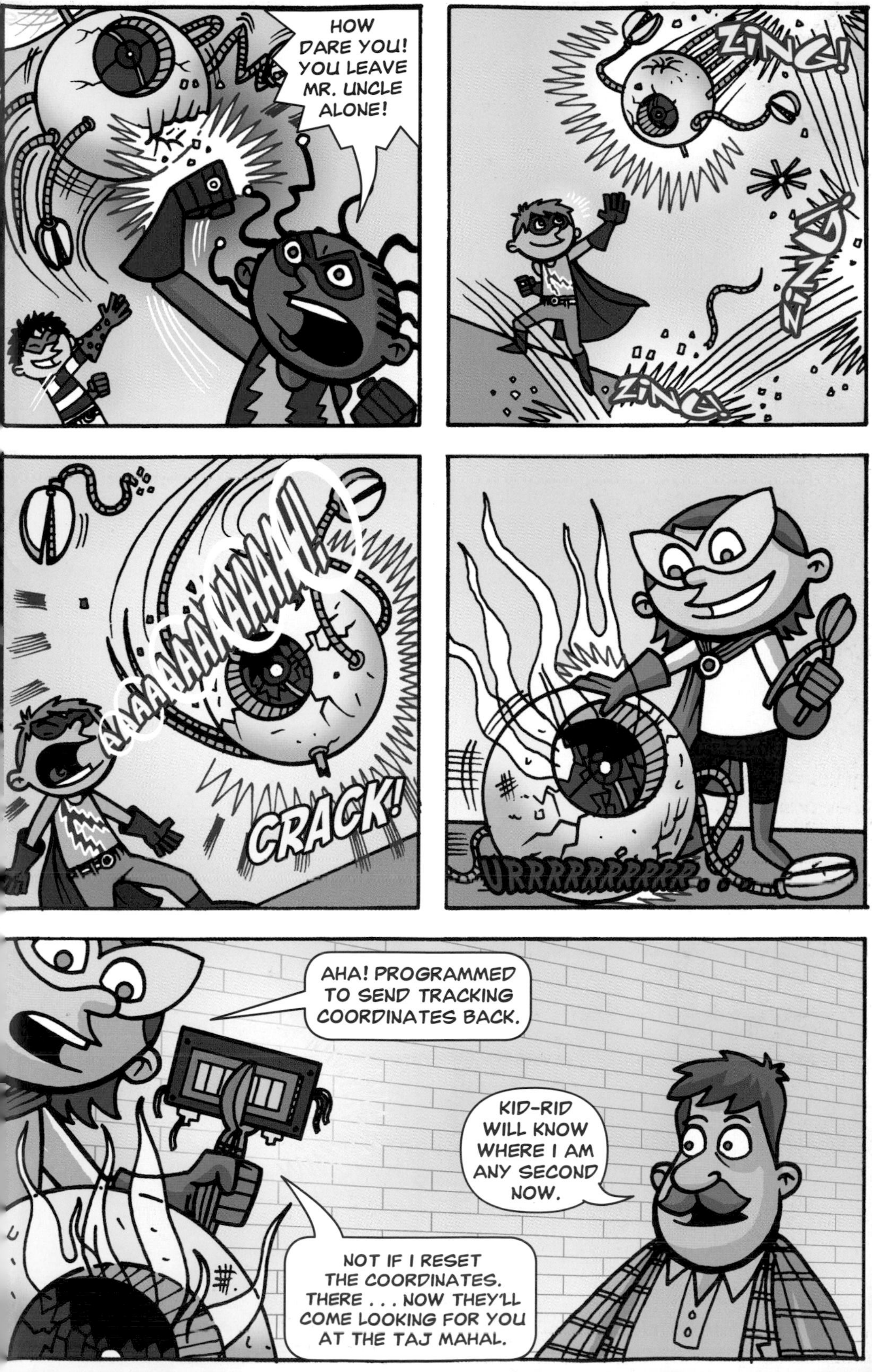

HOW DARE YOU! YOU LEAVE MR. UNCLE ALONE!
ZING!
ZING!
ZING!
AAAAAAAAAAAAA!
CRACK!
URRRRRRRRRR
AHA! PROGRAMMED TO SEND TRACKING COORDINATES BACK.
KID-RID WILL KNOW WHERE I AM ANY SECOND NOW.
NOT IF I RESET THE COORDINATES. THERE . . . NOW THEY'LL COME LOOKING FOR YOU AT THE TAJ MAHAL.

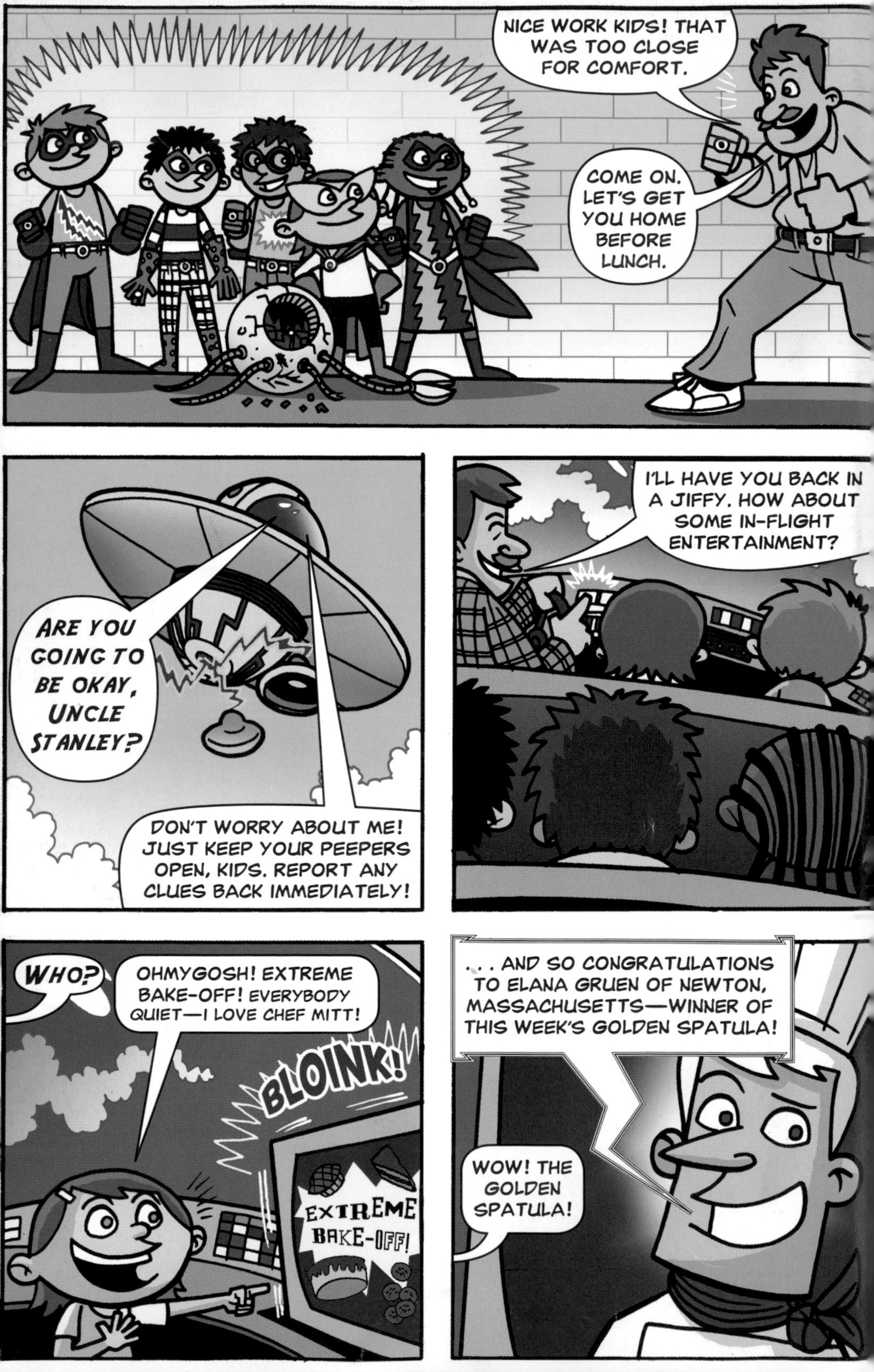
NICE WORK KIDS! THAT WAS TOO CLOSE FOR COMFORT.
COME ON. LET'S GET YOU HOME BEFORE LUNCH.
ARE YOU GOING TO BE OKAY, UNCLE STANLEY?
DON'T WORRY ABOUT ME! JUST KEEP YOUR PEEPERS OPEN, KIDS. REPORT ANY CLUES BACK IMMEDIATELY!
I'LL HAVE YOU BACK IN A JIFFY. HOW ABOUT SOME IN-FLIGHT ENTERTAINMENT?
WHO?
OHMYGOSH! EXTREME BAKE-OFF! EVERYBODY QUIET—I LOVE CHEF MITT!
BLOINK!
EXTREME BAKE-OFF!
. . . AND SO CONGRATULATIONS TO ELANA GRUEN OF NEWTON, MASSACHUSETTS—WINNER OF THIS WEEK'S GOLDEN SPATULA!
WOW! THE GOLDEN SPATULA!

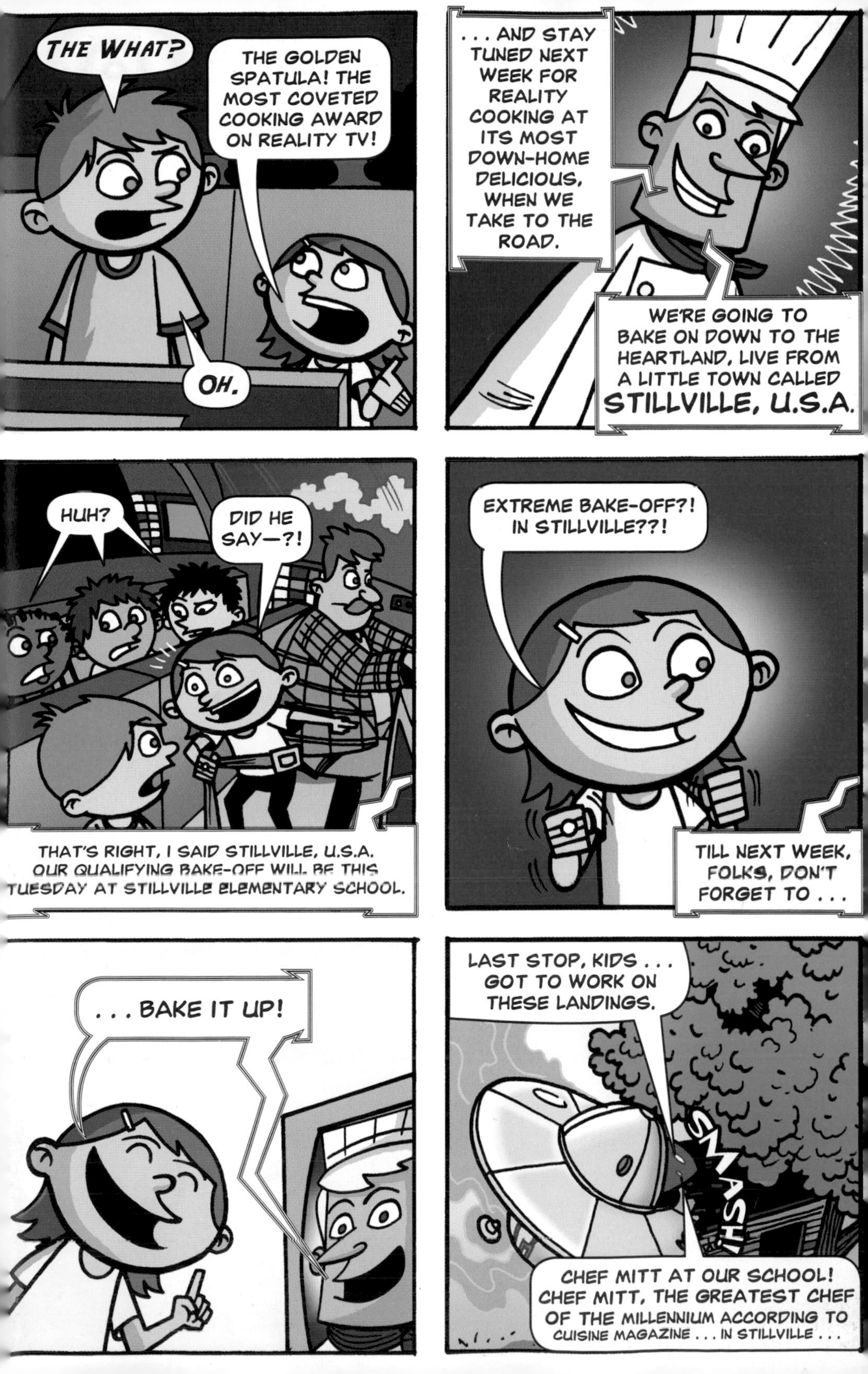
THE WHAT?
THE GOLDEN SPATULA! THE MOST COVETED COOKING AWARD ON REALITY TV!
OH.
. . . AND STAY TUNED NEXT WEEK FOR REALITY COOKING AT ITS MOST DOWN-HOME DELICIOUS, WHEN WE TAKE TO THE ROAD.
WE'RE GOING TO BAKE ON DOWN TO THE HEARTLAND, LIVE FROM A LITTLE TOWN CALLED STILLVILLE, U.S.A.
HUH?
DID HE SAY—?!
THAT'S RIGHT, I SAID STILLVILLE, U.S.A. OUR QUALIFYING BAKE-OFF WILL BE THIS TUESDAY AT STILLVILLE ELEMENTARY SCHOOL.
EXTREME BAKE-OFF?! IN STILLVILLE??!
TILL NEXT WEEK, FOLKS, DON'T FORGET TO . . .
. . . BAKE IT UP!
LAST STOP, KIDS . . . GOT TO WORK ON THESE LANDINGS.
SMASH!
CHEF MITT AT OUR SCHOOL! CHEF MITT, THE GREATEST CHEF OF THE MILLENNIUM ACCORDING TO CUISINE MAGAZINE . . . IN STILLVILLE . . .

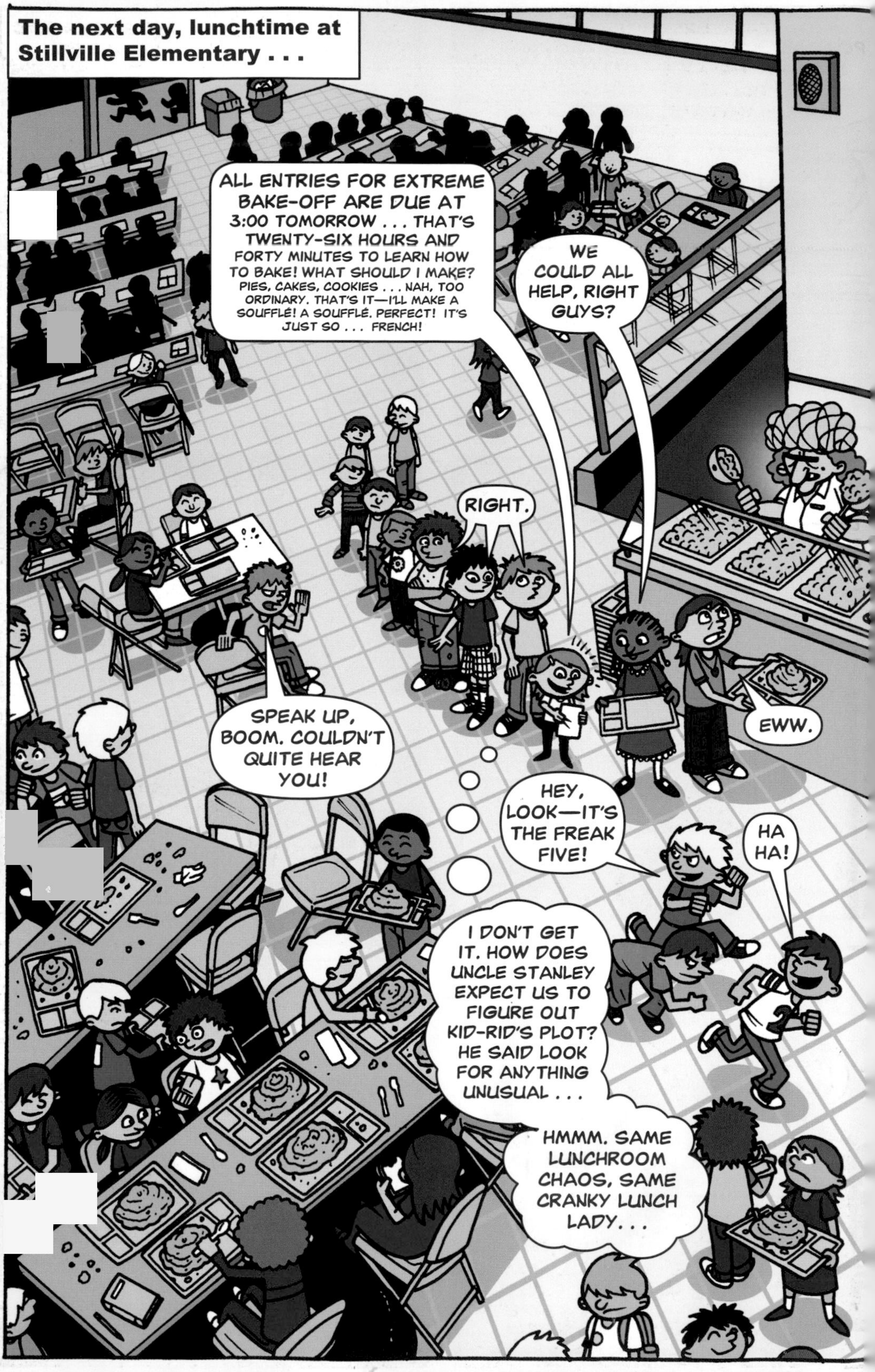
The next day, lunchtime at Stillville Elementary . . .
ALL ENTRIES FOR EXTREME BAKE-OFF ARE DUE AT 3:00 TOMORROW . . . THAT'S TWENTY-SIX HOURS AND FORTY MINUTES TO LEARN HOW TO BAKE! WHAT SHOULD I MAKE? PIES, CAKES, COOKIES . . . NAH, TOO ORDINARY. THAT'S IT—I'LL MAKE A SOUFFLÉ! A SOUFFLÉ. PERFECT! IT'S JUST SO . . . FRENCH!
WE COULD ALL HELP, RIGHT GUYS?
RIGHT.
SPEAK UP, BOOM. COULDN'T QUITE HEAR YOU!
EWW.
HEY, LOOK—IT'S THE FREAK FIVE!
HA HA!
I DON'T GET IT. HOW DOES UNCLE STANLEY EXPECT US TO FIGURE OUT KID-RID'S PLOT? HE SAID LOOK FOR ANYTHING UNUSUAL . . .
HMMM. SAME LUNCHROOM CHAOS, SAME CRANKY LUNCH LADY . . .

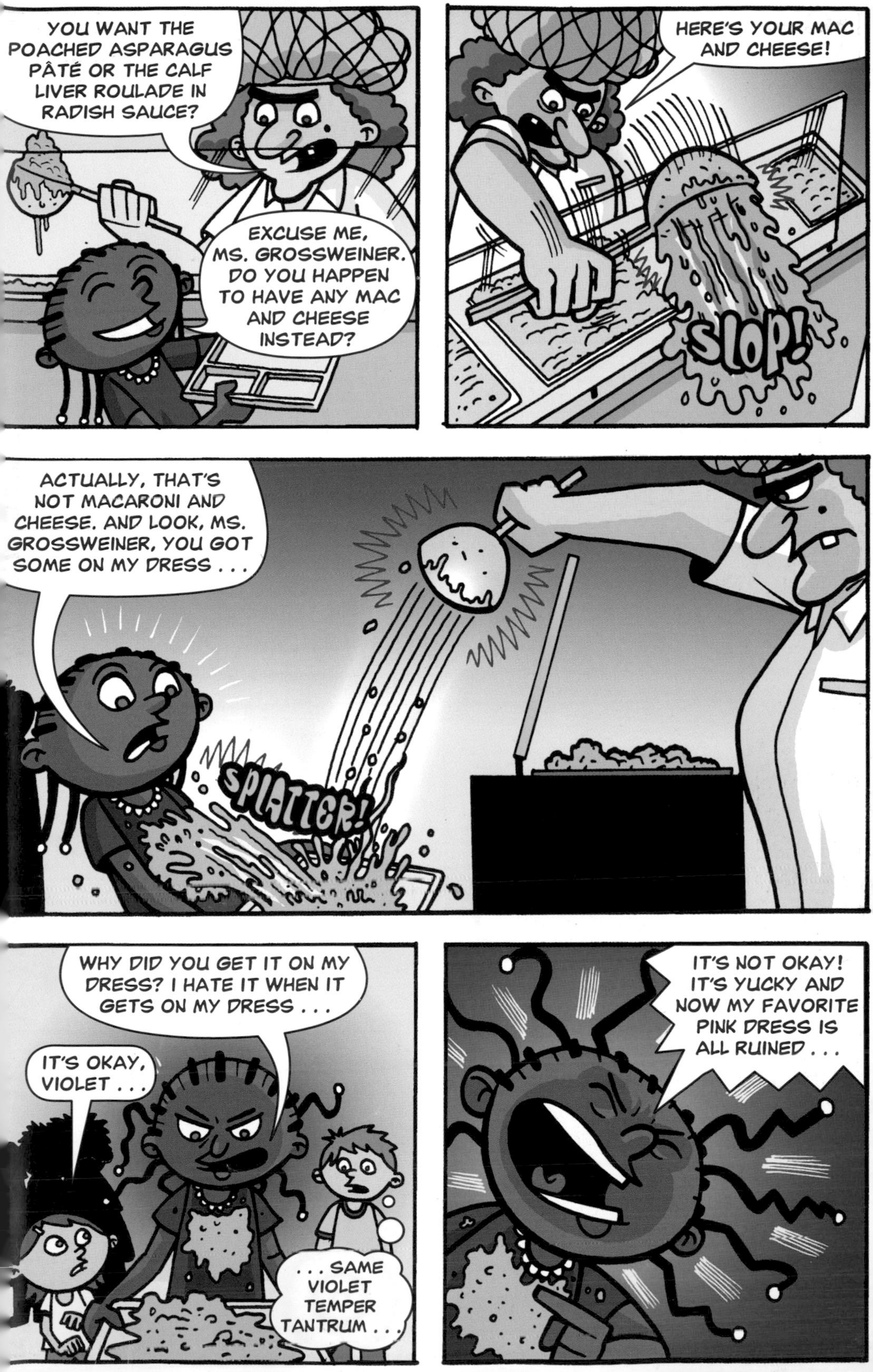
YOU WANT THE POACHED ASPARAGUS PÂTÉ OR THE CALF LIVER ROULADE IN RADISH SAUCE?
EXCUSE ME, MS. GROSSWEINER. DO YOU HAPPEN TO HAVE ANY MAC AND CHEESE INSTEAD?
HERE'S YOUR MAC AND CHEESE!
SLOP!
ACTUALLY, THAT'S NOT MACARONI AND CHEESE. AND LOOK, MS. GROSSWEINER, YOU GOT SOME ON MY DRESS . . .
SPLATTER!
WHY DID YOU GET IT ON MY DRESS? I HATE IT WHEN IT GETS ON MY DRESS . . .
IT'S OKAY, VIOLET . . .
. . . SAME VIOLET TEMPER TANTRUM . . .
IT'S NOT OKAY! IT'S YUCKY AND NOW MY FAVORITE PINK DRESS IS ALL RUINED . . .

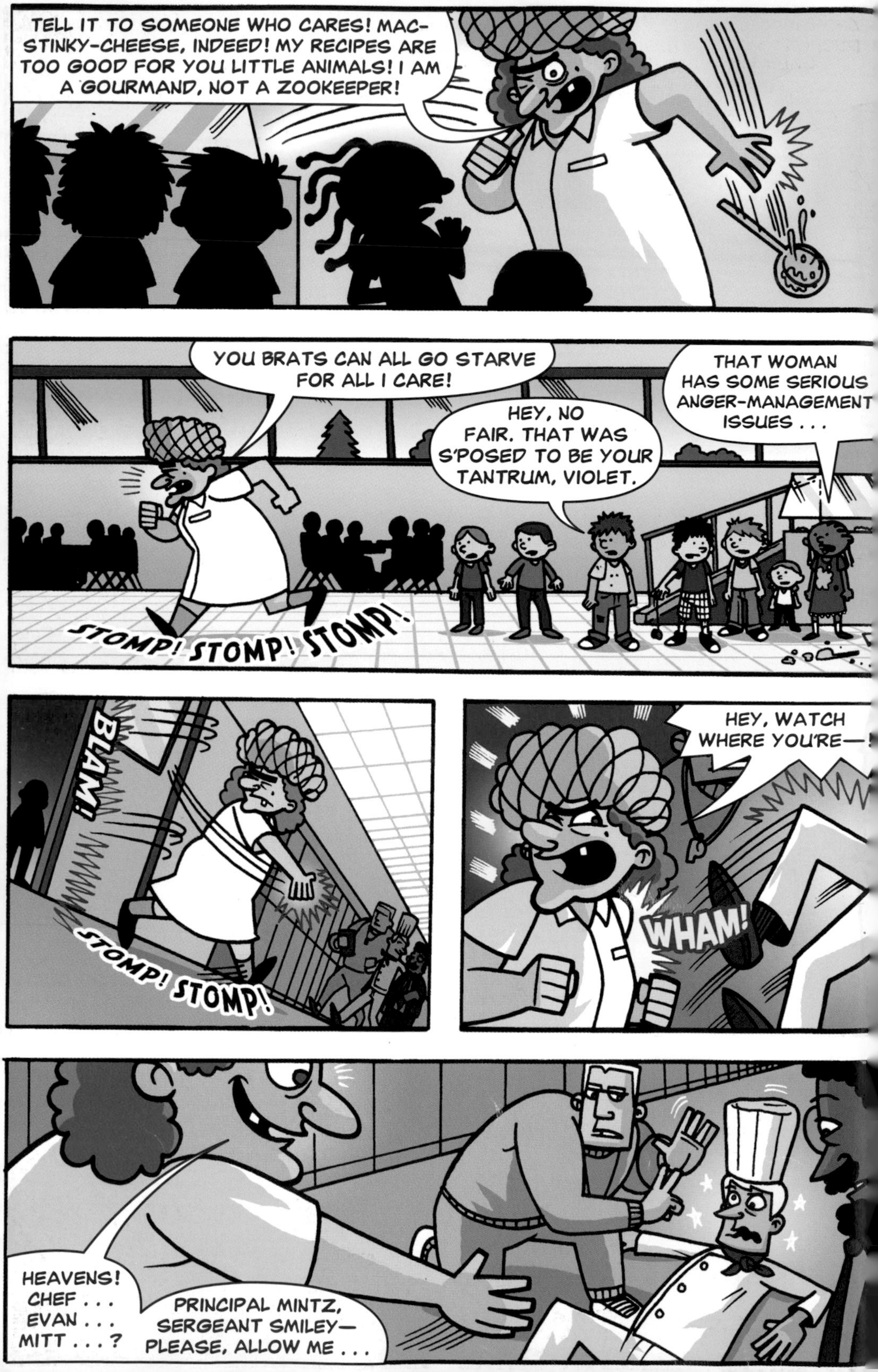

TELL IT TO SOMEONE WHO CARES! MAC-STINKY-CHEESE, INDEED! MY RECIPES ARE TOO GOOD FOR YOU LITTLE ANIMALS! I AM A GOURMAND, NOT A ZOOKEEPER!
YOU BRATS CAN ALL GO STARVE FOR ALL I CARE!
HEY, NO FAIR. THAT WAS S'POSED TO BE YOUR TANTRUM, VIOLET.
THAT WOMAN HAS SOME SERIOUS ANGER-MANAGEMENT ISSUES . . .
STOMP! STOMP! STOMP!
BLAM!
STOMP! STOMP!
HEY, WATCH WHERE YOU'RE—
WHAM!
HEAVENS! CHEF . . . EVAN . . . MITT . . . ?
PRINCIPAL MINTZ, SERGEANT SMILEY—PLEASE, ALLOW ME . . .

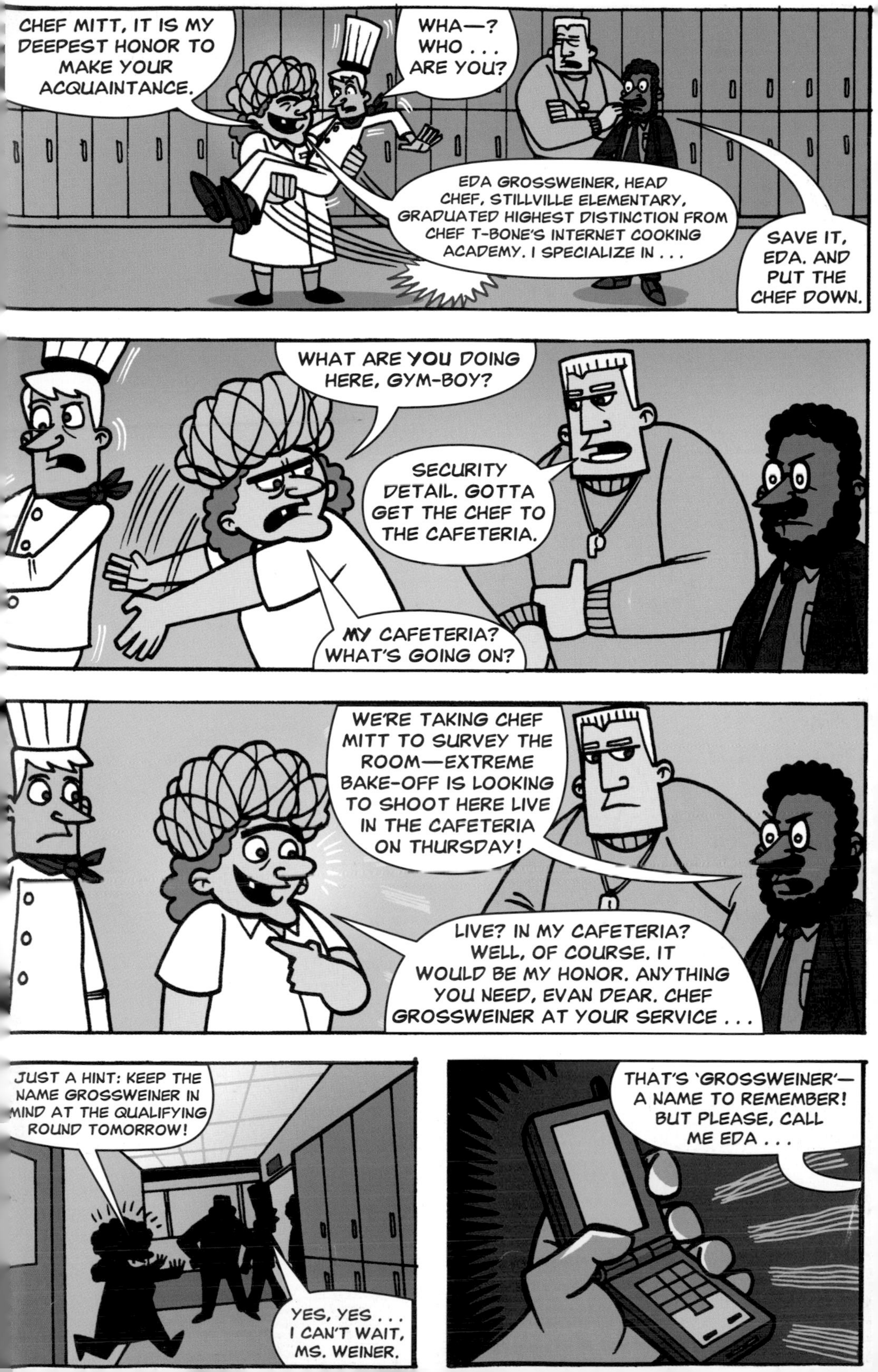
CHEF MITT, IT IS MY DEEPEST HONOR TO MAKE YOUR ACQUAINTANCE.
WHA—? WHO . . . ARE YOU?
EDA GROSSWEINER, HEAD CHEF, STILLVILLE ELEMENTARY, GRADUATED HIGHEST DISTINCTION FROM CHEF T-BONE'S INTERNET COOKING ACADEMY. I SPECIALIZE IN . . .
SAVE IT, EDA. AND PUT THE CHEF DOWN.
WHAT ARE YOU DOING HERE, GYM-BOY?
SECURITY DETAIL. GOTTA GET THE CHEF TO THE CAFETERIA.
MY CAFETERIA? WHAT'S GOING ON?
WE'RE TAKING CHEF MITT TO SURVEY THE ROOM—EXTREME BAKE-OFF IS LOOKING TO SHOOT HERE LIVE IN THE CAFETERIA ON THURSDAY!
LIVE? IN MY CAFETERIA? WELL, OF COURSE. IT WOULD BE MY HONOR. ANYTHING YOU NEED, EVAN DEAR. CHEF GROSSWEINER AT YOUR SERVICE . . .
JUST A HINT: KEEP THE NAME GROSSWEINER IN MIND AT THE QUALIFYING ROUND TOMORROW!
YES, YES . . . I CAN'T WAIT, MS. WEINER.
THAT'S 'GROSSWEINER'— A NAME TO REMEMBER! BUT PLEASE, CALL ME EDA . . .

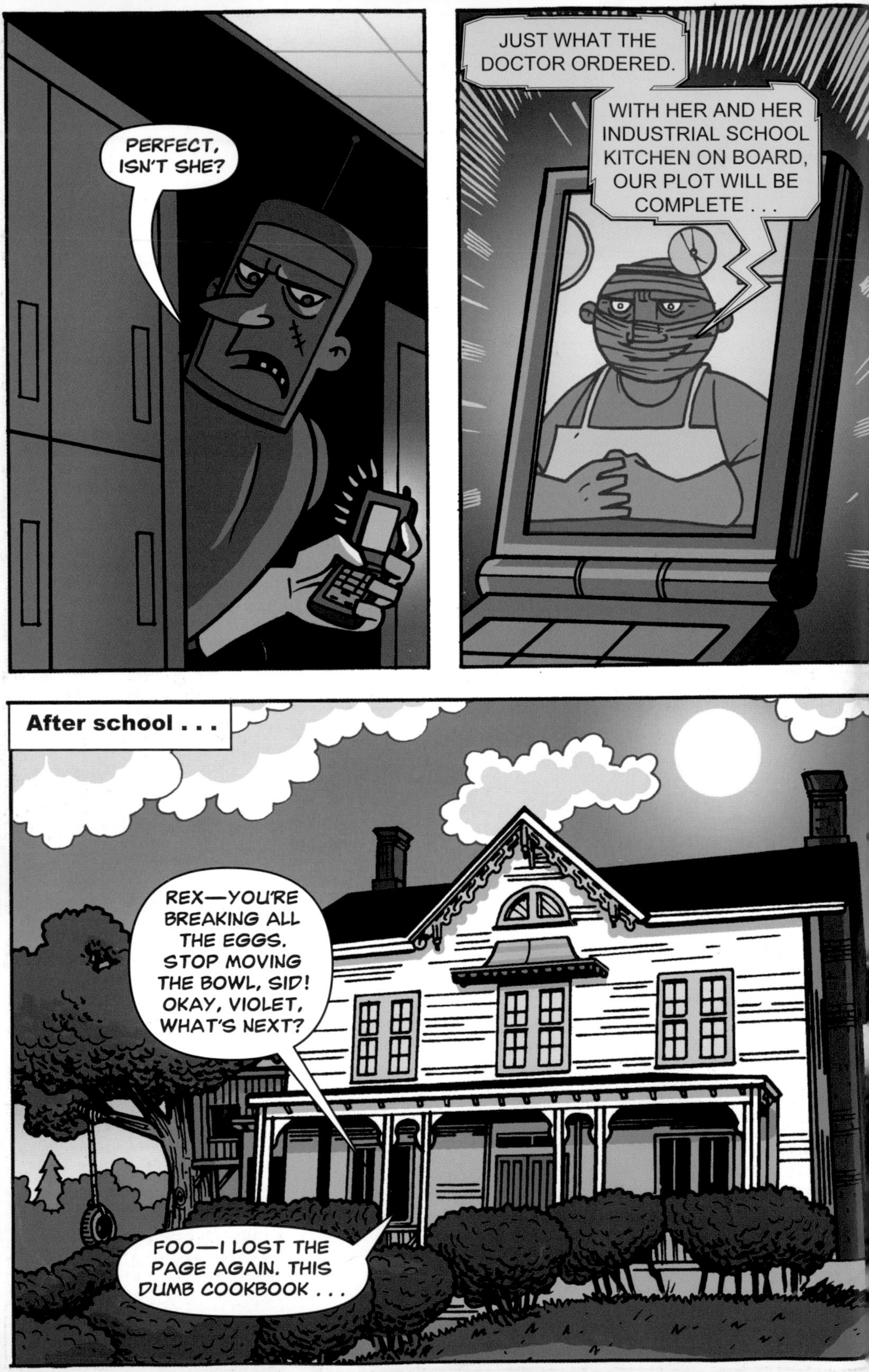
PERFECT, ISN'T SHE?
JUST WHAT THE DOCTOR ORDERED.
WITH HER AND HER INDUSTRIAL SCHOOL KITCHEN ON BOARD, OUR PLOT WILL BE COMPLETE . . .
After school . . .
REX—YOU'RE BREAKING ALL THE EGGS. STOP MOVING THE BOWL, SID! OKAY, VIOLET, WHAT'S NEXT?
FOO—I LOST THE PAGE AGAIN. THIS DUMB COOKBOOK . . .

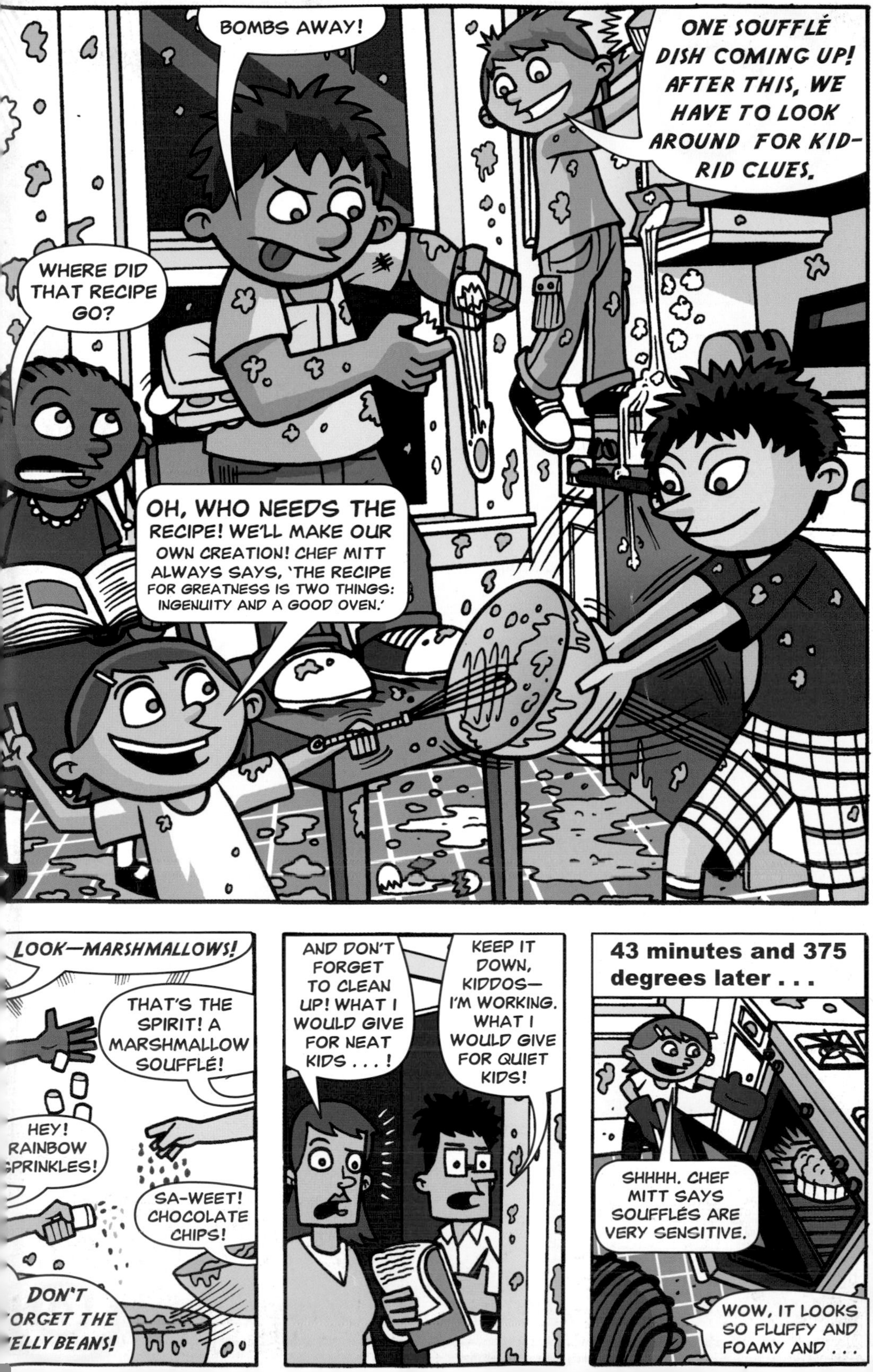
BOMBS AWAY!
ONE SOUFFLÉ DISH COMING UP! AFTER THIS, WE HAVE TO LOOK AROUND FOR KID-RID CLUES.
WHERE DID THAT RECIPE GO?
OH, WHO NEEDS THE RECIPE! WE'LL MAKE OUR OWN CREATION! CHEF MITT ALWAYS SAYS, 'THE RECIPE FOR GREATNESS IS TWO THINGS: INGENUITY AND A GOOD OVEN.'
LOOK—MARSHMALLOWS!
THAT'S THE SPIRIT! A MARSHMALLOW SOUFFLÉ!
HEY! RAINBOW SPRINKLES!
SA-WEET! CHOCOLATE CHIPS!
DON'T FORGET THE JELLYBEANS!
AND DON'T FORGET TO CLEAN UP! WHAT I WOULD GIVE FOR NEAT KIDS . . . !
KEEP IT DOWN, KIDDOS— I'M WORKING. WHAT I WOULD GIVE FOR QUIET KIDS!
43 minutes and 375 degrees later . . .
SHHHH. CHEF MITT SAYS SOUFFLÉS ARE VERY SENSITIVE.
WOW, IT LOOKS SO FLUFFY AND FOAMY AND . . .

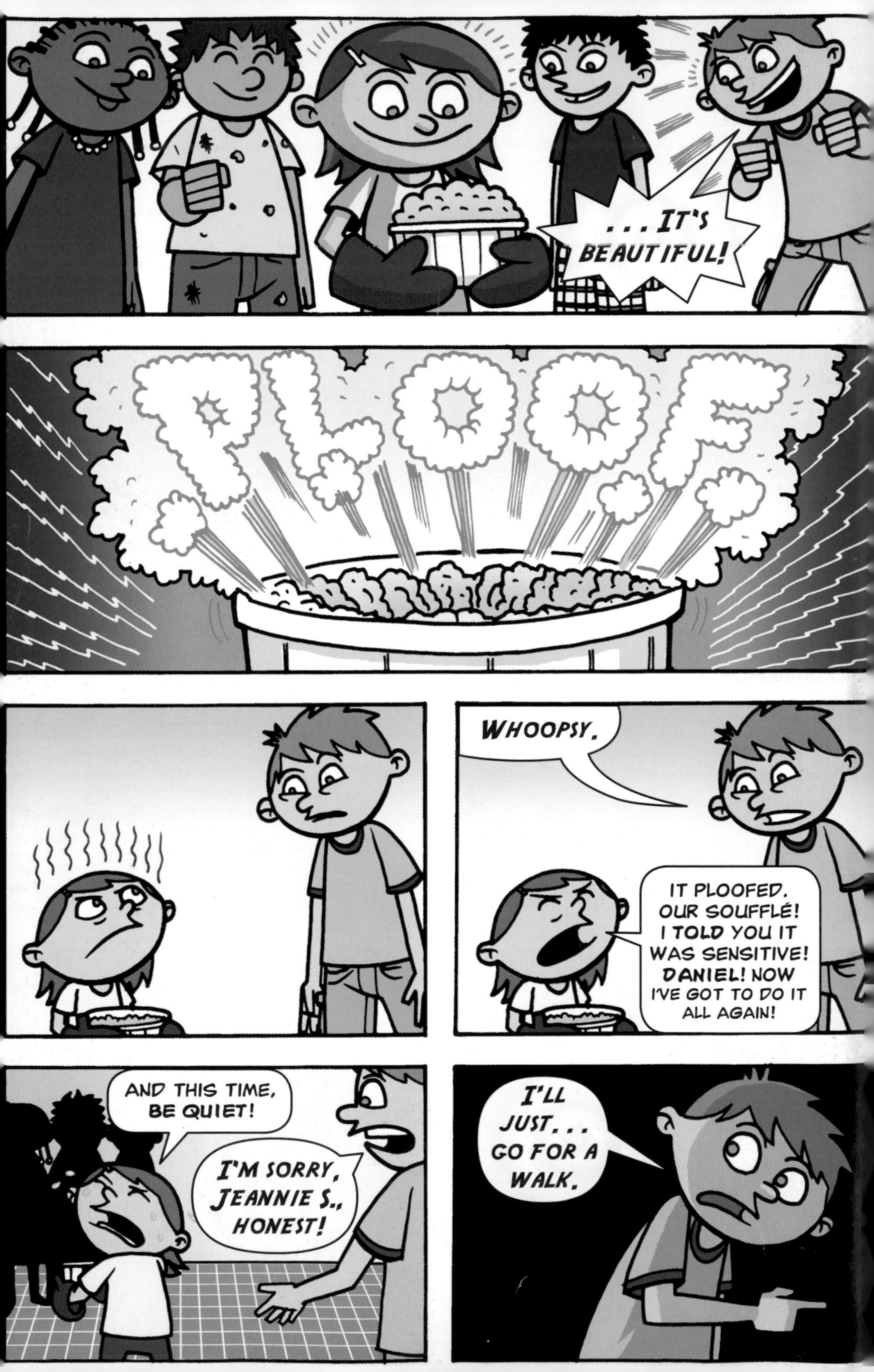

. . . IT'S BEAUTIFUL!
PLOOF
WHOOPSY.
IT PLOOFED. OUR SOUFFLÉ! I TOLD YOU IT WAS SENSITIVE! DANIEL! NOW I'VE GOT TO DO IT ALL AGAIN!
AND THIS TIME, BE QUIET!
I'M SORRY, JEANNIE S., HONEST!
I'LL JUST. . . GO FOR A WALK.

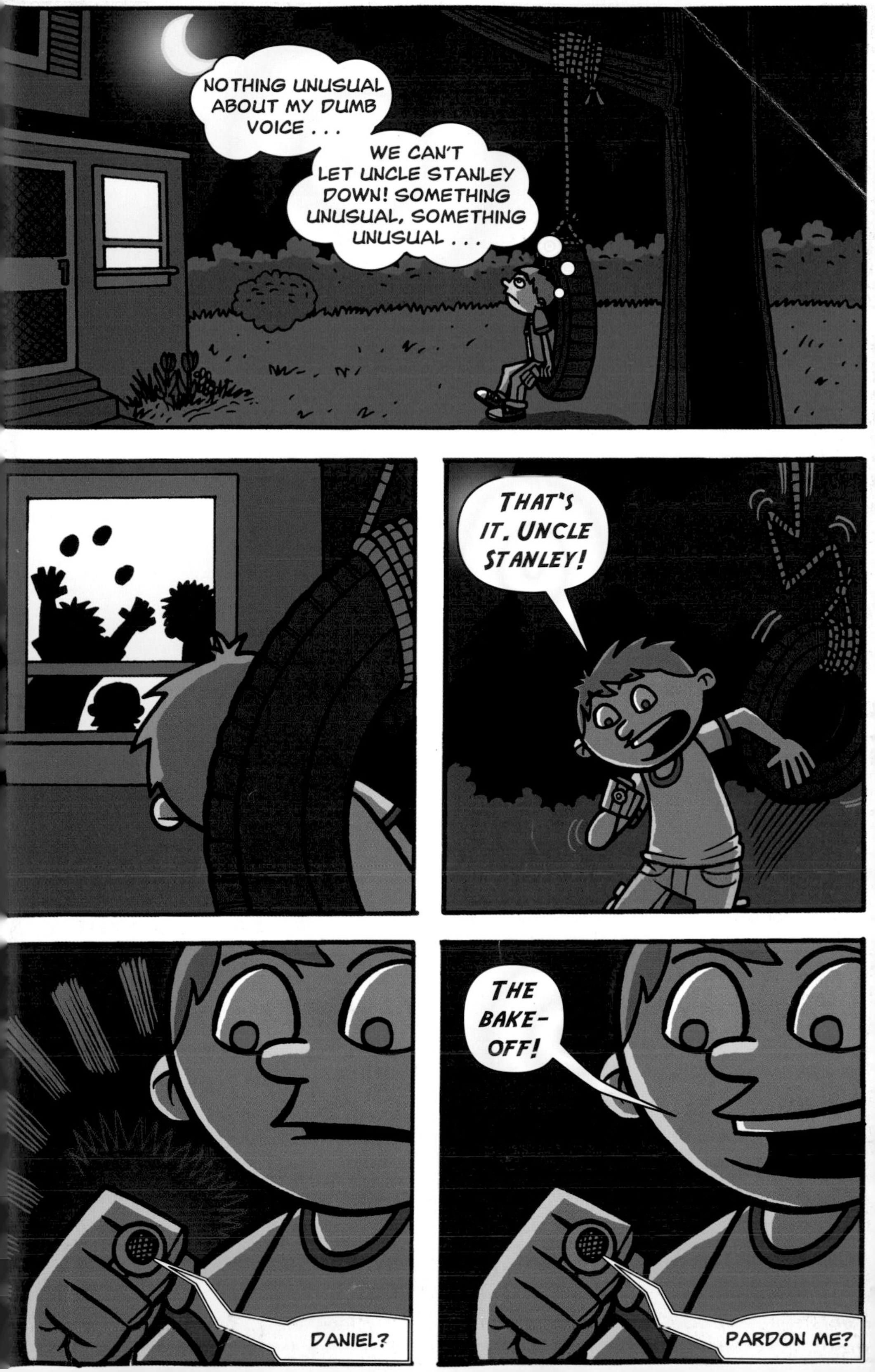
NOTHING UNUSUAL ABOUT MY DUMB VOICE . . .
WE CAN'T LET UNCLE STANLEY DOWN! SOMETHING UNUSUAL, SOMETHING UNUSUAL . . .
THAT'S IT. UNCLE STANLEY!
DANIEL?
THE BAKE-OFF!
PARDON ME?

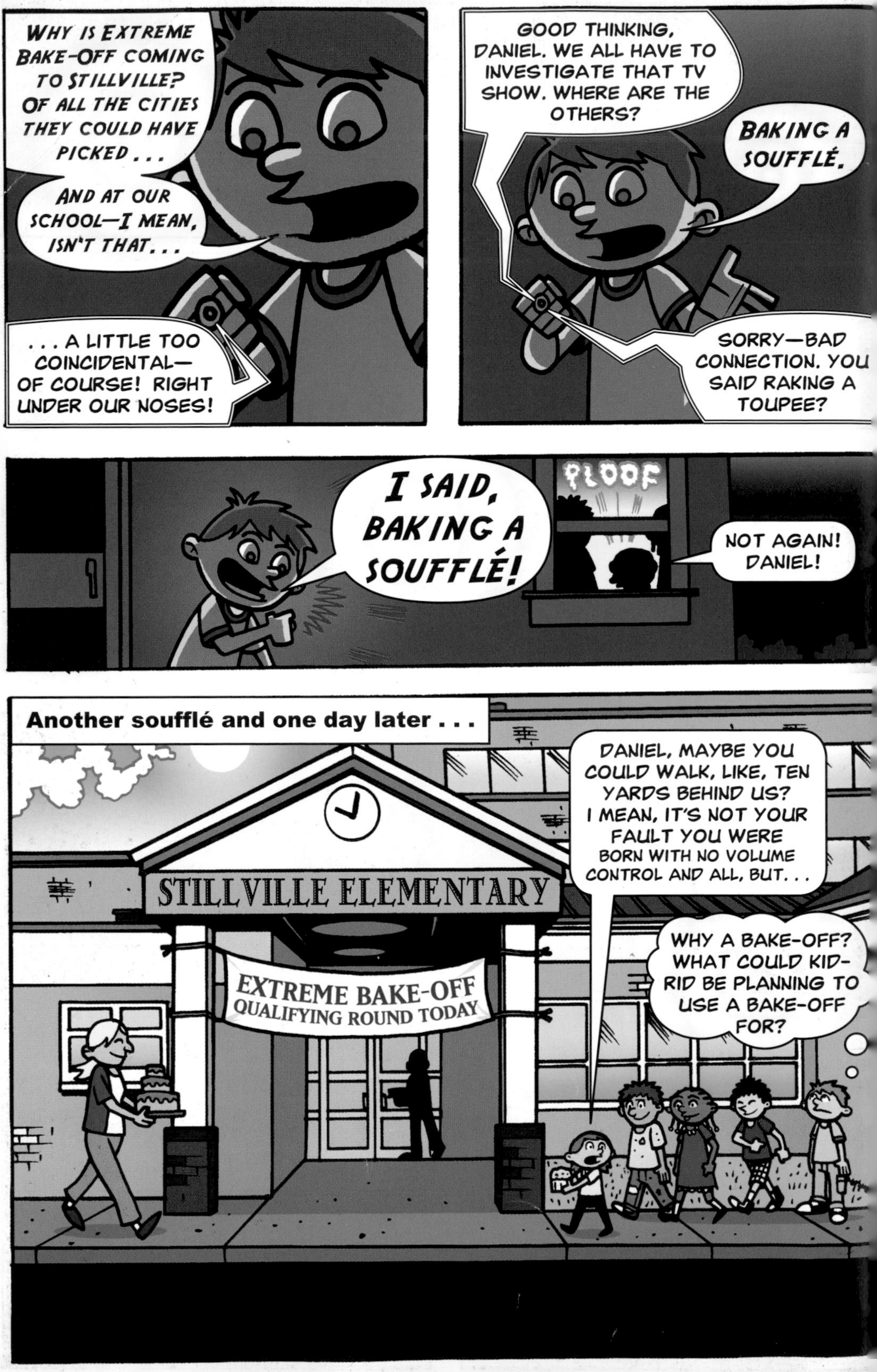
WHY IS EXTREME BAKE-OFF COMING TO STILLVILLE? OF ALL THE CITIES THEY COULD HAVE PICKED . . .
AND AT OUR SCHOOL—I MEAN, ISN'T THAT . . .
. . . A LITTLE TOO COINCIDENTAL—OF COURSE! RIGHT UNDER OUR NOSES!
GOOD THINKING, DANIEL. WE ALL HAVE TO INVESTIGATE THAT TV SHOW. WHERE ARE THE OTHERS?
BAKING A SOUFFLÉ.
SORRY—BAD CONNECTION. YOU SAID RAKING A TOUPEE?
I SAID, BAKING A SOUFFLÉ!
PLOOF
NOT AGAIN! DANIEL!
Another soufflé and one day later . . .
STILLVILLE ELEMENTARY
EXTREME BAKE-OFF QUALIFYING ROUND TODAY
DANIEL, MAYBE YOU COULD WALK, LIKE, TEN YARDS BEHIND US? I MEAN, IT'S NOT YOUR FAULT YOU WERE BORN WITH NO VOLUME CONTROL AND ALL, BUT. . .
WHY A BAKE-OFF? WHAT COULD KID-RID BE PLANNING TO USE A BAKE-OFF FOR?

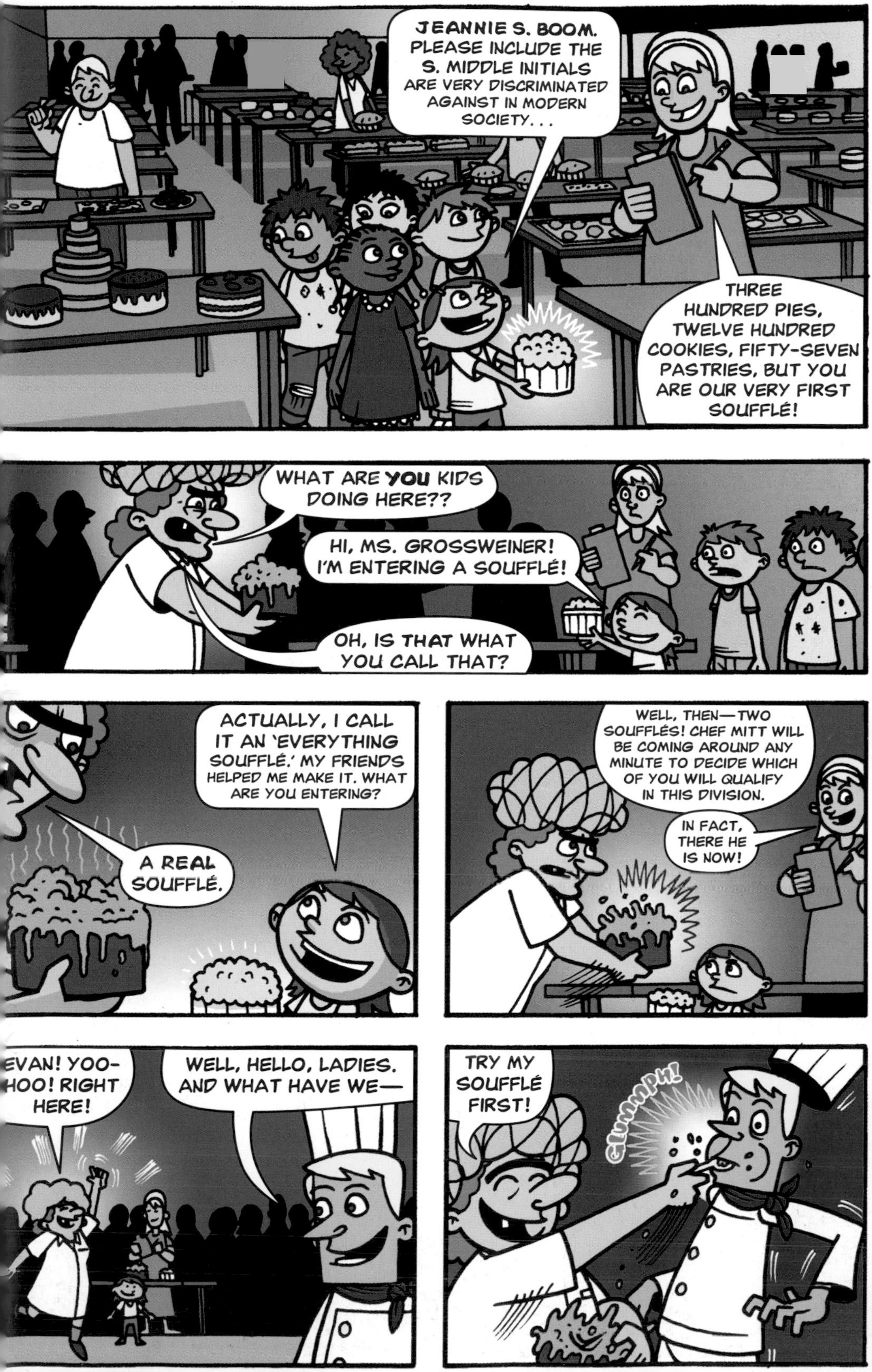
JEANNIE S. BOOM. PLEASE INCLUDE THE S. MIDDLE INITIALS ARE VERY DISCRIMINATED AGAINST IN MODERN SOCIETY. . .
THREE HUNDRED PIES, TWELVE HUNDRED COOKIES, FIFTY-SEVEN PASTRIES, BUT YOU ARE OUR VERY FIRST SOUFFLÉ!
WHAT ARE **YOU** KIDS DOING HERE??
HI, MS. GROSSWEINER! I'M ENTERING A SOUFFLÉ!
OH, IS THAT WHAT YOU CALL THAT?
ACTUALLY, I CALL IT AN 'EVERYTHING SOUFFLÉ.' MY FRIENDS HELPED ME MAKE IT. WHAT ARE YOU ENTERING?
A REAL SOUFFLÉ.
WELL, THEN—TWO SOUFFLÉS! CHEF MITT WILL BE COMING AROUND ANY MINUTE TO DECIDE WHICH OF YOU WILL QUALIFY IN THIS DIVISION.
IN FACT, THERE HE IS NOW!
EVAN! YOO-HOO! RIGHT HERE!
WELL, HELLO, LADIES. AND WHAT HAVE WE—
TRY MY SOUFFLÉ FIRST!
GLUMMPH!

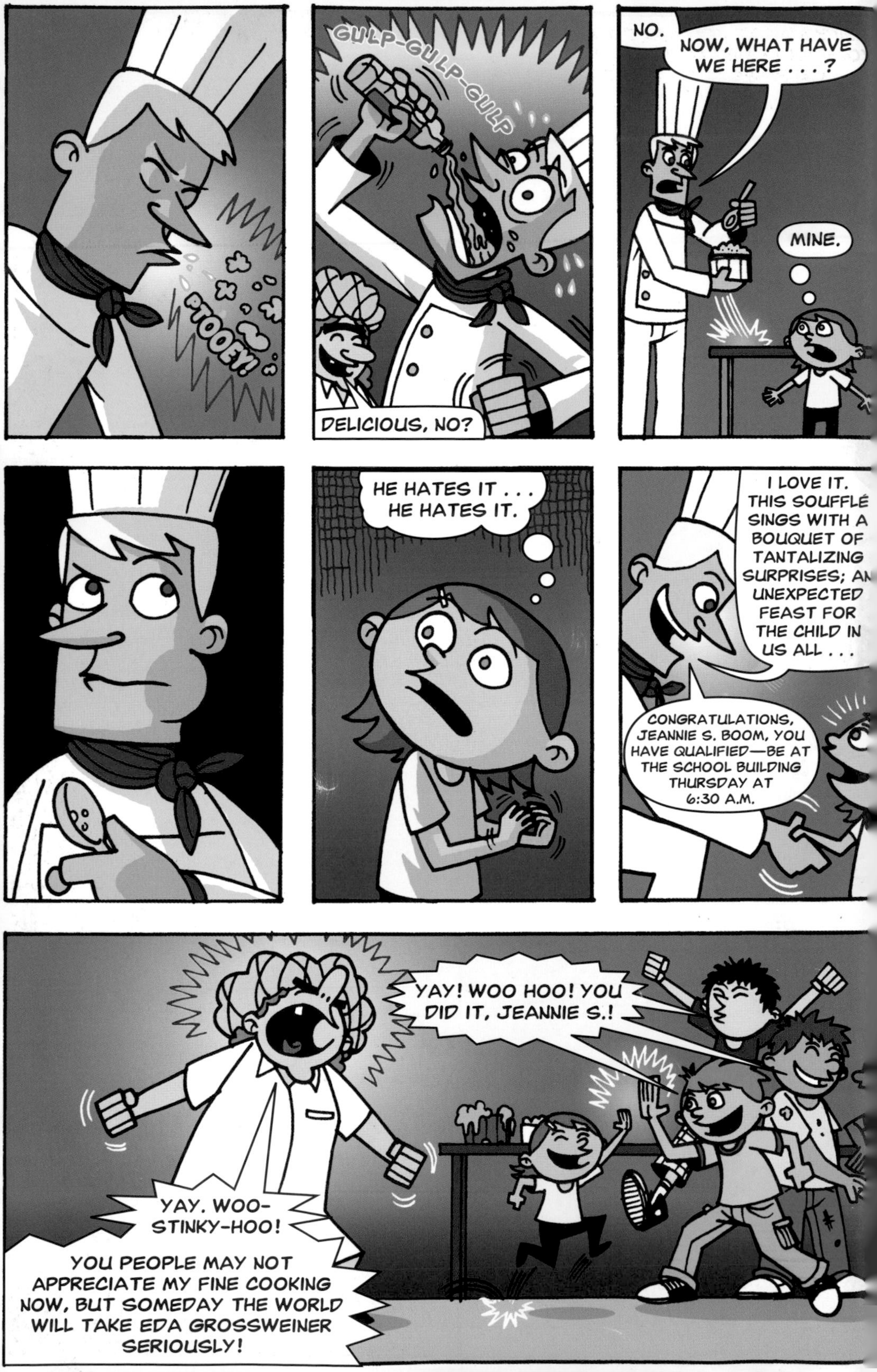
PTOOEY!
GULP-GULP-GULP-GULP
DELICIOUS, NO?
NO.
NOW, WHAT HAVE WE HERE . . . ?
MINE.
HE HATES IT . . . HE HATES IT.
I LOVE IT. THIS SOUFFLÉ SINGS WITH A BOUQUET OF TANTALIZING SURPRISES; AN UNEXPECTED FEAST FOR THE CHILD IN US ALL . . .
CONGRATULATIONS, JEANNIE S. BOOM, YOU HAVE QUALIFIED—BE AT THE SCHOOL BUILDING THURSDAY AT 6:30 A.M.
YAY! WOO HOO! YOU DID IT, JEANNIE S.!
YAY. WOO-STINKY-HOO!
YOU PEOPLE MAY NOT APPRECIATE MY FINE COOKING NOW, BUT SOMEDAY THE WORLD WILL TAKE EDA GROSSWEINER SERIOUSLY!

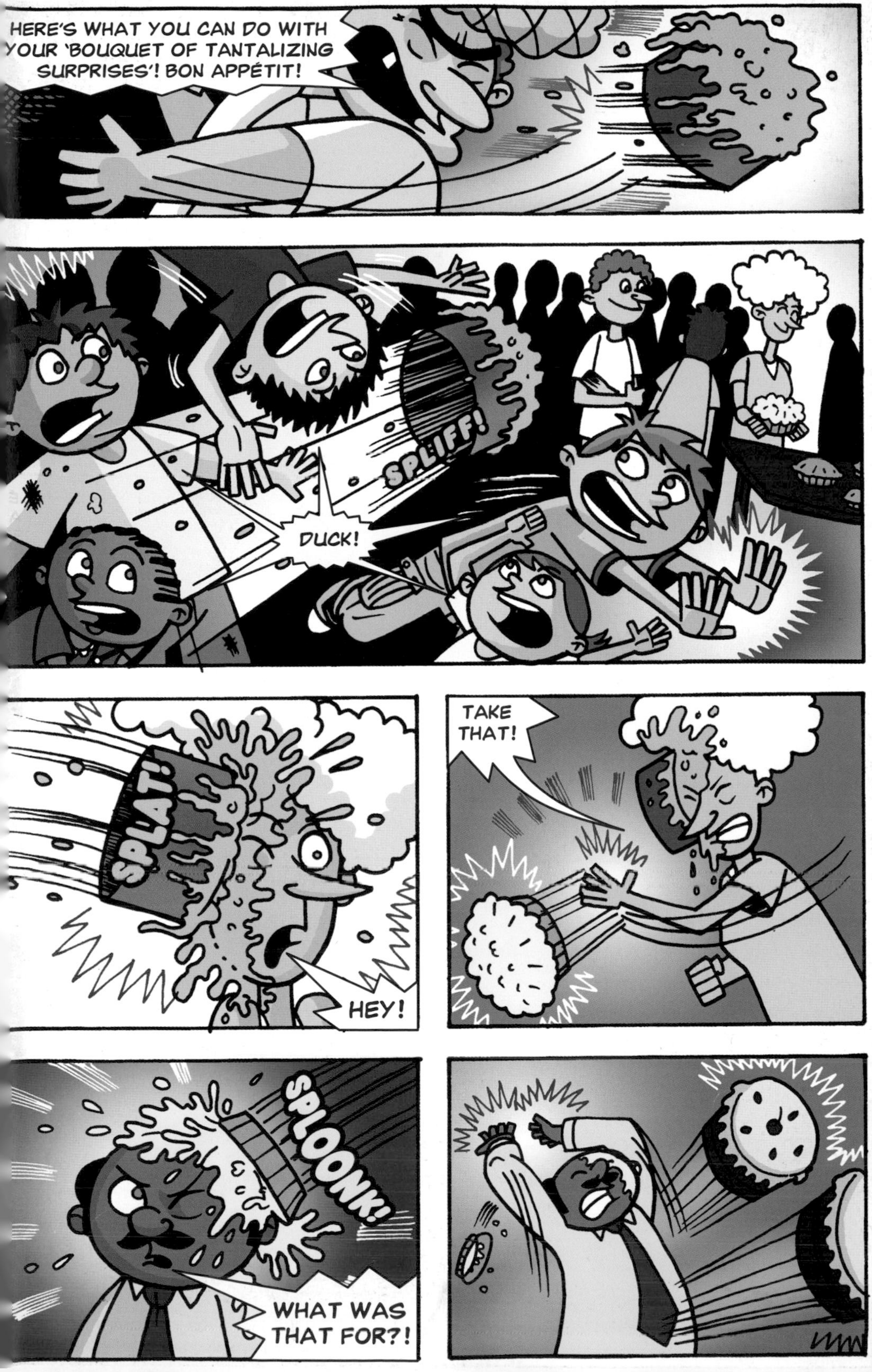
HERE'S WHAT YOU CAN DO WITH YOUR 'BOUQUET OF TANTALIZING SURPRISES'! BON APPÉTIT!
SPLIFF!
DUCK!
SPLAT!
HEY!
TAKE THAT!
SPLOONK!
WHAT WAS THAT FOR?!

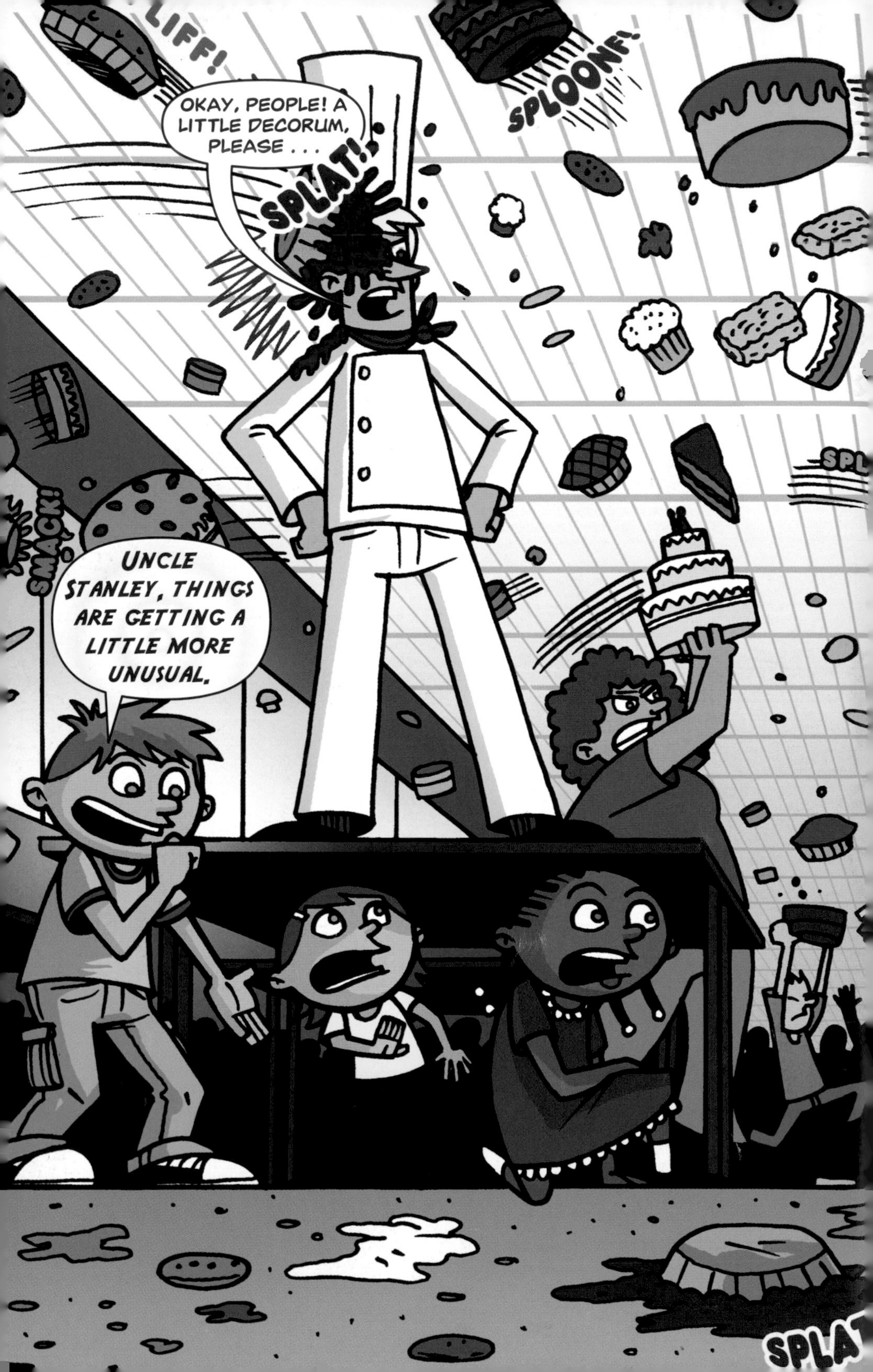
LIFF!
SPLOONF!
OKAY, PEOPLE! A LITTLE DECORUM, PLEASE . . .
SPLAT!
SMACK!
UNCLE STANLEY, THINGS ARE GETTING A LITTLE MORE UNUSUAL.
SPLAT

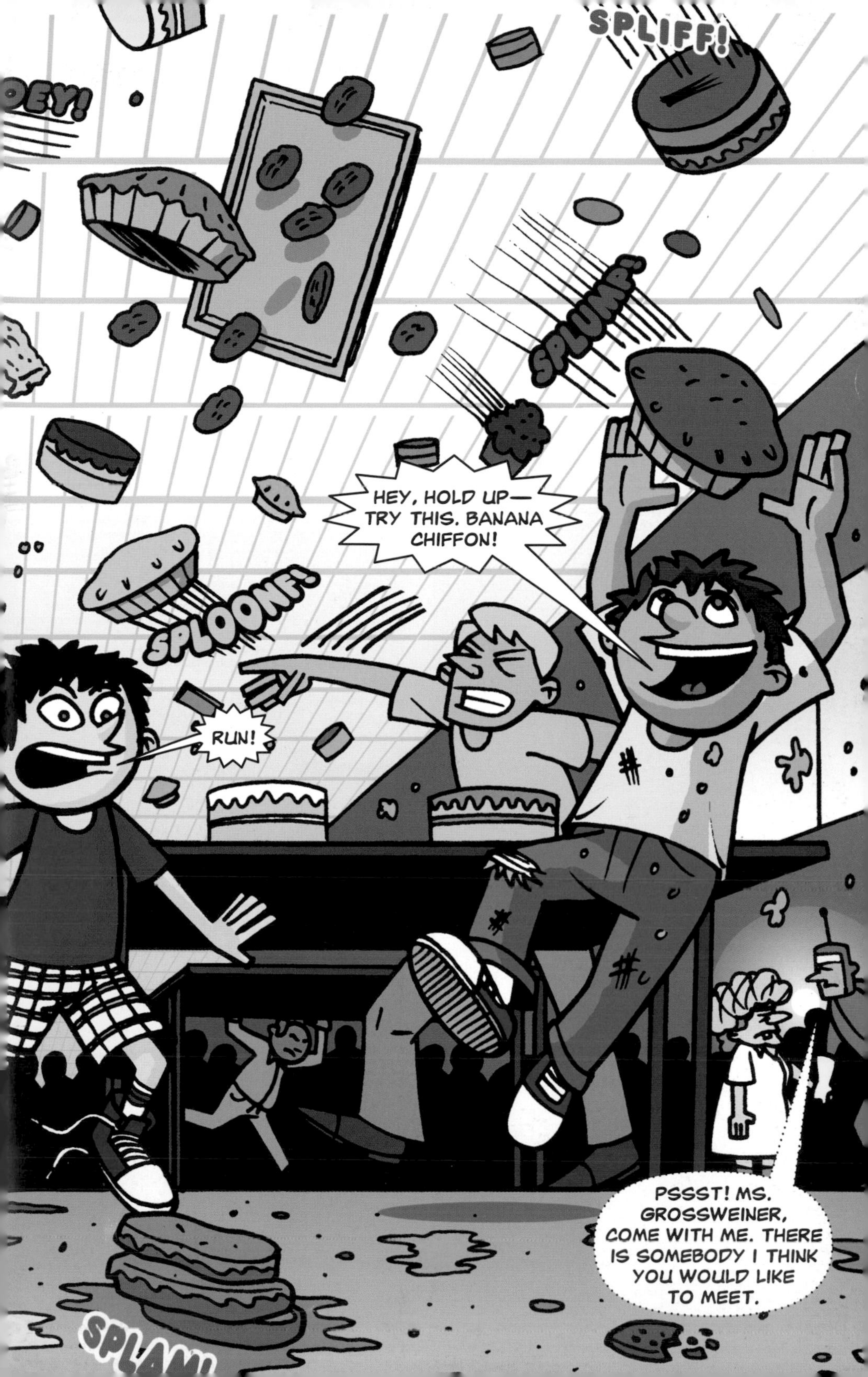
SPLIFF!
OEY!
SPLUMP!
HEY, HOLD UP—
TRY THIS. BANANA
CHIFFON!
SPLOONF!
RUN!
PSSST! MS. GROSSWEINER, COME WITH ME. THERE IS SOMEBODY I THINK YOU WOULD LIKE TO MEET.
SPLAM!

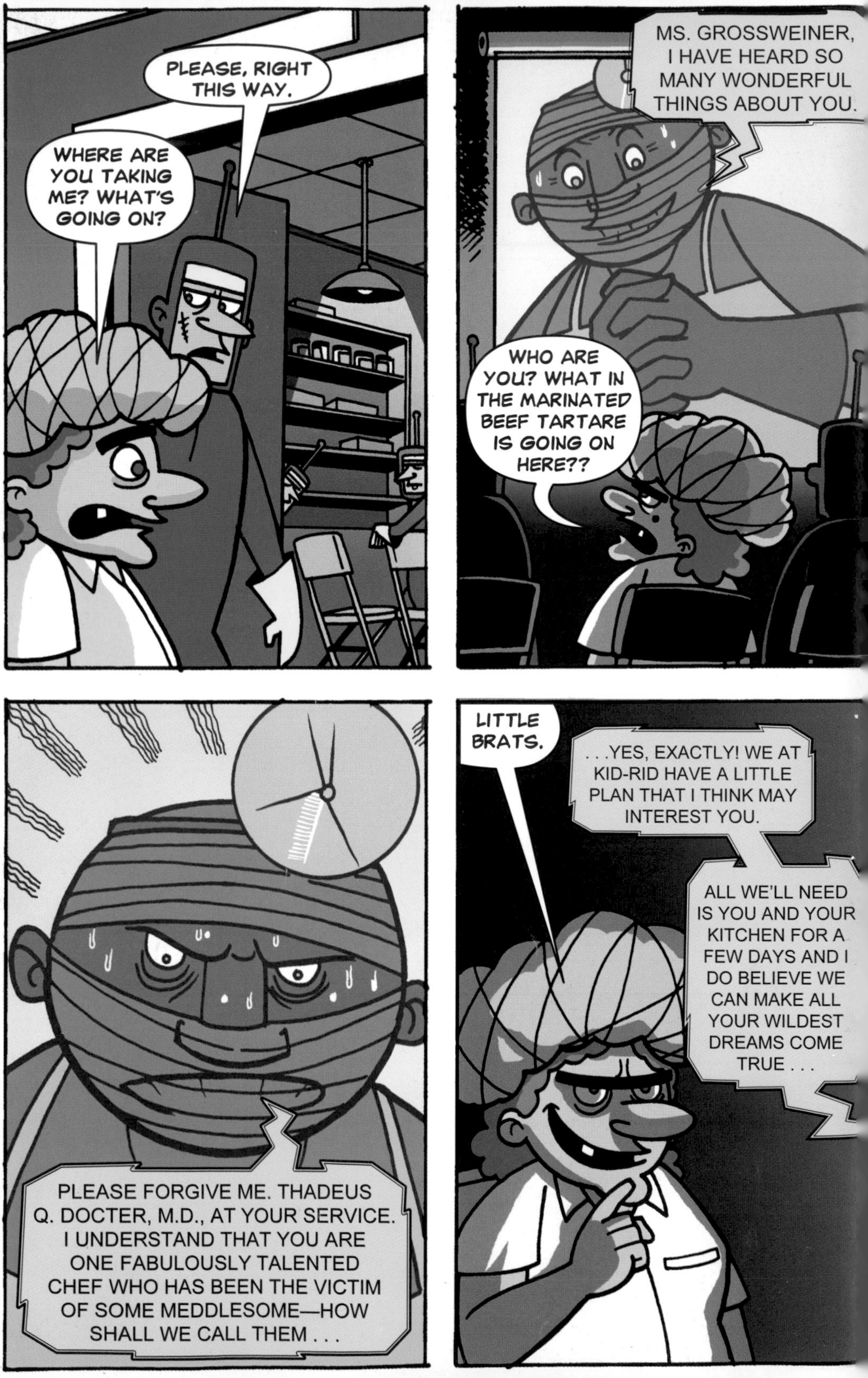

PLEASE, RIGHT THIS WAY.
WHERE ARE YOU TAKING ME? WHAT'S GOING ON?
MS. GROSSWEINER, I HAVE HEARD SO MANY WONDERFUL THINGS ABOUT YOU.
WHO ARE YOU? WHAT IN THE MARINATED BEEF TARTARE IS GOING ON HERE??
PLEASE FORGIVE ME. THADEUS Q. DOCTER, M.D., AT YOUR SERVICE. I UNDERSTAND THAT YOU ARE ONE FABULOUSLY TALENTED CHEF WHO HAS BEEN THE VICTIM OF SOME MEDDLESOME—HOW SHALL WE CALL THEM . . .
LITTLE BRATS.
. . .YES, EXACTLY! WE AT KID-RID HAVE A LITTLE PLAN THAT I THINK MAY INTEREST YOU.
ALL WE'LL NEED IS YOU AND YOUR KITCHEN FOR A FEW DAYS AND I DO BELIEVE WE CAN MAKE ALL YOUR WILDEST DREAMS COME TRUE . . .

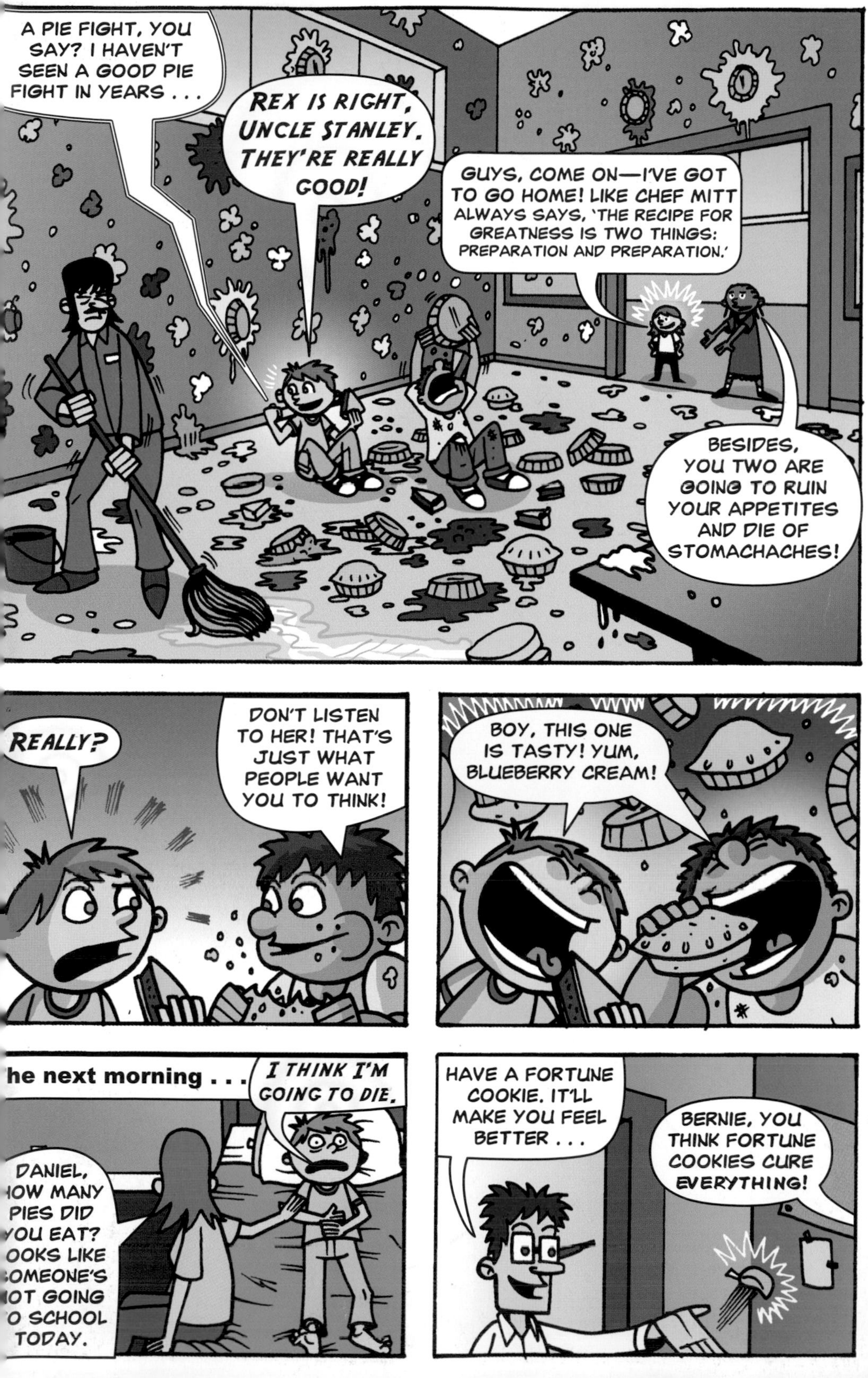
A PIE FIGHT, YOU SAY? I HAVEN'T SEEN A GOOD PIE FIGHT IN YEARS . . .
REX IS RIGHT, UNCLE STANLEY. THEY'RE REALLY GOOD!
GUYS, COME ON—I'VE GOT TO GO HOME! LIKE CHEF MITT ALWAYS SAYS, 'THE RECIPE FOR GREATNESS IS TWO THINGS: PREPARATION AND PREPARATION.'
BESIDES, YOU TWO ARE GOING TO RUIN YOUR APPETITES AND DIE OF STOMACHACHES!
REALLY?
DON'T LISTEN TO HER! THAT'S JUST WHAT PEOPLE WANT YOU TO THINK!
BOY, THIS ONE IS TASTY! YUM, BLUEBERRY CREAM!
he next morning . . .
I THINK I'M GOING TO DIE.
DANIEL, HOW MANY PIES DID YOU EAT? LOOKS LIKE SOMEONE'S NOT GOING TO SCHOOL TODAY.
HAVE A FORTUNE COOKIE. IT'LL MAKE YOU FEEL BETTER . . .
BERNIE, YOU THINK FORTUNE COOKIES CURE EVERYTHING!

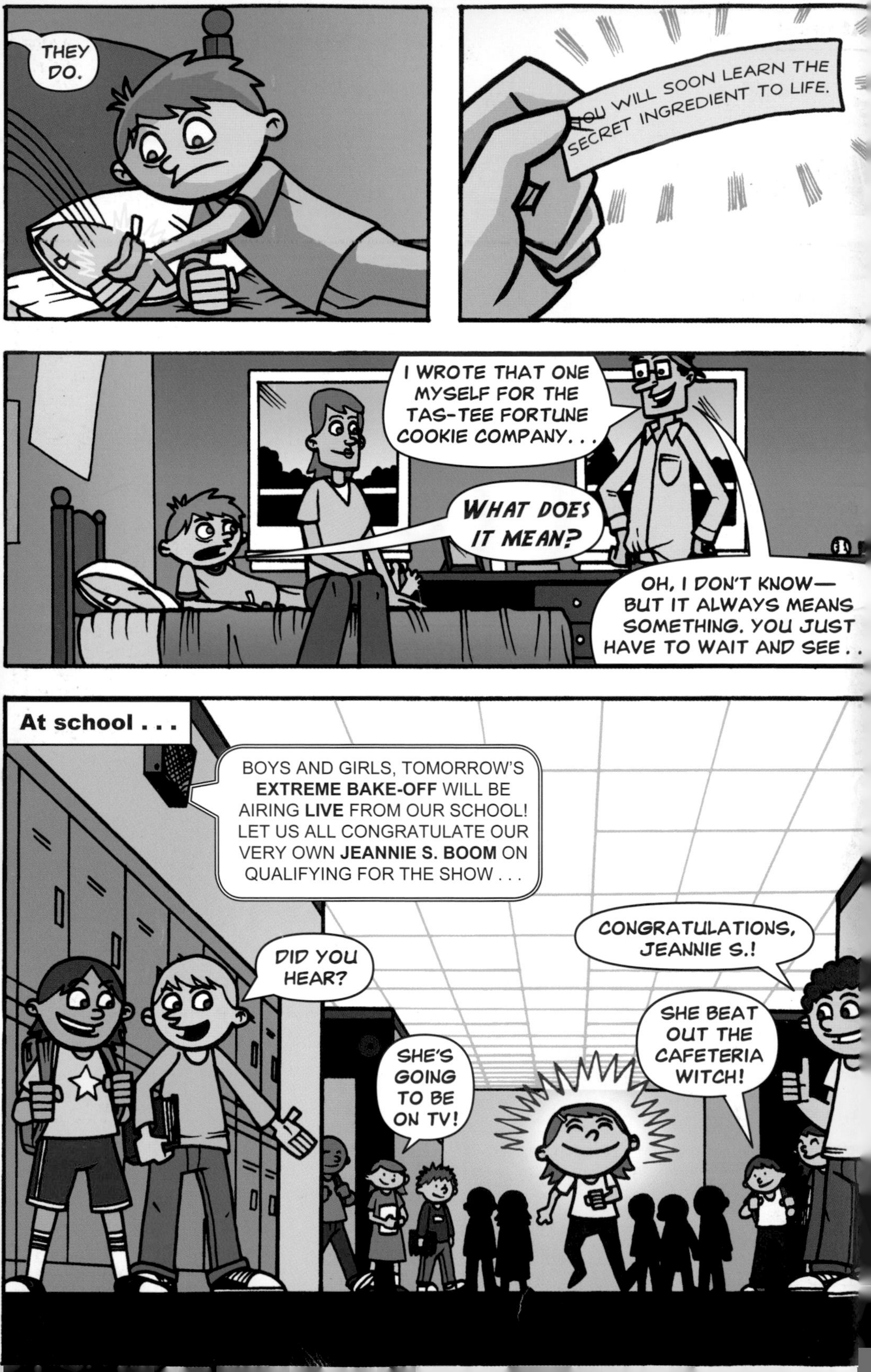

THEY DO.
YOU WILL SOON LEARN THE SECRET INGREDIENT TO LIFE.
I WROTE THAT ONE MYSELF FOR THE TAS-TEE FORTUNE COOKIE COMPANY. . .
WHAT DOES IT MEAN?
OH, I DON'T KNOW— BUT IT ALWAYS MEANS SOMETHING. YOU JUST HAVE TO WAIT AND SEE . .
At school . . .
BOYS AND GIRLS, TOMORROW'S EXTREME BAKE-OFF WILL BE AIRING LIVE FROM OUR SCHOOL! LET US ALL CONGRATULATE OUR VERY OWN JEANNIE S. BOOM ON QUALIFYING FOR THE SHOW . . .
DID YOU HEAR?
SHE'S GOING TO BE ON TV!
SHE BEAT OUT THE CAFETERIA WITCH!
CONGRATULATIONS, JEANNIE S.!

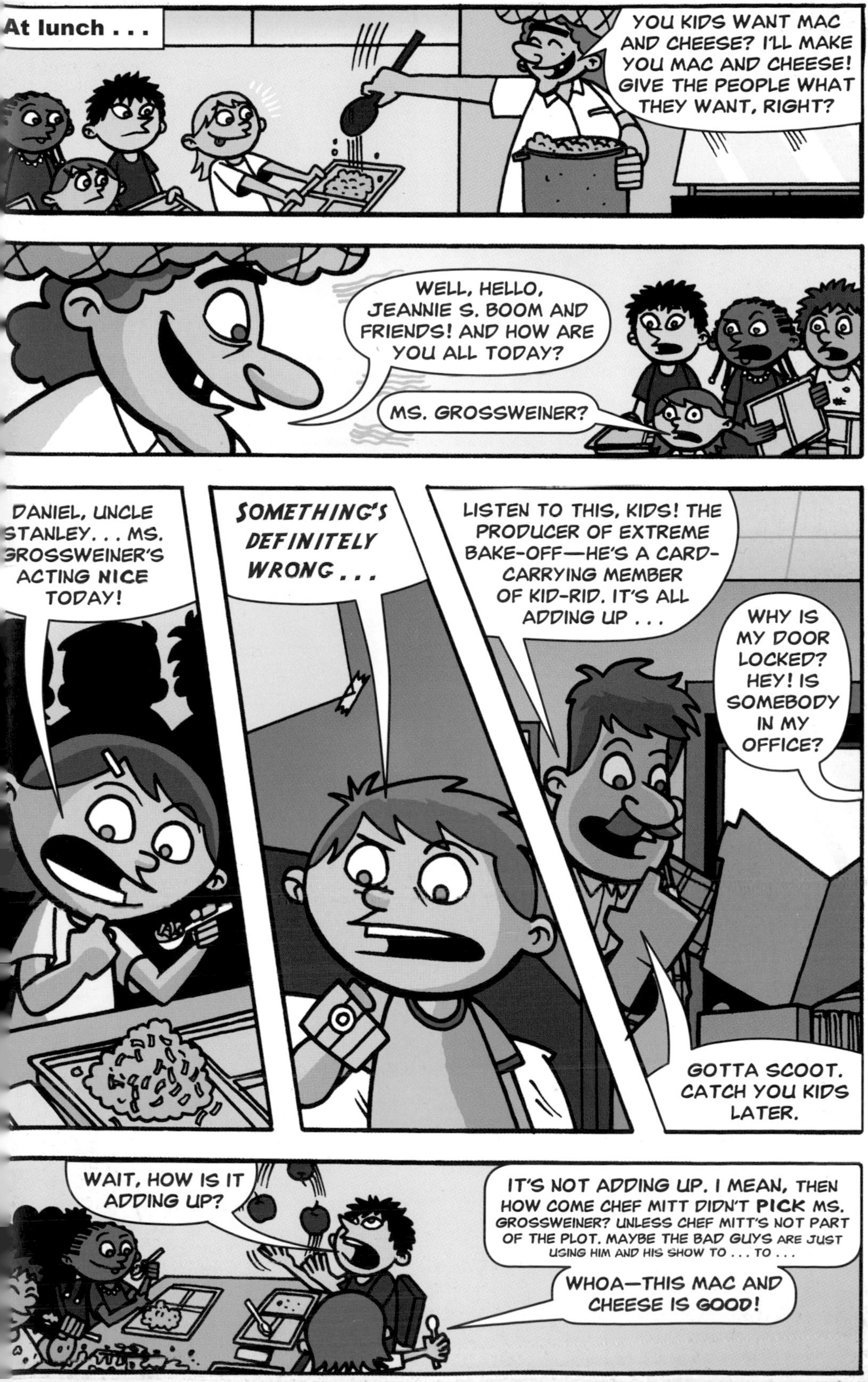
At lunch . . .
YOU KIDS WANT MAC AND CHEESE? I'LL MAKE YOU MAC AND CHEESE! GIVE THE PEOPLE WHAT THEY WANT, RIGHT?
WELL, HELLO, JEANNIE S. BOOM AND FRIENDS! AND HOW ARE YOU ALL TODAY?
MS. GROSSWEINER?
DANIEL, UNCLE STANLEY . . . MS. GROSSWEINER'S ACTING NICE TODAY!
SOMETHING'S DEFINITELY WRONG . . .
LISTEN TO THIS, KIDS! THE PRODUCER OF EXTREME BAKE-OFF—HE'S A CARD-CARRYING MEMBER OF KID-RID. IT'S ALL ADDING UP . . .
WHY IS MY DOOR LOCKED? HEY! IS SOMEBODY IN MY OFFICE?
GOTTA SCOOT. CATCH YOU KIDS LATER.
WAIT, HOW IS IT ADDING UP?
IT'S NOT ADDING UP. I MEAN, THEN HOW COME CHEF MITT DIDN'T PICK MS. GROSSWEINER? UNLESS CHEF MITT'S NOT PART OF THE PLOT. MAYBE THE BAD GUYS ARE JUST USING HIM AND HIS SHOW TO . . . TO . . .
WHOA—THIS MAC AND CHEESE IS GOOD!

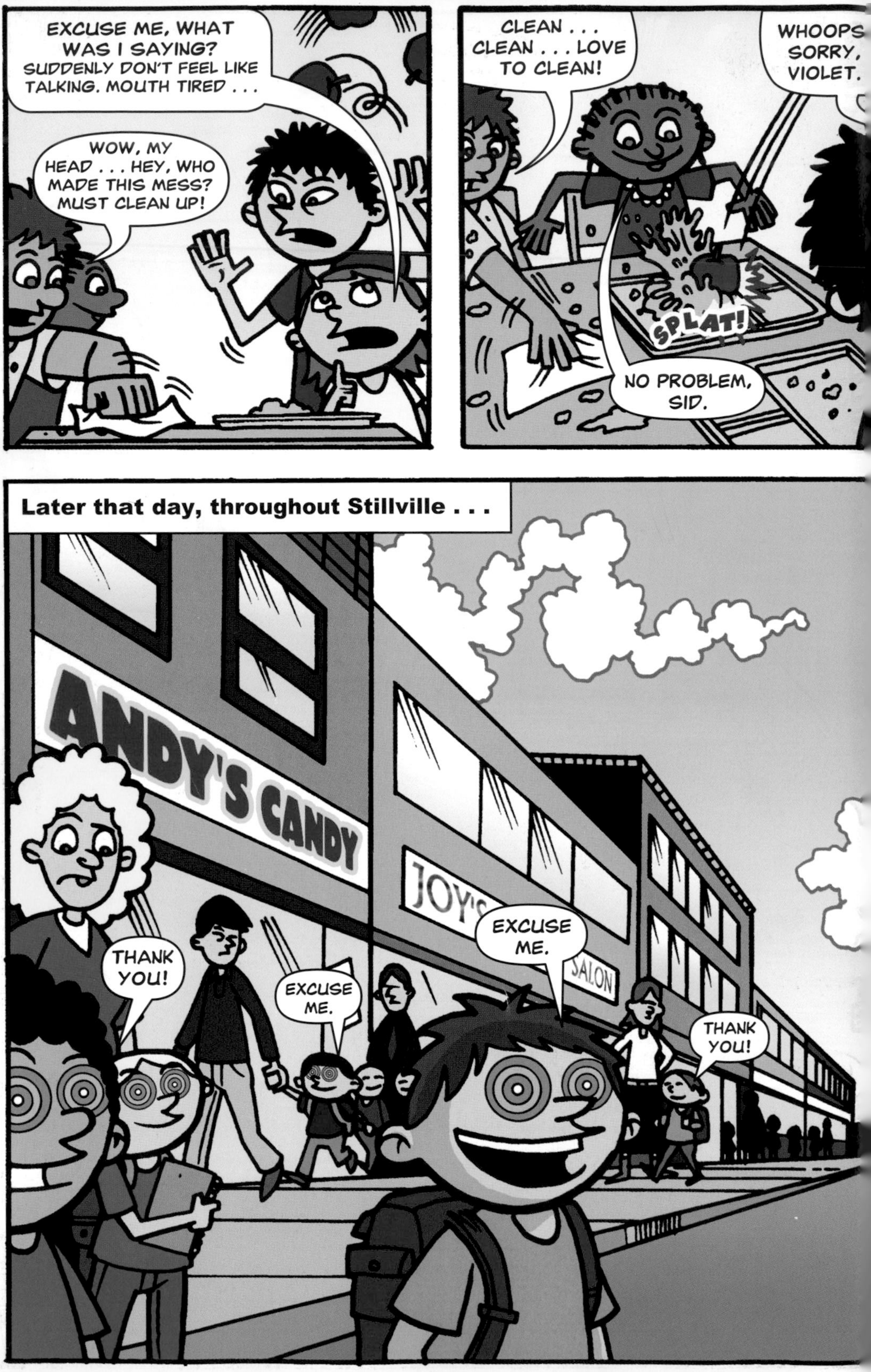
EXCUSE ME, WHAT WAS I SAYING? SUDDENLY DON'T FEEL LIKE TALKING. MOUTH TIRED . . .
WOW, MY HEAD . . . HEY, WHO MADE THIS MESS? MUST CLEAN UP!
CLEAN . . . CLEAN . . . LOVE TO CLEAN!
WHOOPS SORRY, VIOLET.
SPLAT!
NO PROBLEM, SID.
Later that day, throughout Stillville . . .
ANDY'S CANDY
JOY'S
SALON
THANK YOU!
EXCUSE ME.
EXCUSE ME.
THANK YOU!

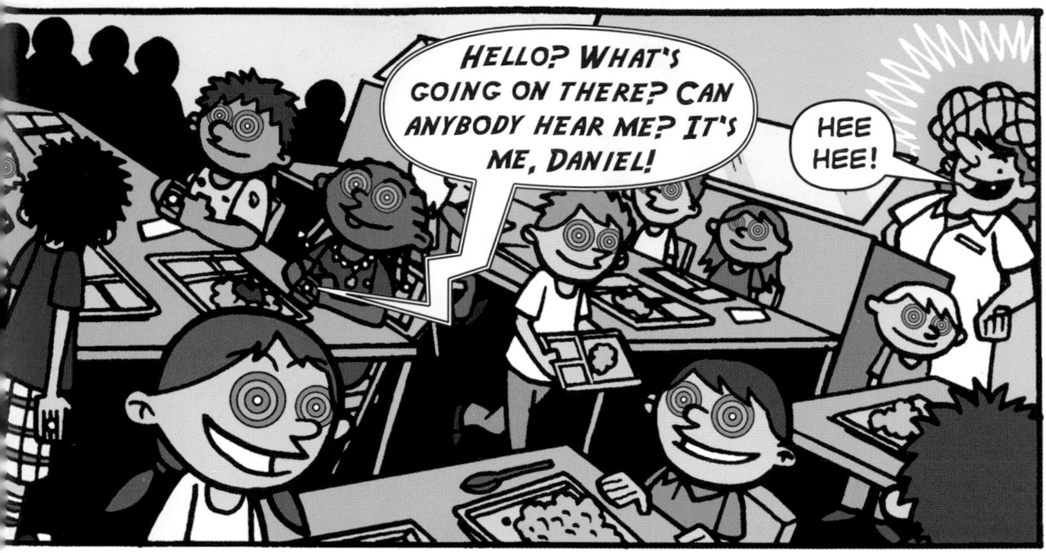
HELLO? WHAT'S GOING ON THERE? CAN ANYBODY HEAR ME? IT'S ME, DANIEL!
HEE HEE!
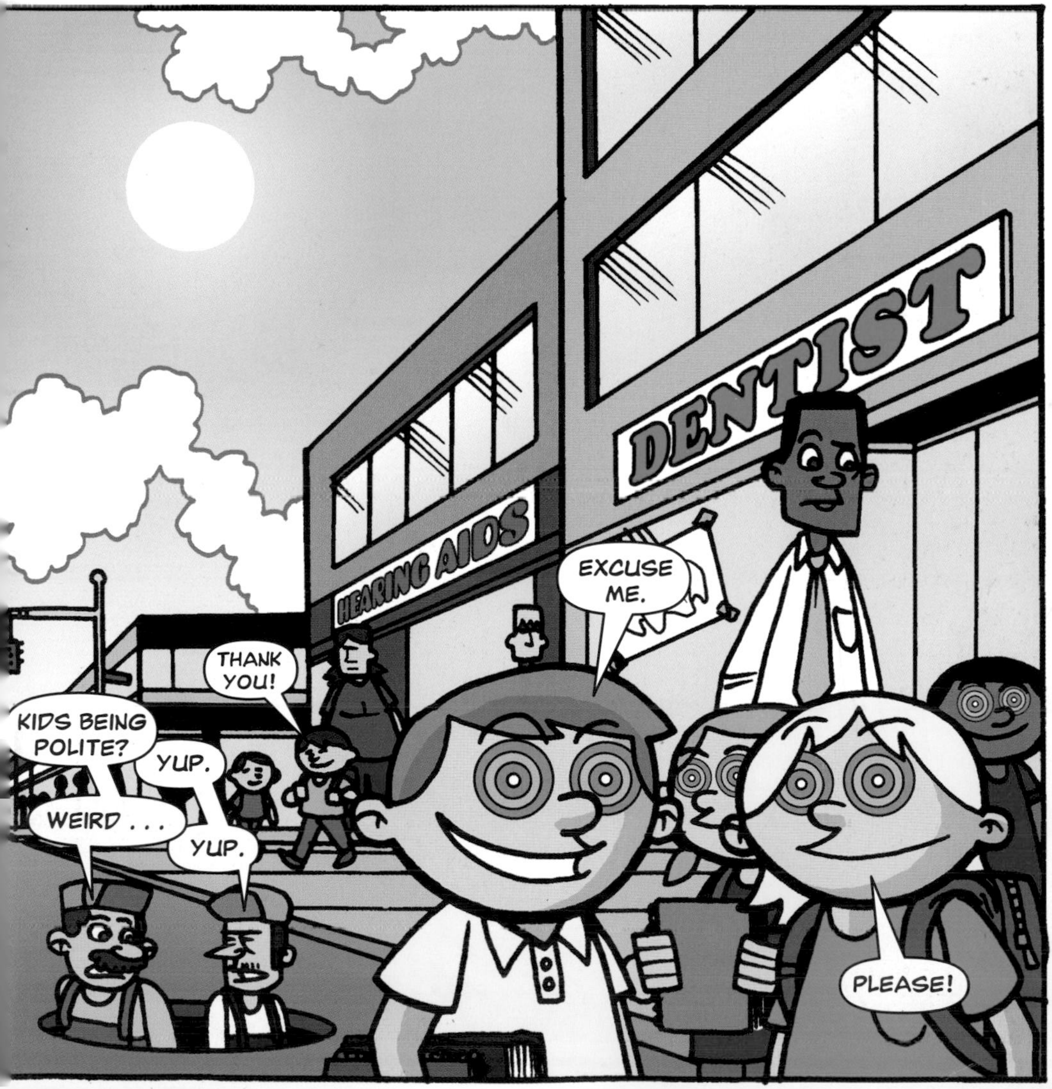
DENTIST
HEARING AIDS
EXCUSE ME.
THANK YOU!
KIDS BEING POLITE?
YUP.
WEIRD . . .
YUP.
PLEASE!

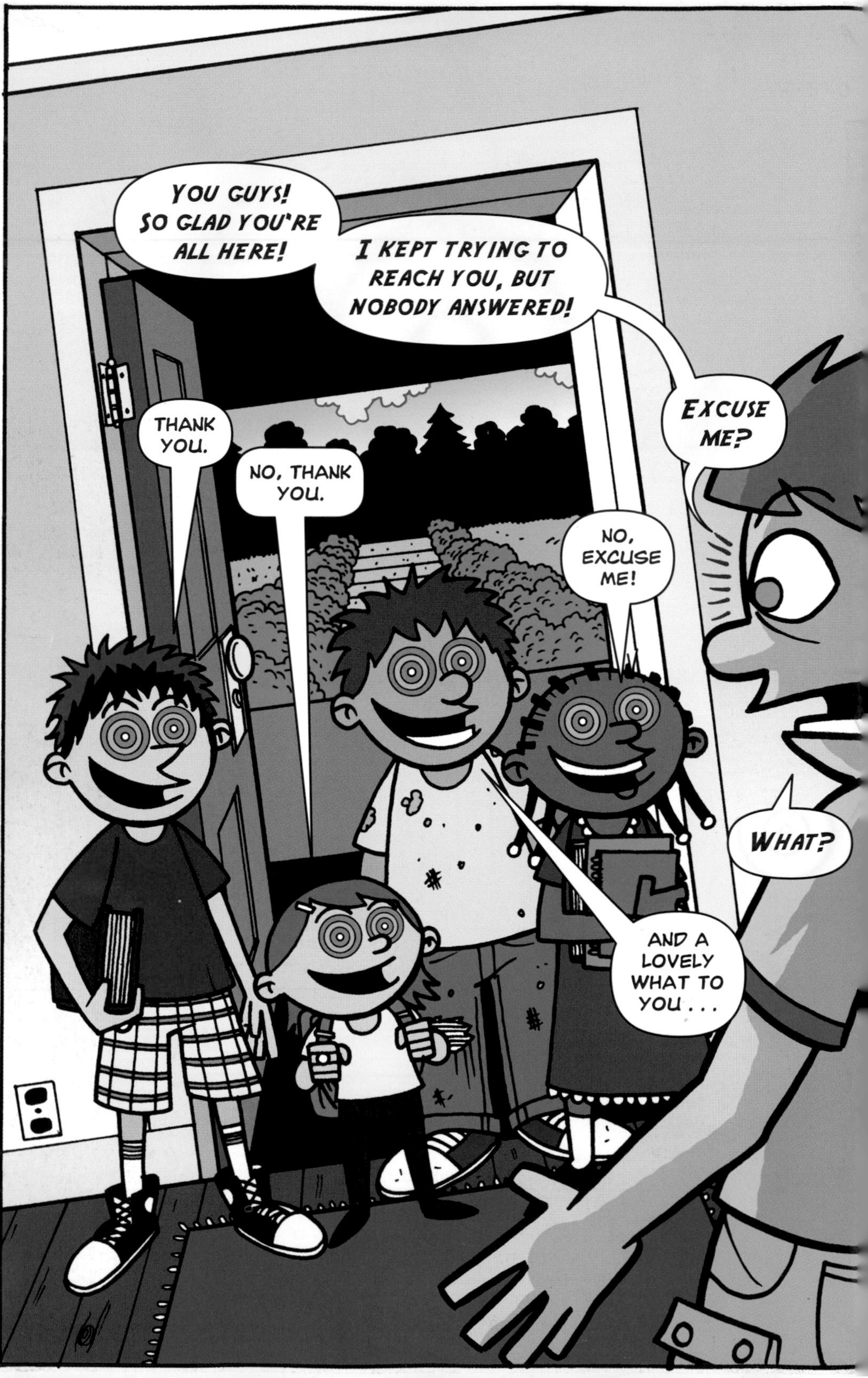
YOU GUYS! SO GLAD YOU'RE ALL HERE!
I KEPT TRYING TO REACH YOU, BUT NOBODY ANSWERED!
EXCUSE ME?
THANK YOU.
NO, THANK YOU.
NO, EXCUSE ME!
WHAT?
AND A LOVELY WHAT TO YOU . . .

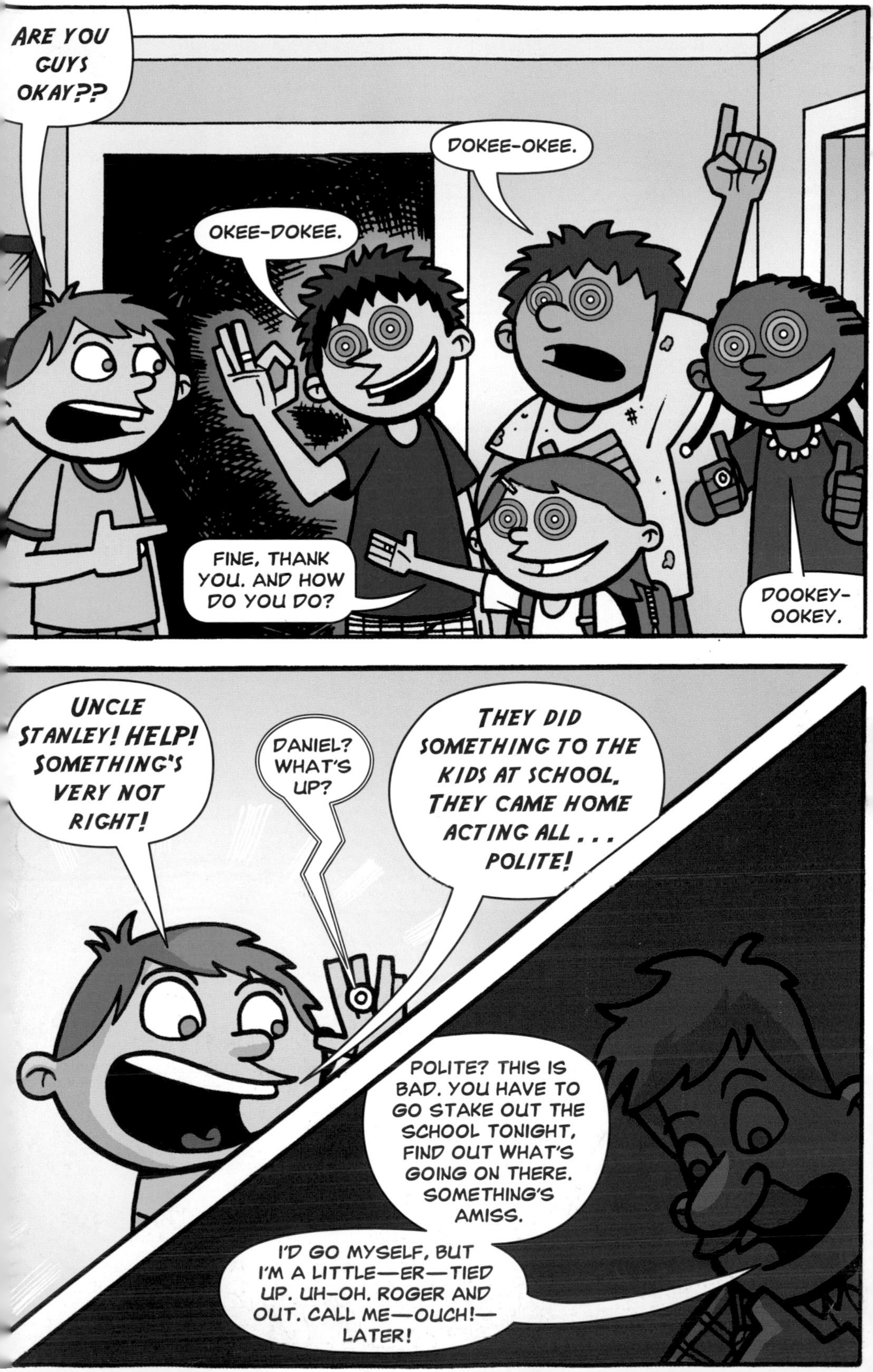
ARE YOU GUYS OKAY??
OKEE-DOKEE.
DOKEE-OKEE.
FINE, THANK YOU. AND HOW DO YOU DO?
DOOKEY-OOKEY.
UNCLE STANLEY! HELP! SOMETHING'S VERY NOT RIGHT!
DANIEL? WHAT'S UP?
THEY DID SOMETHING TO THE KIDS AT SCHOOL. THEY CAME HOME ACTING ALL . . . POLITE!
POLITE? THIS IS BAD. YOU HAVE TO GO STAKE OUT THE SCHOOL TONIGHT, FIND OUT WHAT'S GOING ON THERE. SOMETHING'S AMISS.
I'D GO MYSELF, BUT I'M A LITTLE—ER—TIED UP. UH-OH. ROGER AND OUT. CALL ME—OUCH!—LATER!

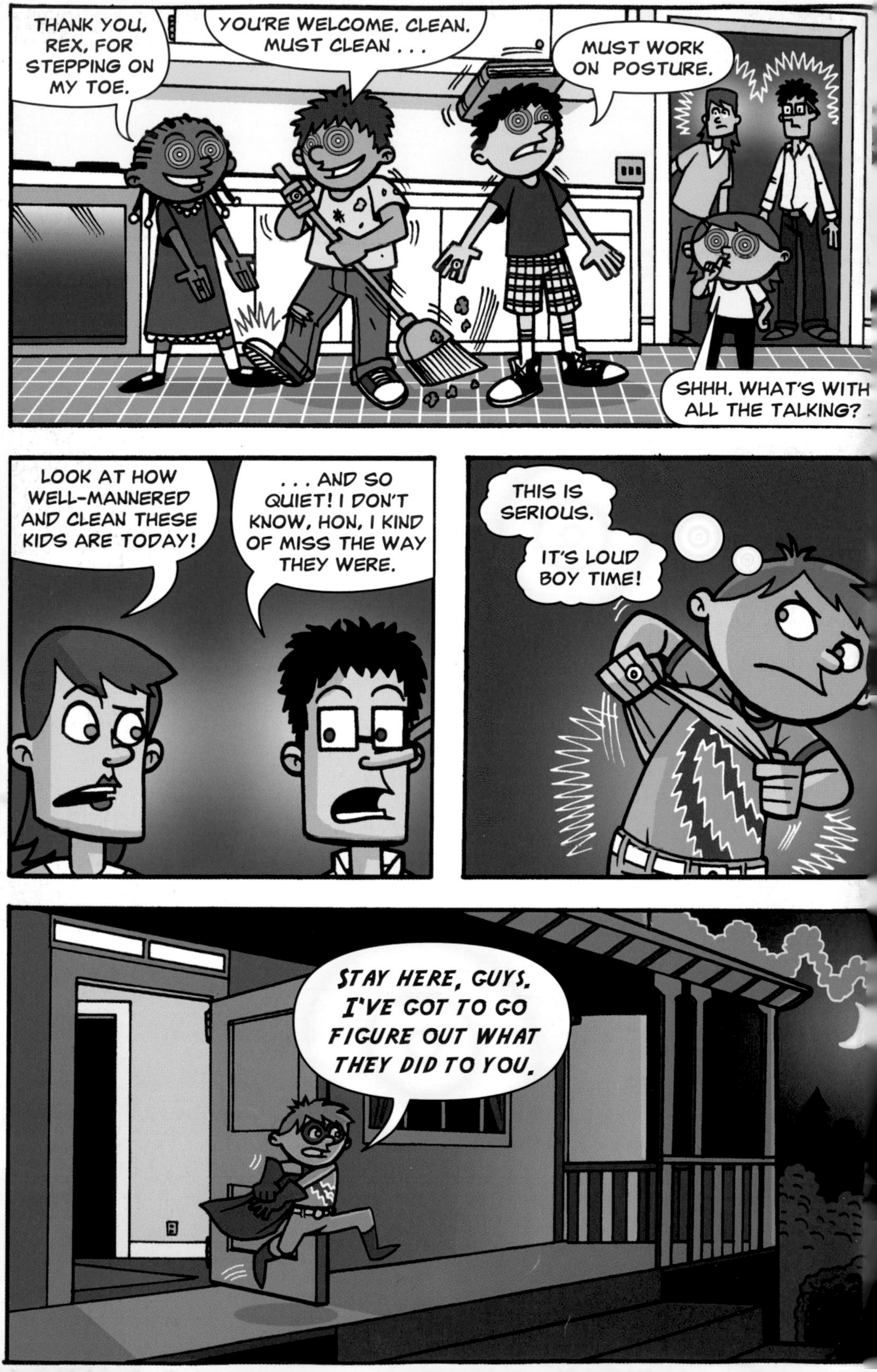
THANK YOU, REX, FOR STEPPING ON MY TOE.
YOU'RE WELCOME. CLEAN. MUST CLEAN . . .
MUST WORK ON POSTURE.
SHHH. WHAT'S WITH ALL THE TALKING?
LOOK AT HOW WELL-MANNERED AND CLEAN THESE KIDS ARE TODAY!
. . . AND SO QUIET! I DON'T KNOW, HON, I KIND OF MISS THE WAY THEY WERE.
THIS IS SERIOUS.
IT'S LOUD BOY TIME!
STAY HERE, GUYS. I'VE GOT TO GO FIGURE OUT WHAT THEY DID TO YOU.

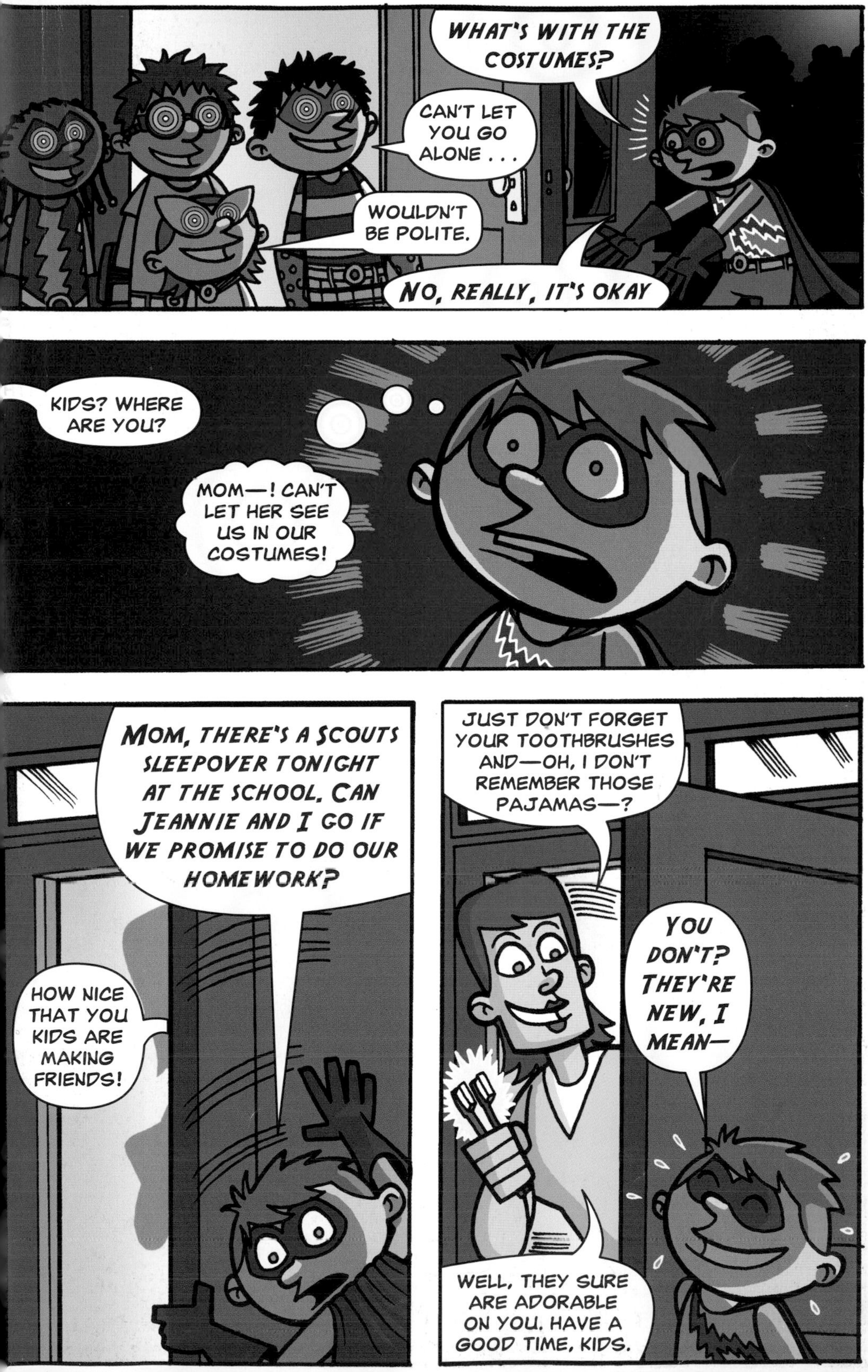
WHAT'S WITH THE COSTUMES?
CAN'T LET YOU GO ALONE . . .
WOULDN'T BE POLITE.
NO, REALLY, IT'S OKAY
KIDS? WHERE ARE YOU?
MOM—! CAN'T LET HER SEE US IN OUR COSTUMES!
MOM, THERE'S A SCOUTS SLEEPOVER TONIGHT AT THE SCHOOL. CAN JEANNIE AND I GO IF WE PROMISE TO DO OUR HOMEWORK?
HOW NICE THAT YOU KIDS ARE MAKING FRIENDS!
JUST DON'T FORGET YOUR TOOTHBRUSHES AND—OH, I DON'T REMEMBER THOSE PAJAMAS—?
YOU DON'T? THEY'RE NEW, I MEAN—
WELL, THEY SURE ARE ADORABLE ON YOU. HAVE A GOOD TIME, KIDS.

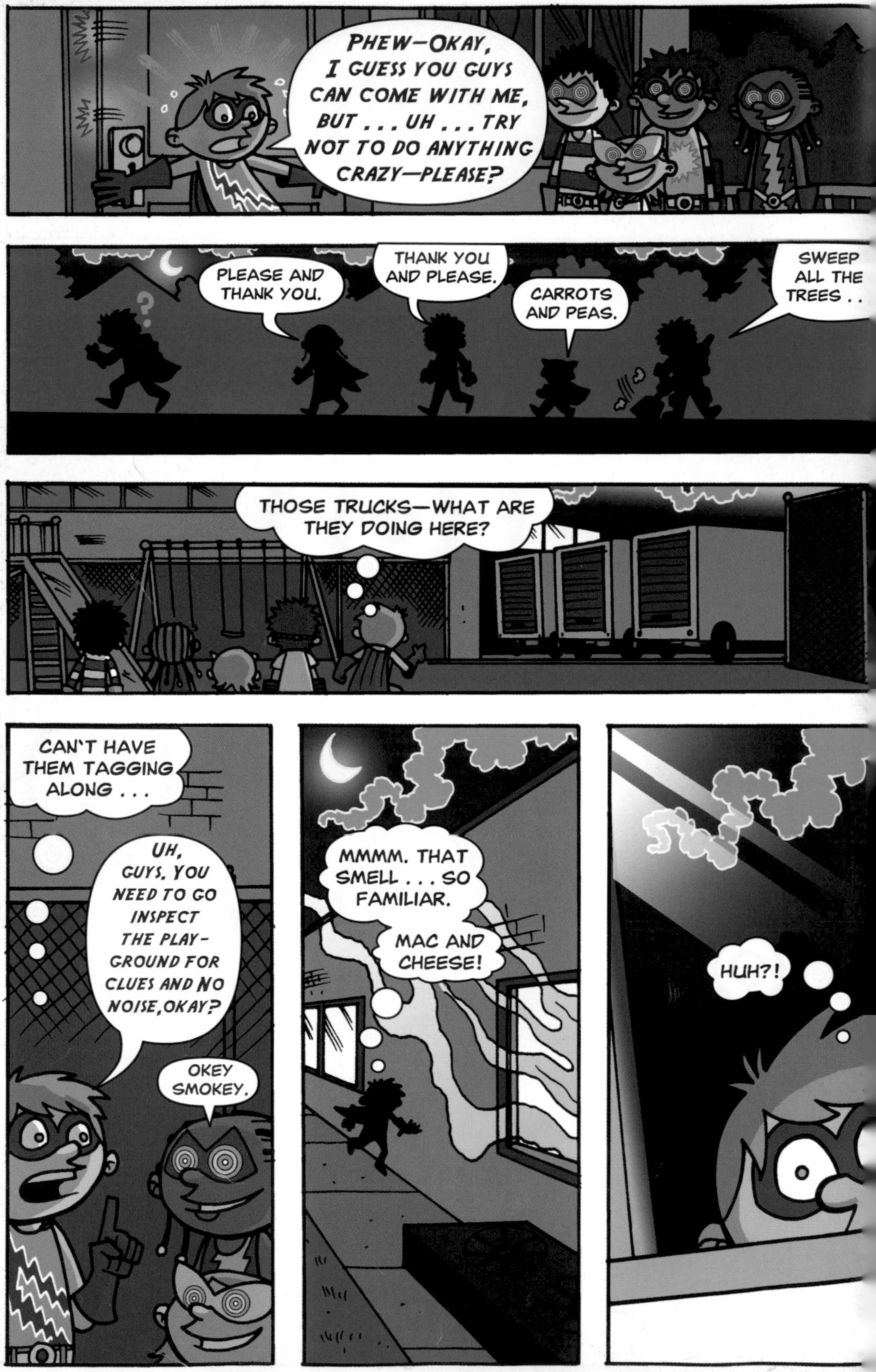
PHEW—OKAY, I GUESS YOU GUYS CAN COME WITH ME, BUT . . . UH . . . TRY NOT TO DO ANYTHING CRAZY—PLEASE?
PLEASE AND THANK YOU.
THANK YOU AND PLEASE.
CARROTS AND PEAS.
SWEEP ALL THE TREES . .
THOSE TRUCKS—WHAT ARE THEY DOING HERE?
CAN'T HAVE THEM TAGGING ALONG . . .
UH, GUYS, YOU NEED TO GO INSPECT THE PLAY-GROUND FOR CLUES AND NO NOISE, OKAY?
OKEY SMOKEY.
MMMM. THAT SMELL . . . SO FAMILIAR.
MAC AND CHEESE!
HUH?!

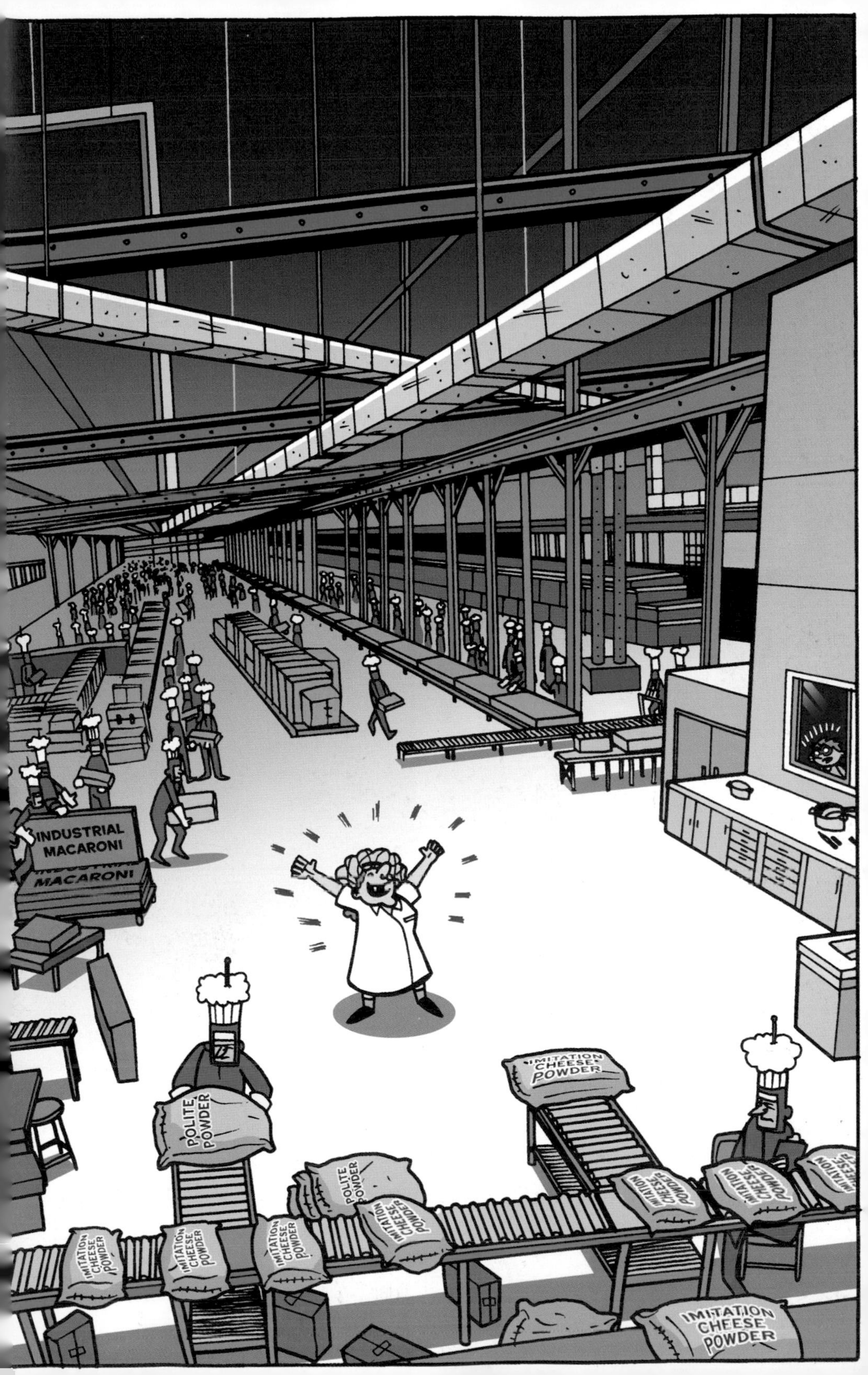

INDUSTRIAL MACARONI
MACARONI
POLITE POWDER
IMITATION CHEESE POWDER
POLITE POWDER
IMITATION CHEESE POWDER
IMITATION CHEESE POWDER
IMITATION CHEESE POWDER
IMITATION CHEESE POWDER
IMITATION CHEESE POWDER
IMITATION CHEESE POWDER
IMITATION CHEESE POWDER

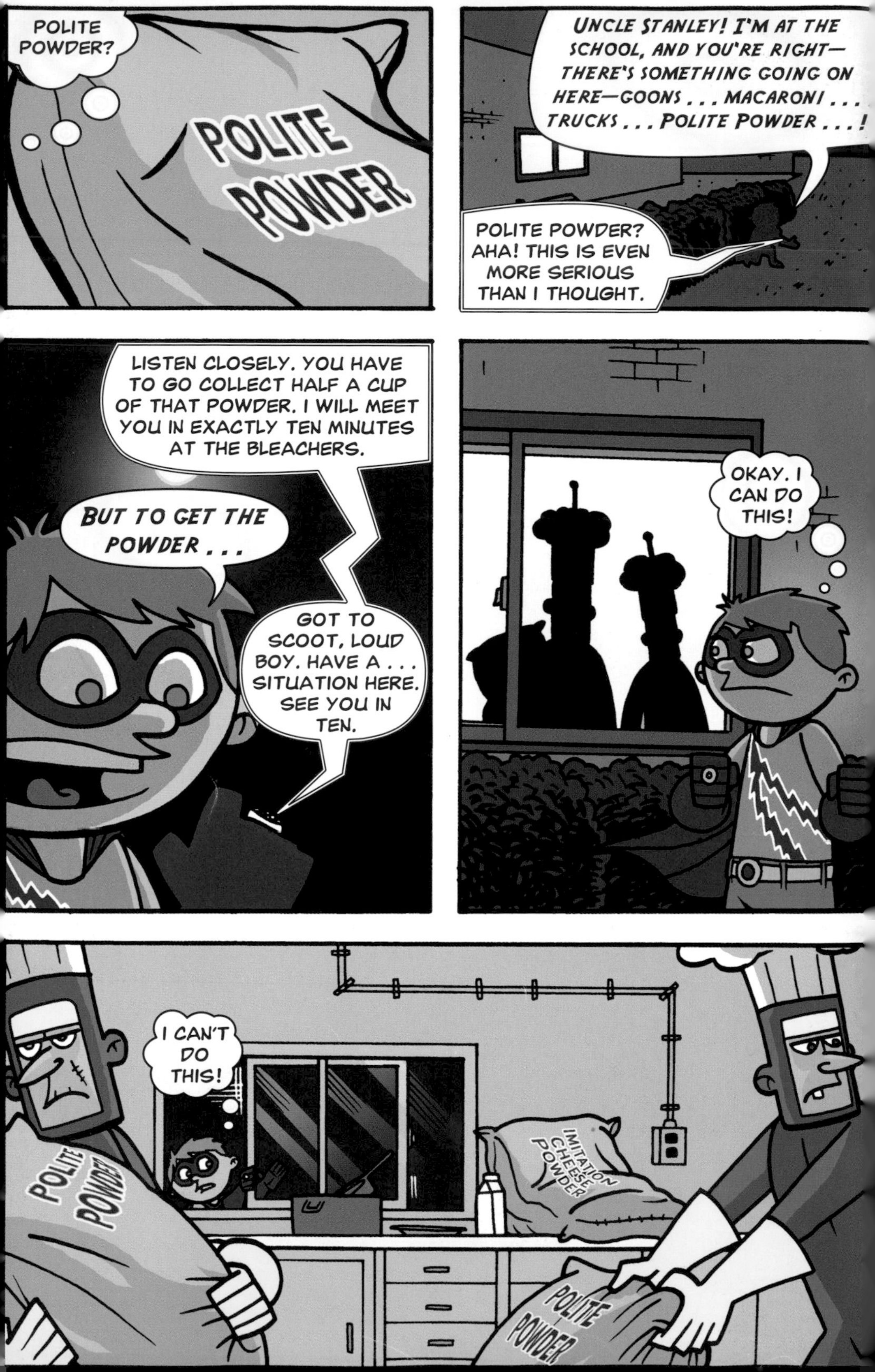
POLITE POWDER?
POLITE POWDER
UNCLE STANLEY! I'M AT THE SCHOOL, AND YOU'RE RIGHT— THERE'S SOMETHING GOING ON HERE—GOONS . . . MACARONI . . . TRUCKS . . . POLITE POWDER . . . !
POLITE POWDER? AHA! THIS IS EVEN MORE SERIOUS THAN I THOUGHT.
LISTEN CLOSELY. YOU HAVE TO GO COLLECT HALF A CUP OF THAT POWDER. I WILL MEET YOU IN EXACTLY TEN MINUTES AT THE BLEACHERS.
BUT TO GET THE POWDER . . .
GOT TO SCOOT, LOUD BOY. HAVE A . . . SITUATION HERE. SEE YOU IN TEN.
OKAY. I CAN DO THIS!
I CAN'T DO THIS!
POLITE POWDER
IMITATION CHEESE POWDER
POLITE POWDER

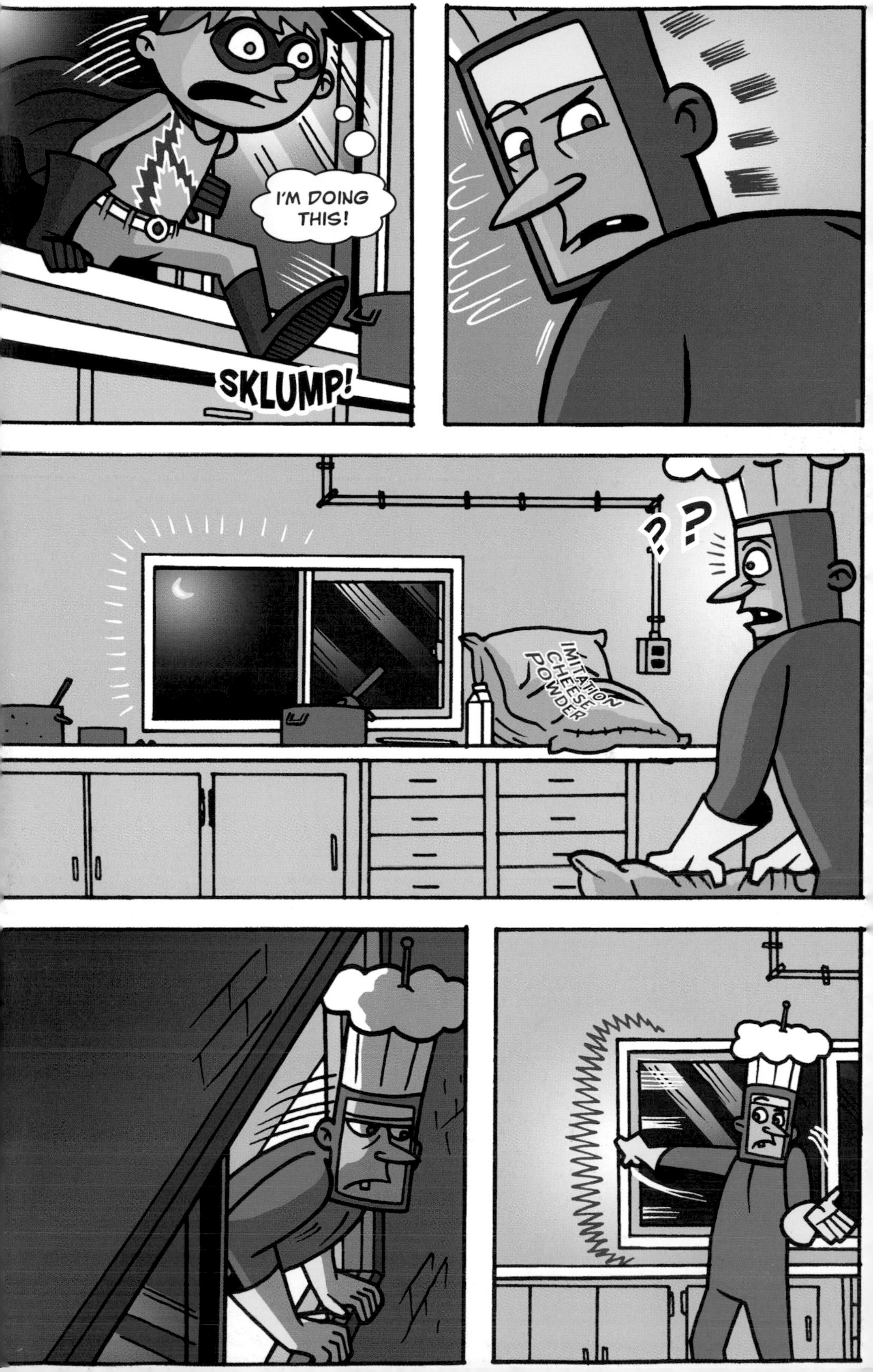
I'M DOING THIS!
SKLUMP!
IMITATION CHEESE POWDER
??

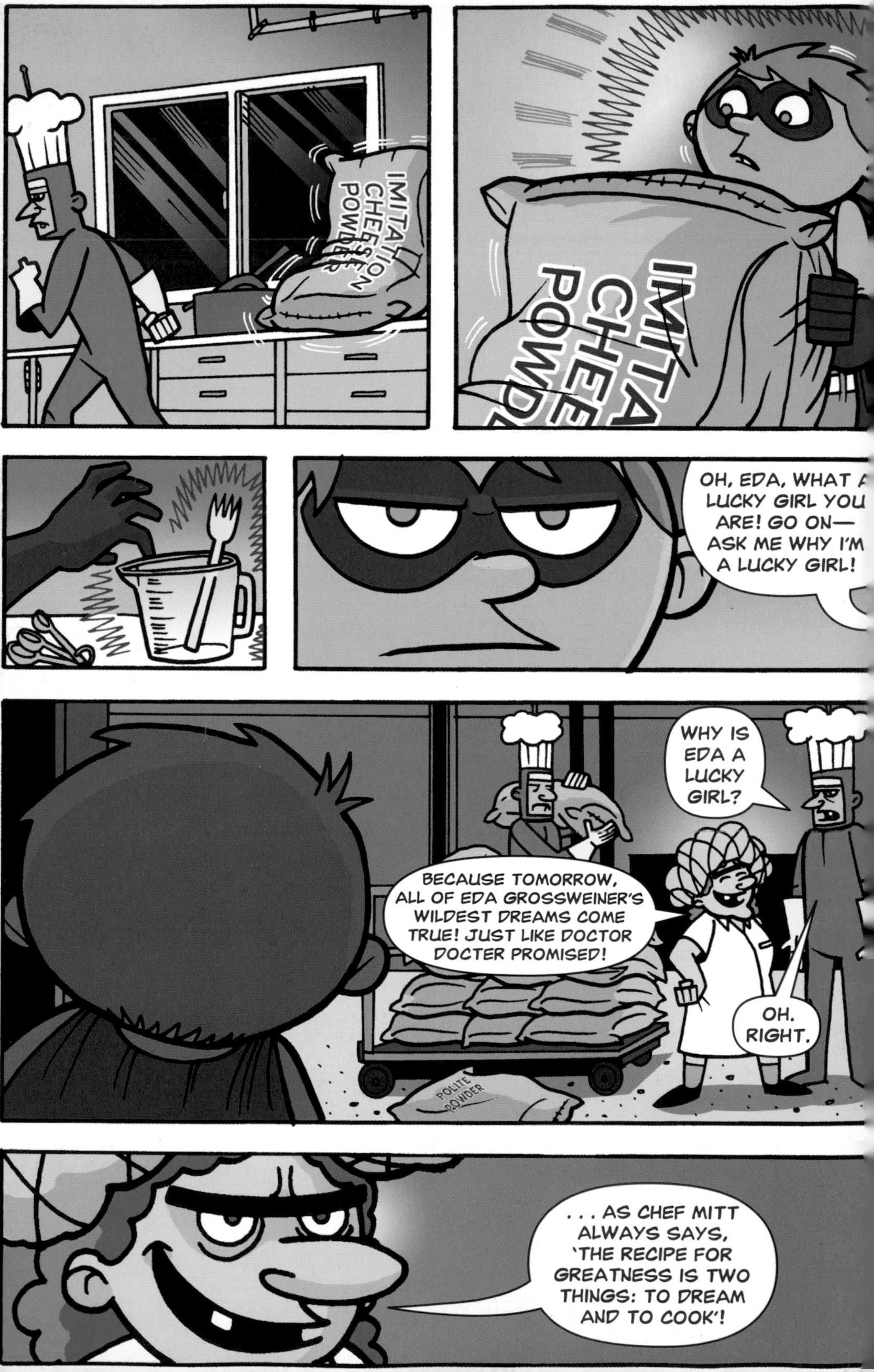
IMITATION CHEESE POWDER
IMITATION CHEESE POWDER
OH, EDA, WHAT A LUCKY GIRL YOU ARE! GO ON— ASK ME WHY I'M A LUCKY GIRL!
WHY IS EDA A LUCKY GIRL?
BECAUSE TOMORROW, ALL OF EDA GROSSWEINER'S WILDEST DREAMS COME TRUE! JUST LIKE DOCTOR DOCTER PROMISED!
OH. RIGHT.
POLITE POWDER
. . . AS CHEF MITT ALWAYS SAYS, 'THE RECIPE FOR GREATNESS IS TWO THINGS: TO DREAM AND TO COOK'!

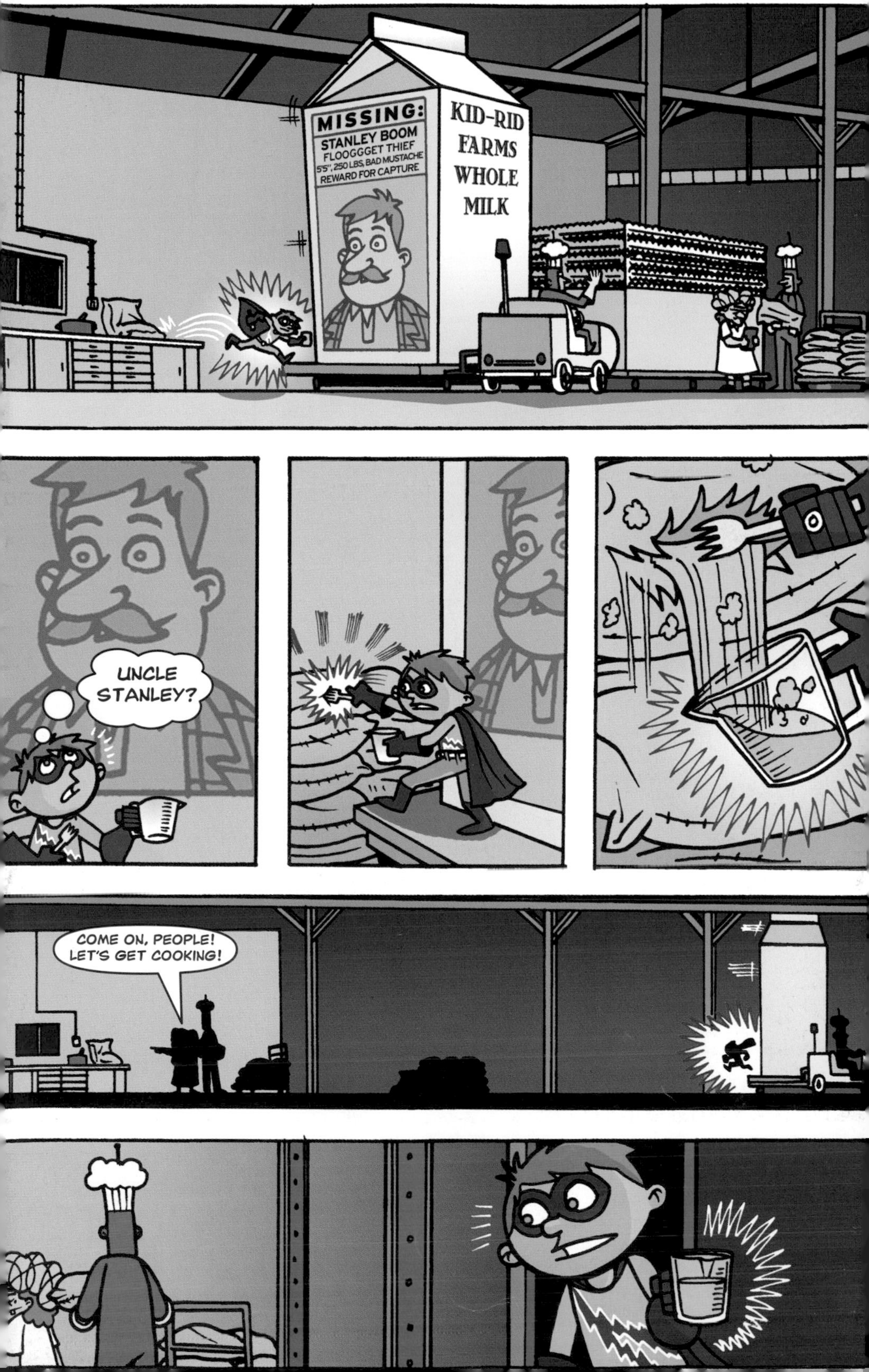
MISSING:
STANLEY BOOM
FLOOGGGET THIEF
5'5", 250 LBS, BAD MUSTACHE
REWARD FOR CAPTURE
KID-RID FARMS WHOLE MILK
UNCLE STANLEY?
COME ON, PEOPLE! LET'S GET COOKING!

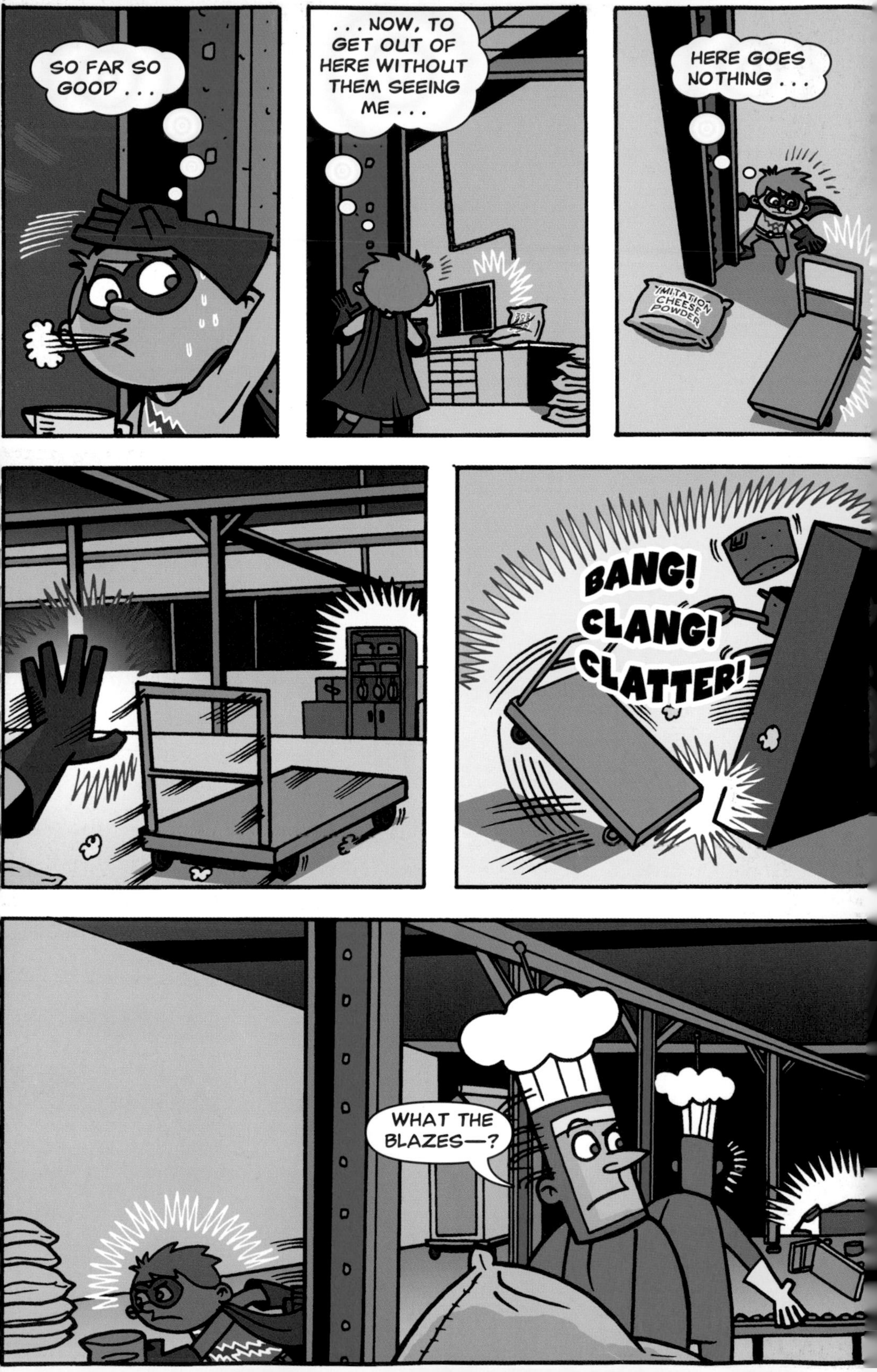
SO FAR SO GOOD . . .
. . . NOW, TO GET OUT OF HERE WITHOUT THEM SEEING ME . . .
HERE GOES NOTHING . . .
IMITATION CHEESE POWDER
BANG!
CLANG!
CLATTER!
WHAT THE BLAZES—?

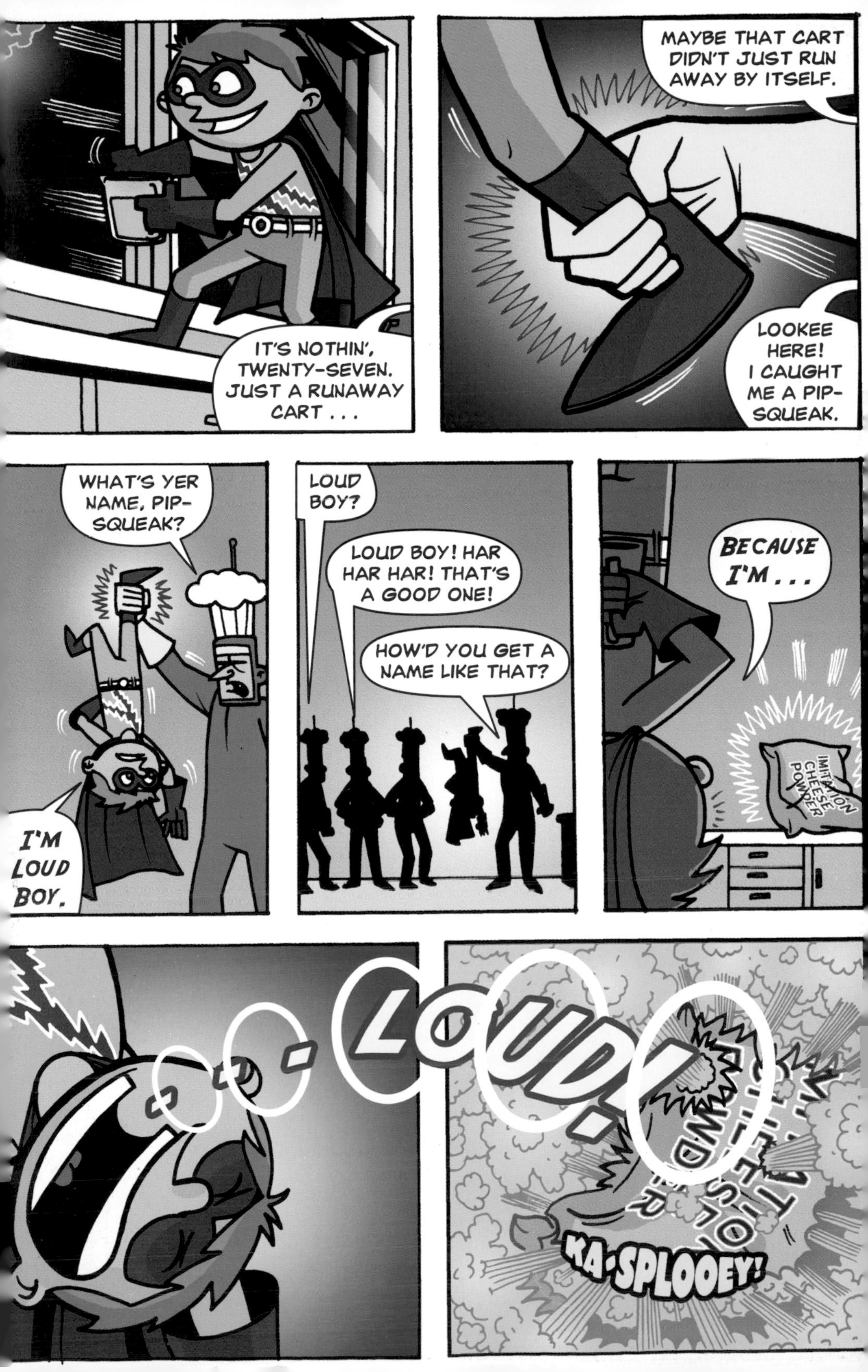

IT'S NOTHIN', TWENTY-SEVEN. JUST A RUNAWAY CART . . .
MAYBE THAT CART DIDN'T JUST RUN AWAY BY ITSELF.
LOOKEE HERE! I CAUGHT ME A PIP-SQUEAK.
WHAT'S YER NAME, PIP-SQUEAK?
I'M LOUD BOY.
LOUD BOY?
LOUD BOY! HAR HAR HAR! THAT'S A GOOD ONE!
HOW'D YOU GET A NAME LIKE THAT?
BECAUSE I'M . . .
IMITATION CHEESE POWDER
- LOUD!
KA-SPLOOEY!

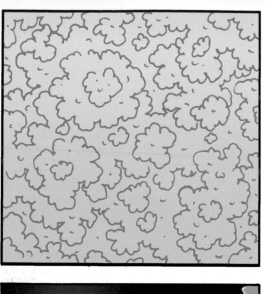

HUH? WHERE'D HE GO?

PHEW.

UNCLE STANLEY SAID TEN MINUTES. HE SHOULD BE HERE.

UNCLE STANLEY?

GZZZZZZ...

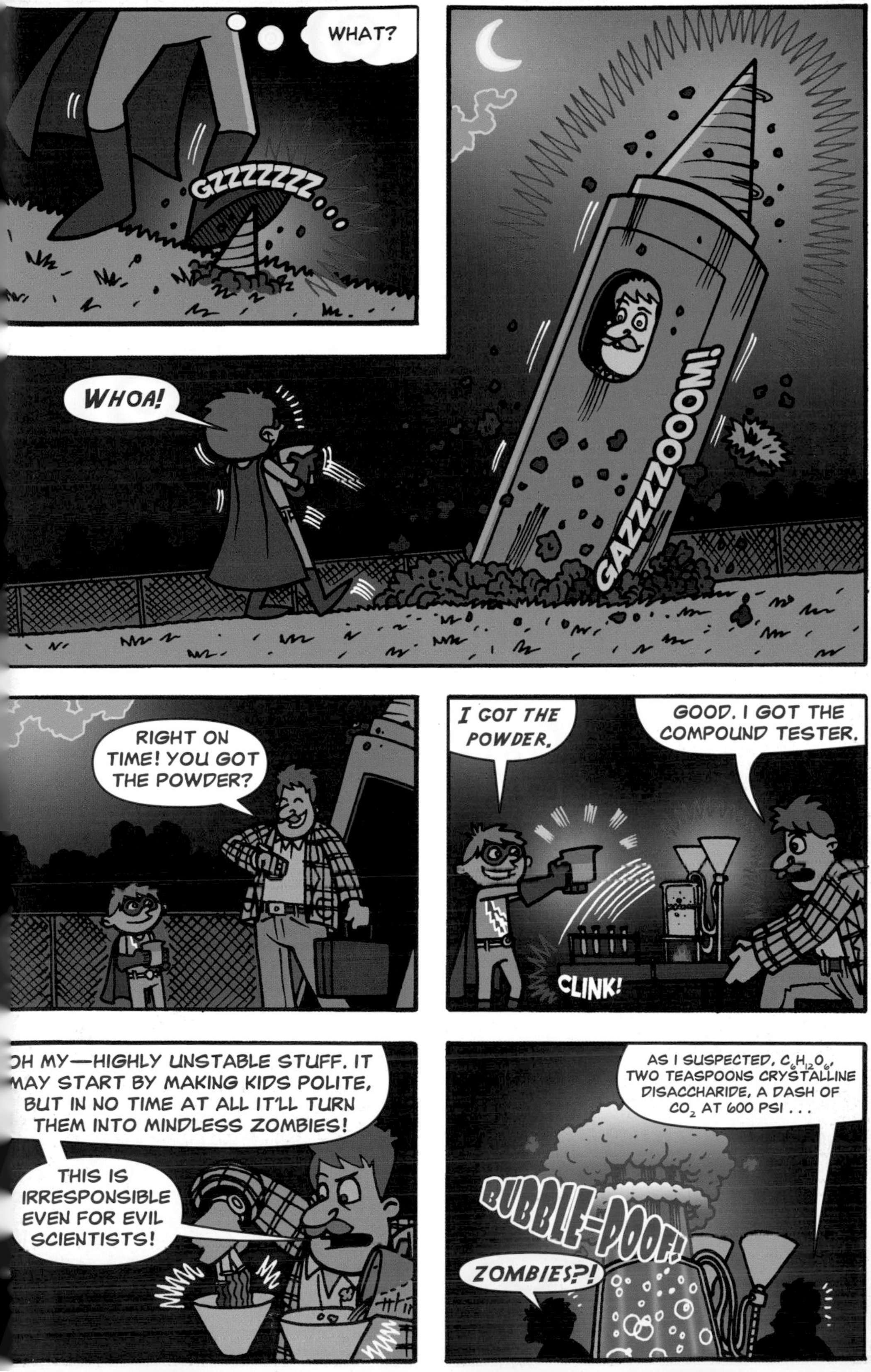
WHAT?
GZZZZZZZ...
WHOA!
GAZZZZOOOM!
RIGHT ON TIME! YOU GOT THE POWDER?
I GOT THE POWDER.
GOOD. I GOT THE COMPOUND TESTER.
CLINK!
OH MY—HIGHLY UNSTABLE STUFF. IT MAY START BY MAKING KIDS POLITE, BUT IN NO TIME AT ALL IT'LL TURN THEM INTO MINDLESS ZOMBIES!
THIS IS IRRESPONSIBLE EVEN FOR EVIL SCIENTISTS!
AS I SUSPECTED, $C_6H_{12}O_6$, TWO TEASPOONS CRYSTALLINE DISACCHARIDE, A DASH OF $CO_2$ AT 600 PSI . . .
BUBBLE-POOF!
ZOMBIES?!

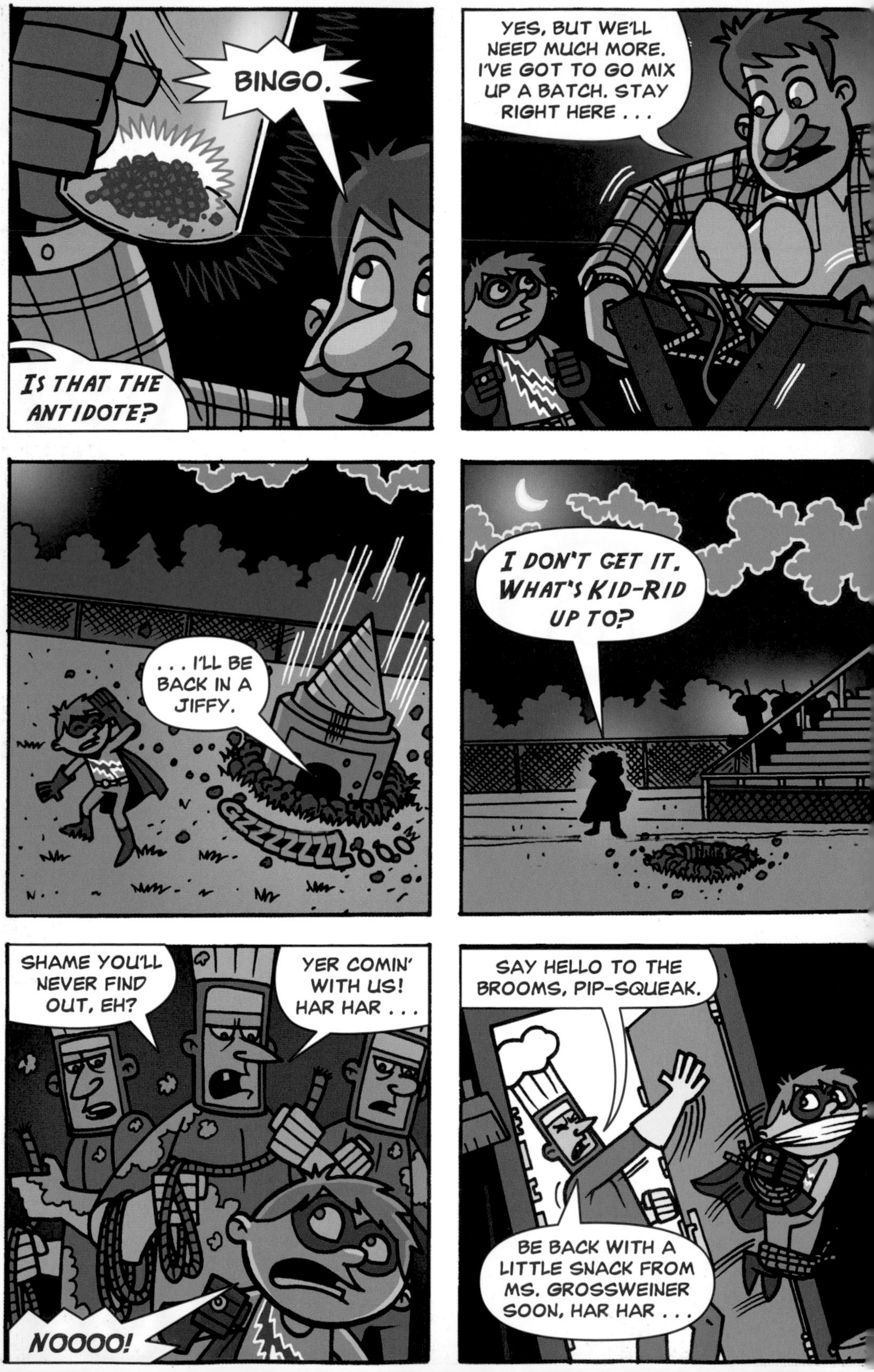
BINGO.
IS THAT THE ANTIDOTE?
YES, BUT WE'LL NEED MUCH MORE. I'VE GOT TO GO MIX UP A BATCH. STAY RIGHT HERE . . .
. . . I'LL BE BACK IN A JIFFY.
GZZZZZZZZOOO
I DON'T GET IT. WHAT'S KID-RID UP TO?
SHAME YOU'LL NEVER FIND OUT, EH?
YER COMIN' WITH US! HAR HAR . . .
NOOOO!
SAY HELLO TO THE BROOMS, PIP-SQUEAK.
BE BACK WITH A LITTLE SNACK FROM MS. GROSSWEINER SOON, HAR HAR . . .

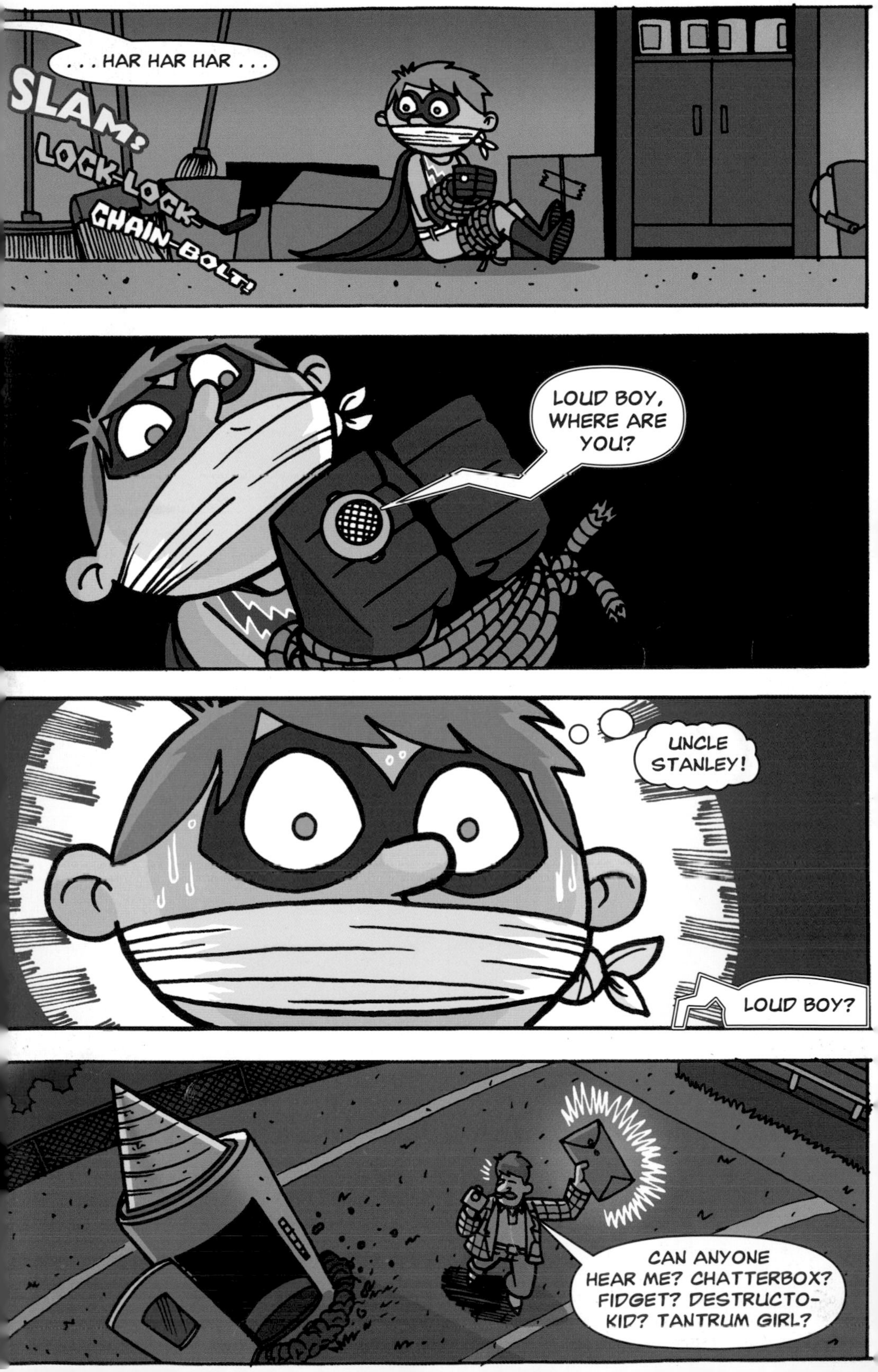
. . . HAR HAR HAR . . .
SLAM!
LOCK-LOCK-
CHAIN-BOLT!
LOUD BOY, WHERE ARE YOU?
UNCLE STANLEY!
LOUD BOY?
CAN ANYONE HEAR ME? CHATTERBOX? FIDGET? DESTRUCTO-KID? TANTRUM GIRL?

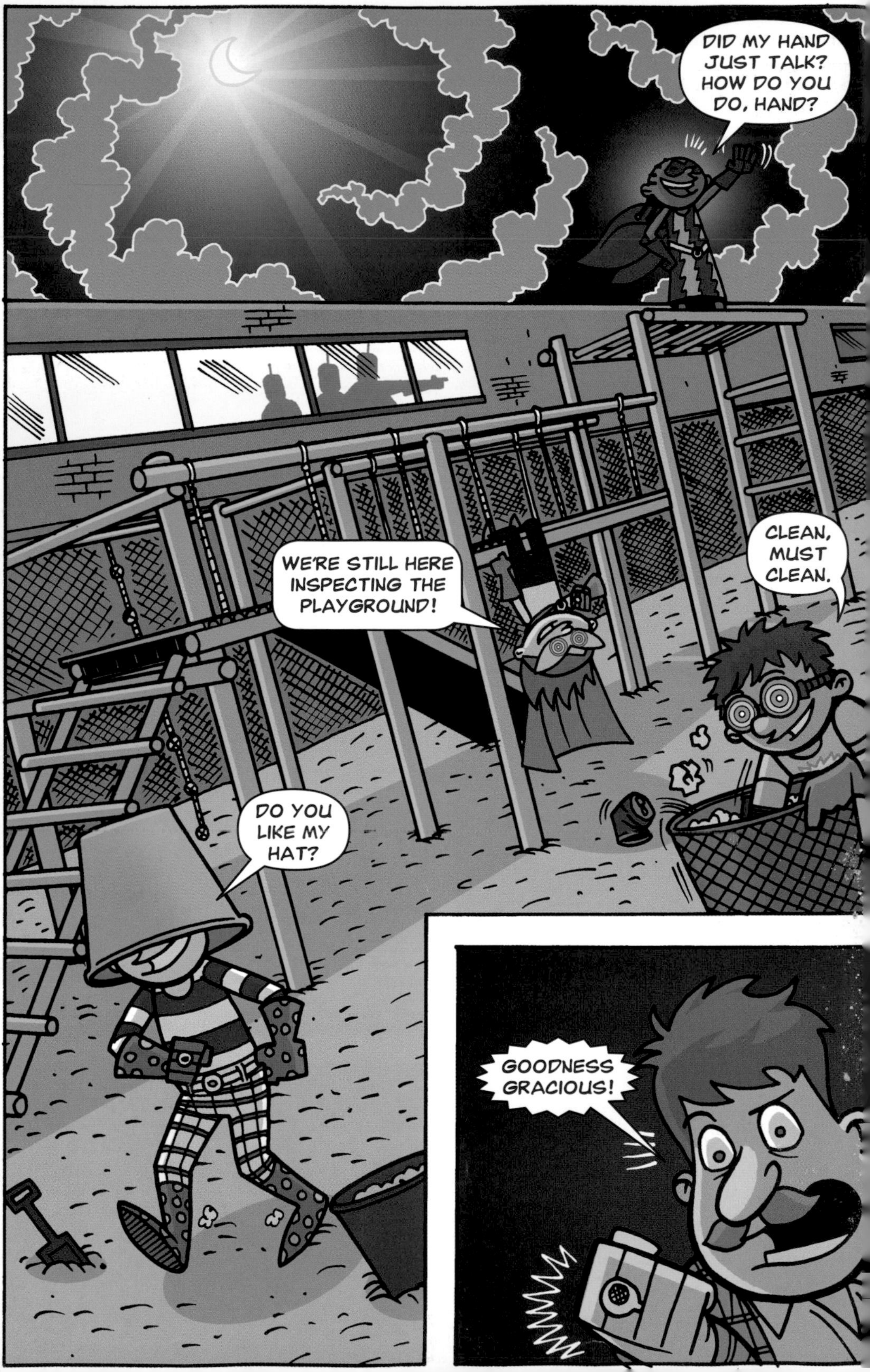
DID MY HAND JUST TALK? HOW DO YOU DO, HAND?
WE'RE STILL HERE INSPECTING THE PLAYGROUND!
CLEAN, MUST CLEAN.
DO YOU LIKE MY HAT?
GOODNESS GRACIOUS!

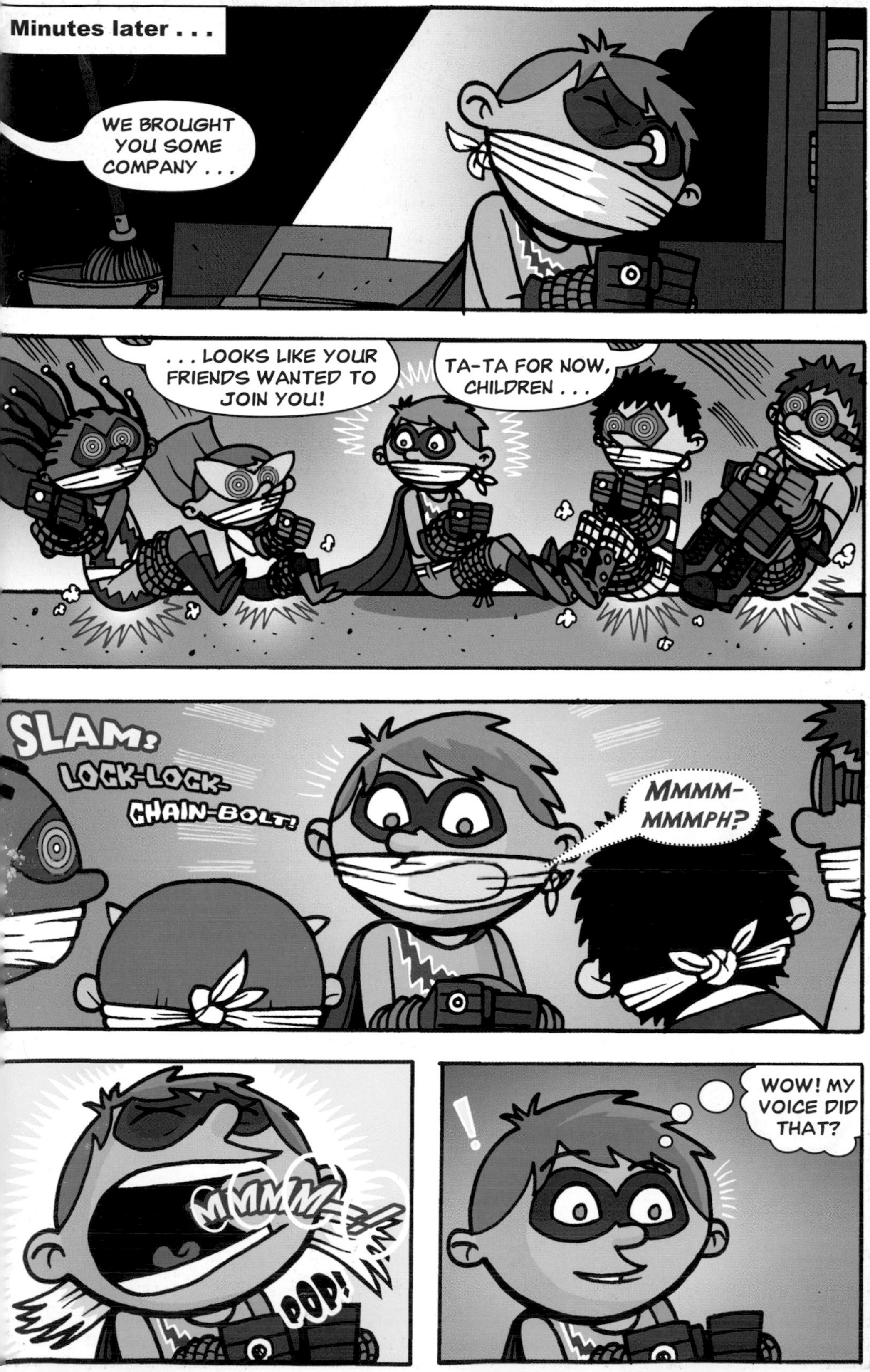
Minutes later . . .
WE BROUGHT YOU SOME COMPANY . . .
. . . LOOKS LIKE YOUR FRIENDS WANTED TO JOIN YOU!
TA-TA FOR NOW, CHILDREN . . .
SLAM!
LOCK-LOCK-
CHAIN-BOLT!
MMMM-MMMPH?
POP!
WOW! MY VOICE DID THAT?

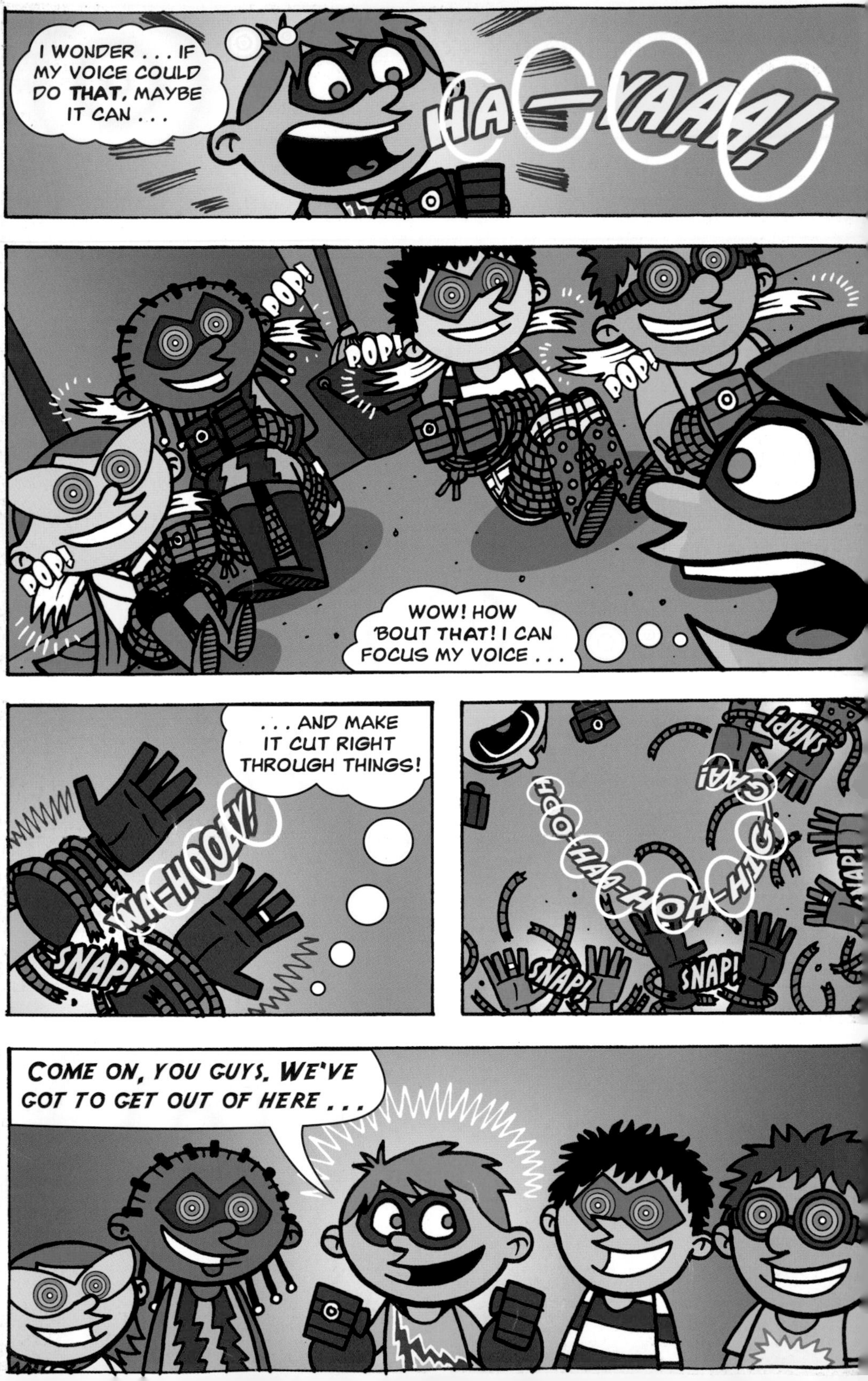
I WONDER . . . IF MY VOICE COULD DO **THAT**, MAYBE IT CAN . . .
HA—YAAA!
POP!
POP!
POP!
POP!
WOW! HOW 'BOUT THAT! I CAN FOCUS MY VOICE . . .
. . . AND MAKE IT CUT RIGHT THROUGH THINGS!
WA-HOOEY!
SNAP!
HOO-HAA-HOH-HIC-GAA!
SNAP!
SNAP!
SNAP!
SNAP!
COME ON, YOU GUYS. WE'VE GOT TO GET OUT OF HERE . . .

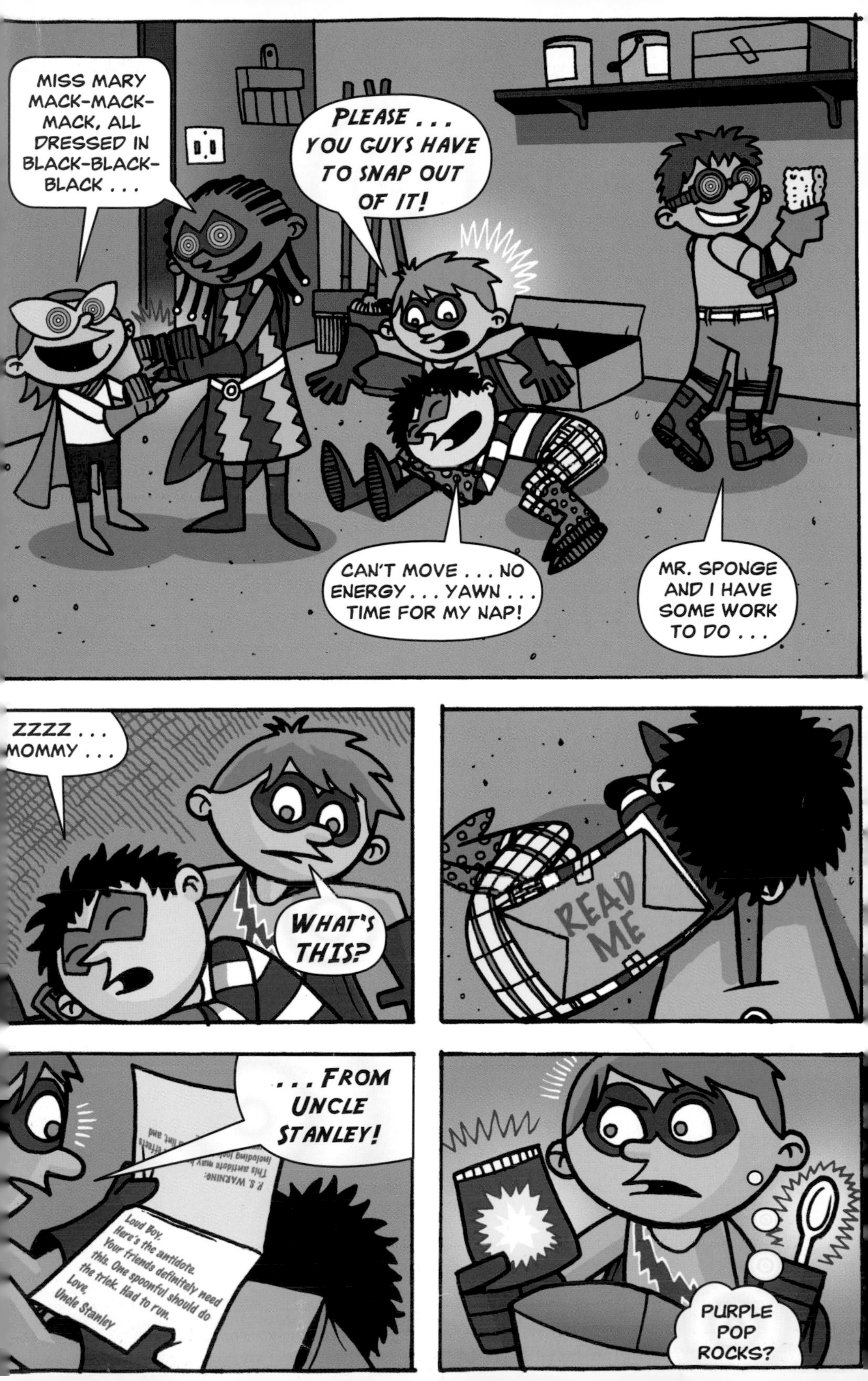
MISS MARY MACK-MACK-MACK, ALL DRESSED IN BLACK-BLACK-BLACK . . .
PLEASE . . . YOU GUYS HAVE TO SNAP OUT OF IT!
CAN'T MOVE . . . NO ENERGY . . . YAWN . . . TIME FOR MY NAP!
MR. SPONGE AND I HAVE SOME WORK TO DO . . .
ZZZZ . . . MOMMY . . .
WHAT'S THIS?
READ ME
. . . FROM UNCLE STANLEY!
P.S. WARNING:
Loud Boy,
Here's the antidote.
Your friends definitely need this. One spoonful should do the trick. Had to run.
Love,
Uncle Stanley
PURPLE POP ROCKS?

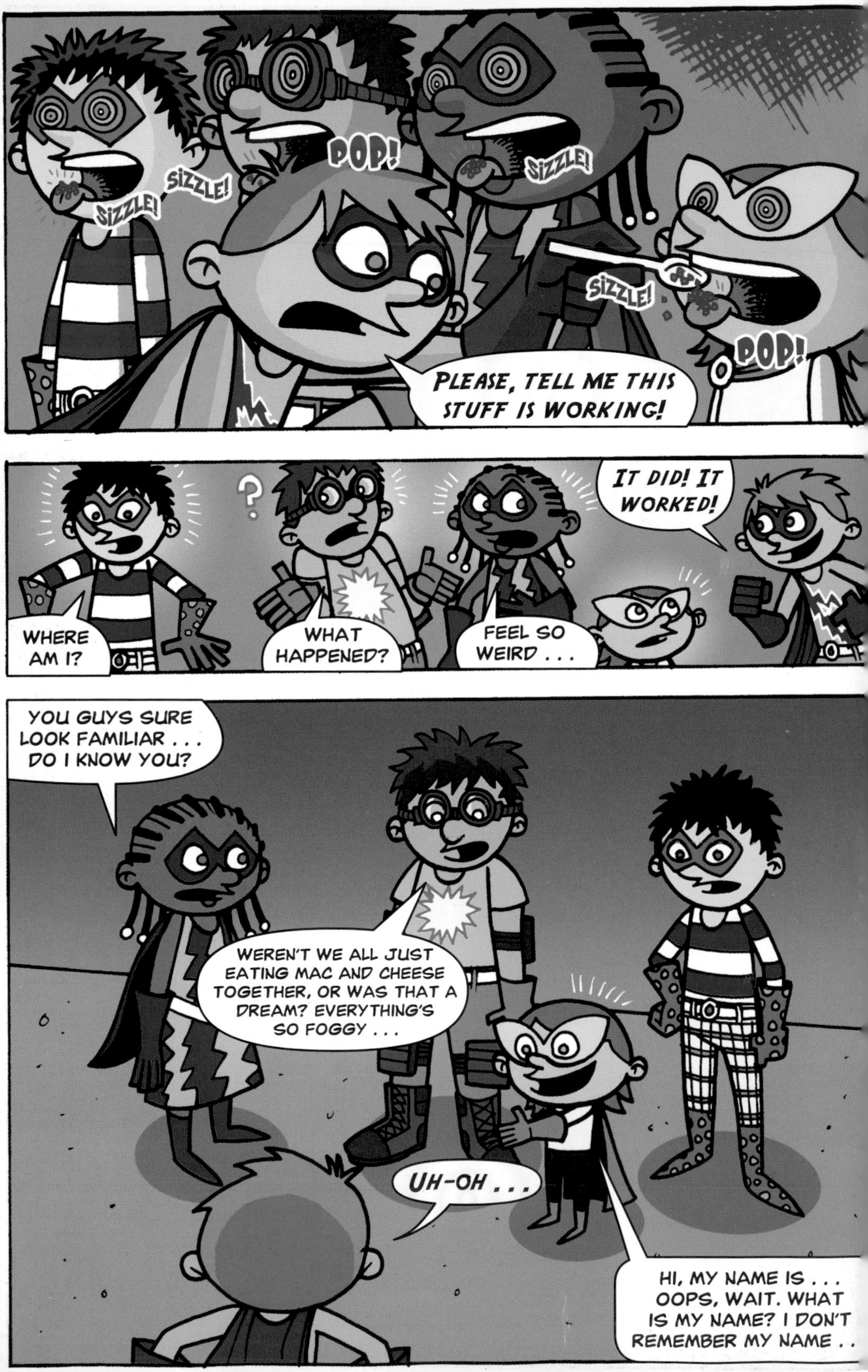

SIZZLE!
SIZZLE!
POP!
SIZZLE!
SIZZLE!
POP!
PLEASE, TELL ME THIS STUFF IS WORKING!
IT DID! IT WORKED!
WHERE AM I?
WHAT HAPPENED?
FEEL SO WEIRD . . .
YOU GUYS SURE LOOK FAMILIAR . . . DO I KNOW YOU?
WEREN'T WE ALL JUST EATING MAC AND CHEESE TOGETHER, OR WAS THAT A DREAM? EVERYTHING'S SO FOGGY . . .
UH-OH . . .
HI, MY NAME IS . . . OOPS, WAIT. WHAT IS MY NAME? I DON'T REMEMBER MY NAME . .

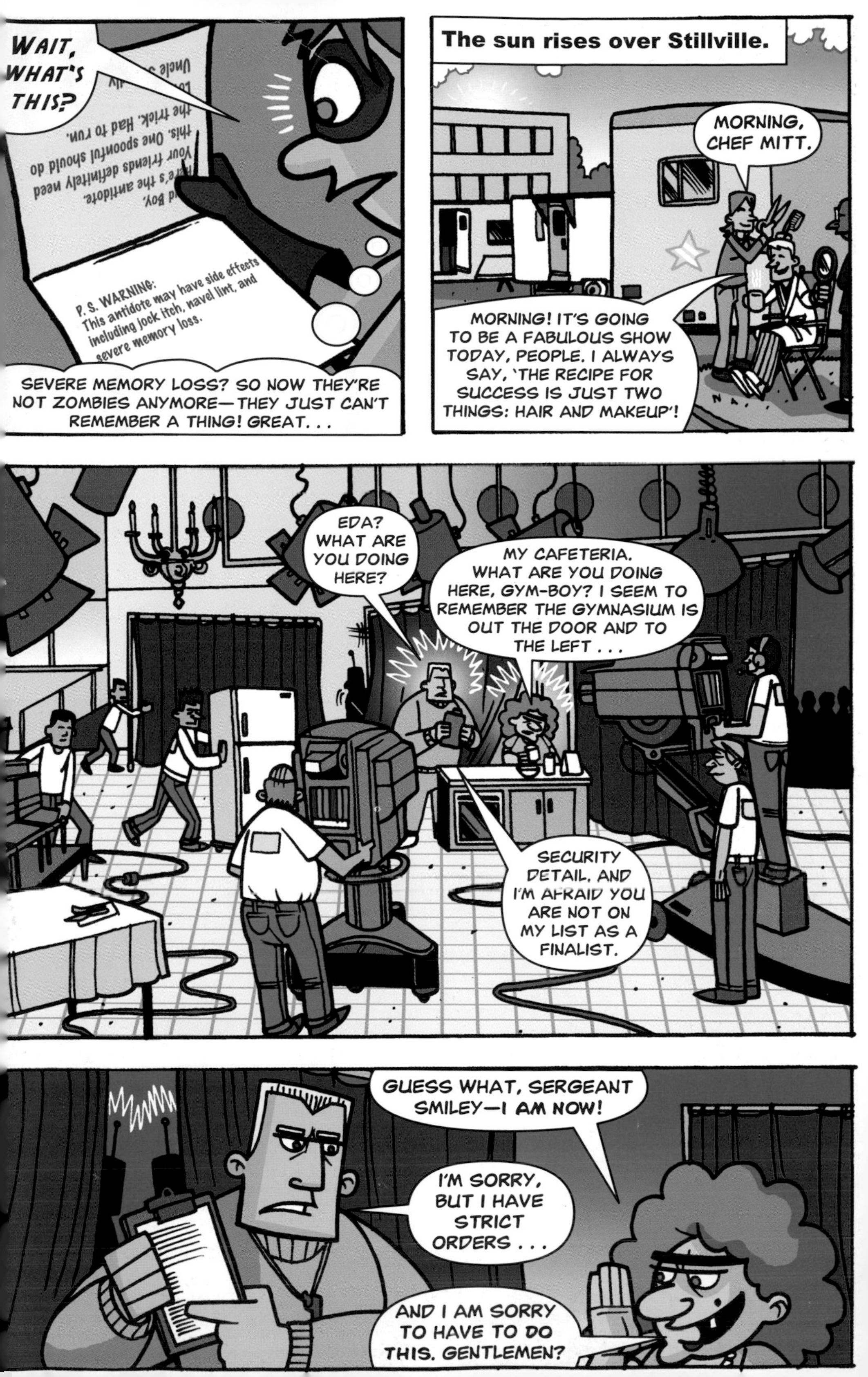

WAIT, WHAT'S THIS?
Your friends definitely need
this. One spoonful should do
the trick. Had to run.
P. S. WARNING:
This antidote may have side effects including jock itch, navel lint, and severe memory loss.
SEVERE MEMORY LOSS? SO NOW THEY'RE NOT ZOMBIES ANYMORE—THEY JUST CAN'T REMEMBER A THING! GREAT. . .
The sun rises over Stillville.
MORNING, CHEF MITT.
MORNING! IT'S GOING TO BE A FABULOUS SHOW TODAY, PEOPLE. I ALWAYS SAY, 'THE RECIPE FOR SUCCESS IS JUST TWO THINGS: HAIR AND MAKEUP'!
EDA? WHAT ARE YOU DOING HERE?
MY CAFETERIA. WHAT ARE YOU DOING HERE, GYM-BOY? I SEEM TO REMEMBER THE GYMNASIUM IS OUT THE DOOR AND TO THE LEFT . . .
SECURITY DETAIL, AND I'M AFRAID YOU ARE NOT ON MY LIST AS A FINALIST.
GUESS WHAT, SERGEANT SMILEY—I AM NOW!
I'M SORRY, BUT I HAVE STRICT ORDERS . . .
AND I AM SORRY TO HAVE TO DO THIS. GENTLEMEN?

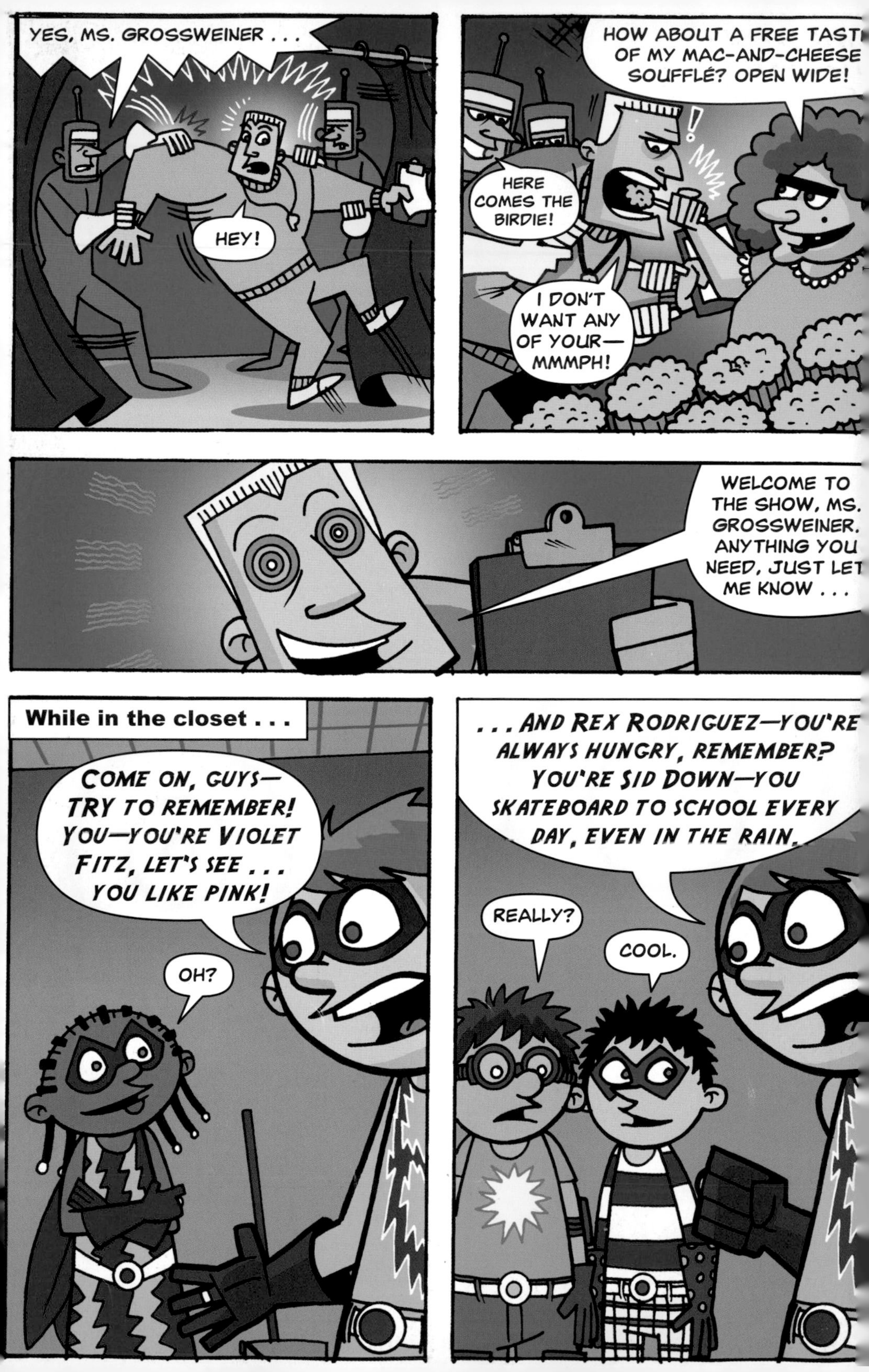
YES, MS. GROSSWEINER . . .
HEY!
HOW ABOUT A FREE TAST[E]
OF MY MAC-AND-CHEESE
SOUFFLÉ? OPEN WIDE!
HERE COMES THE BIRDIE!
I DON'T WANT ANY OF YOUR—MMMPH!
WELCOME TO THE SHOW, MS. GROSSWEINER. ANYTHING YOU NEED, JUST LET ME KNOW . . .
While in the closet . . .
COME ON, GUYS—TRY TO REMEMBER! YOU—YOU'RE VIOLET FITZ, LET'S SEE . . . YOU LIKE PINK!
OH?
. . . AND REX RODRIGUEZ—YOU'RE ALWAYS HUNGRY, REMEMBER? YOU'RE SID DOWN—YOU SKATEBOARD TO SCHOOL EVERY DAY, EVEN IN THE RAIN.
REALLY?
COOL.

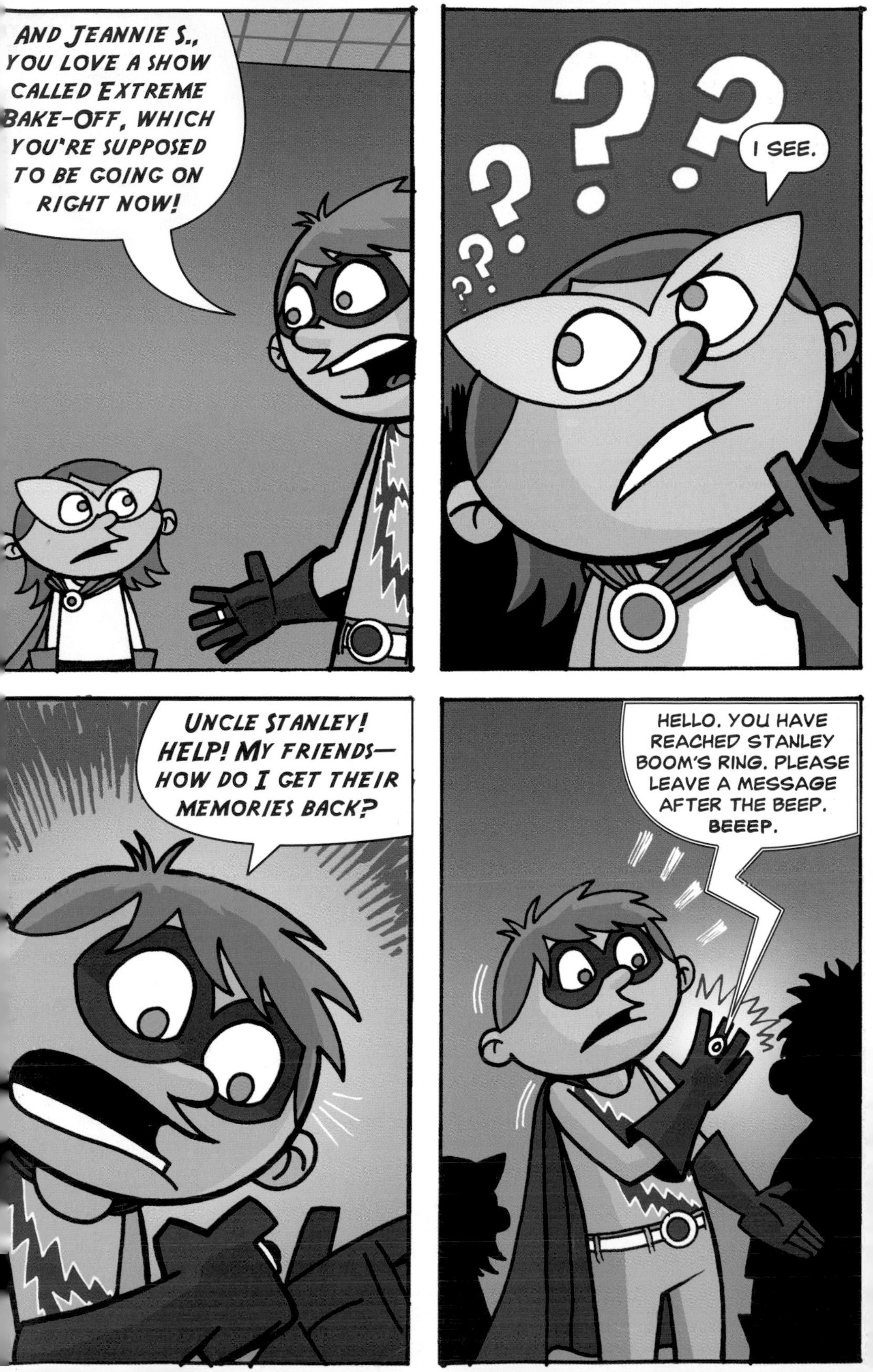
AND JEANNIE S., YOU LOVE A SHOW CALLED EXTREME BAKE-OFF, WHICH YOU'RE SUPPOSED TO BE GOING ON RIGHT NOW!
I SEE.
UNCLE STANLEY! HELP! MY FRIENDS— HOW DO I GET THEIR MEMORIES BACK?
HELLO. YOU HAVE REACHED STANLEY BOOM'S RING. PLEASE LEAVE A MESSAGE AFTER THE BEEP. BEEEP.

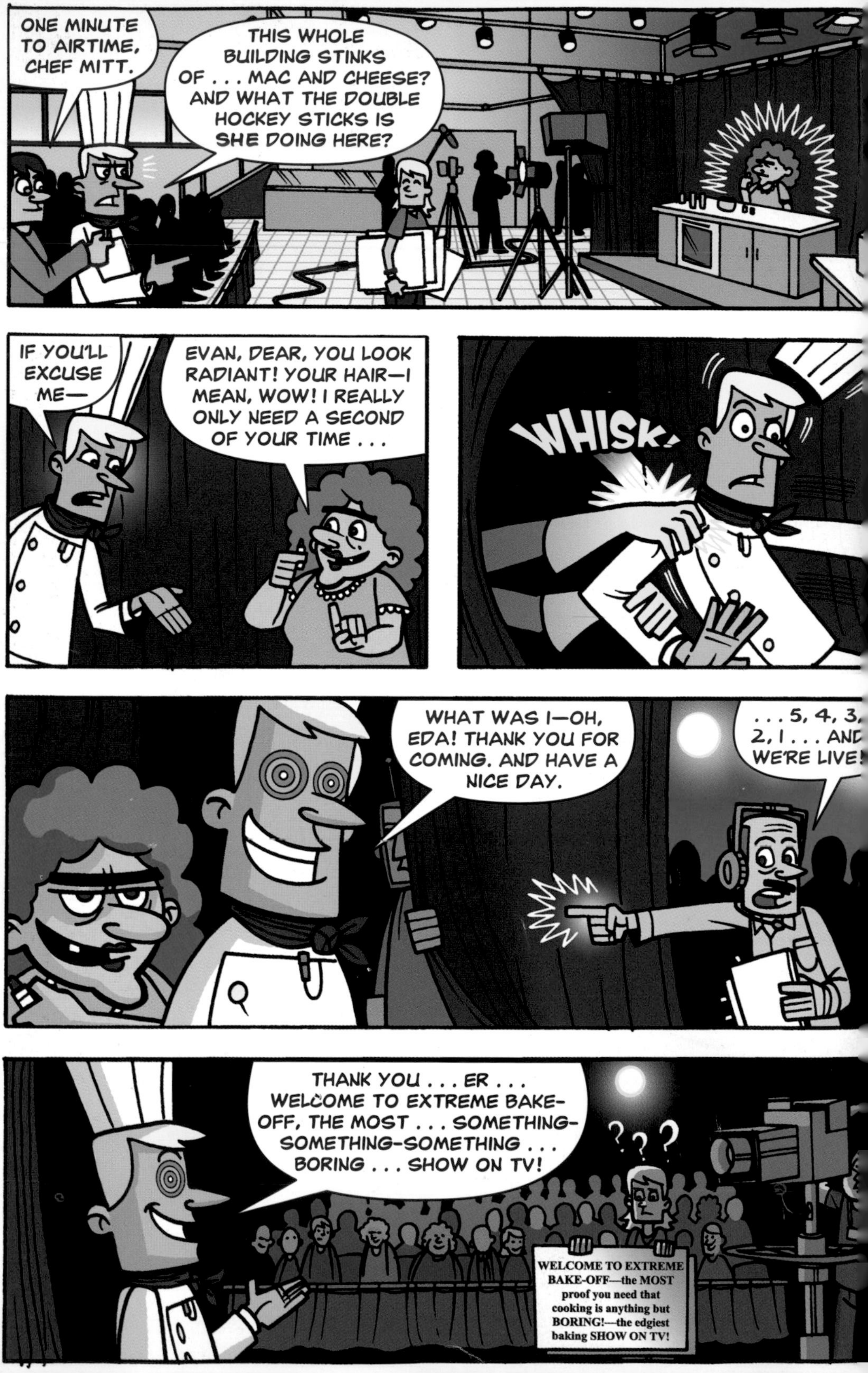

ONE MINUTE TO AIRTIME, CHEF MITT.
THIS WHOLE BUILDING STINKS OF . . . MAC AND CHEESE? AND WHAT THE DOUBLE HOCKEY STICKS IS SHE DOING HERE?
IF YOU'LL EXCUSE ME—
EVAN, DEAR, YOU LOOK RADIANT! YOUR HAIR—I MEAN, WOW! I REALLY ONLY NEED A SECOND OF YOUR TIME . . .
WHISK!
WHAT WAS I—OH, EDA! THANK YOU FOR COMING. AND HAVE A NICE DAY.
. . . 5, 4, 3, 2, 1 . . . AND WE'RE LIVE!
THANK YOU . . . ER . . . WELCOME TO EXTREME BAKE-OFF, THE MOST . . . SOMETHING-SOMETHING-SOMETHING . . . BORING . . . SHOW ON TV!
???
WELCOME TO EXTREME BAKE-OFF—the MOST proof you need that cooking is anything but BORING!—the edgiest baking SHOW ON TV!

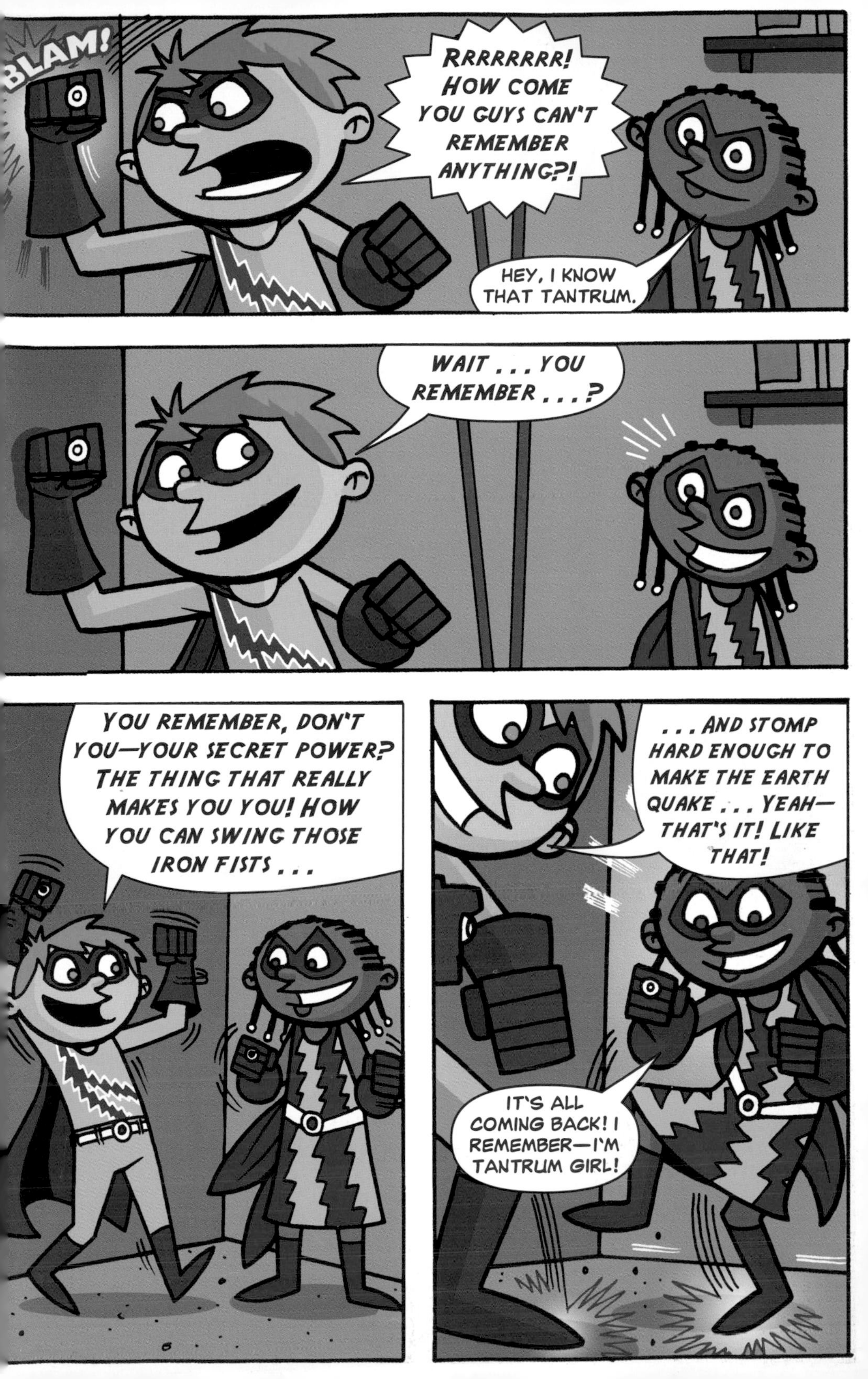
BLAM!
RRRRRRRR! HOW COME YOU GUYS CAN'T REMEMBER ANYTHING?!
HEY, I KNOW THAT TANTRUM.
WAIT . . . YOU REMEMBER . . . ?
YOU REMEMBER, DON'T YOU—YOUR SECRET POWER? THE THING THAT REALLY MAKES YOU YOU! HOW YOU CAN SWING THOSE IRON FISTS . . .
. . . AND STOMP HARD ENOUGH TO MAKE THE EARTH QUAKE . . . YEAH—THAT'S IT! LIKE THAT!
IT'S ALL COMING BACK! I REMEMBER—I'M TANTRUM GIRL!

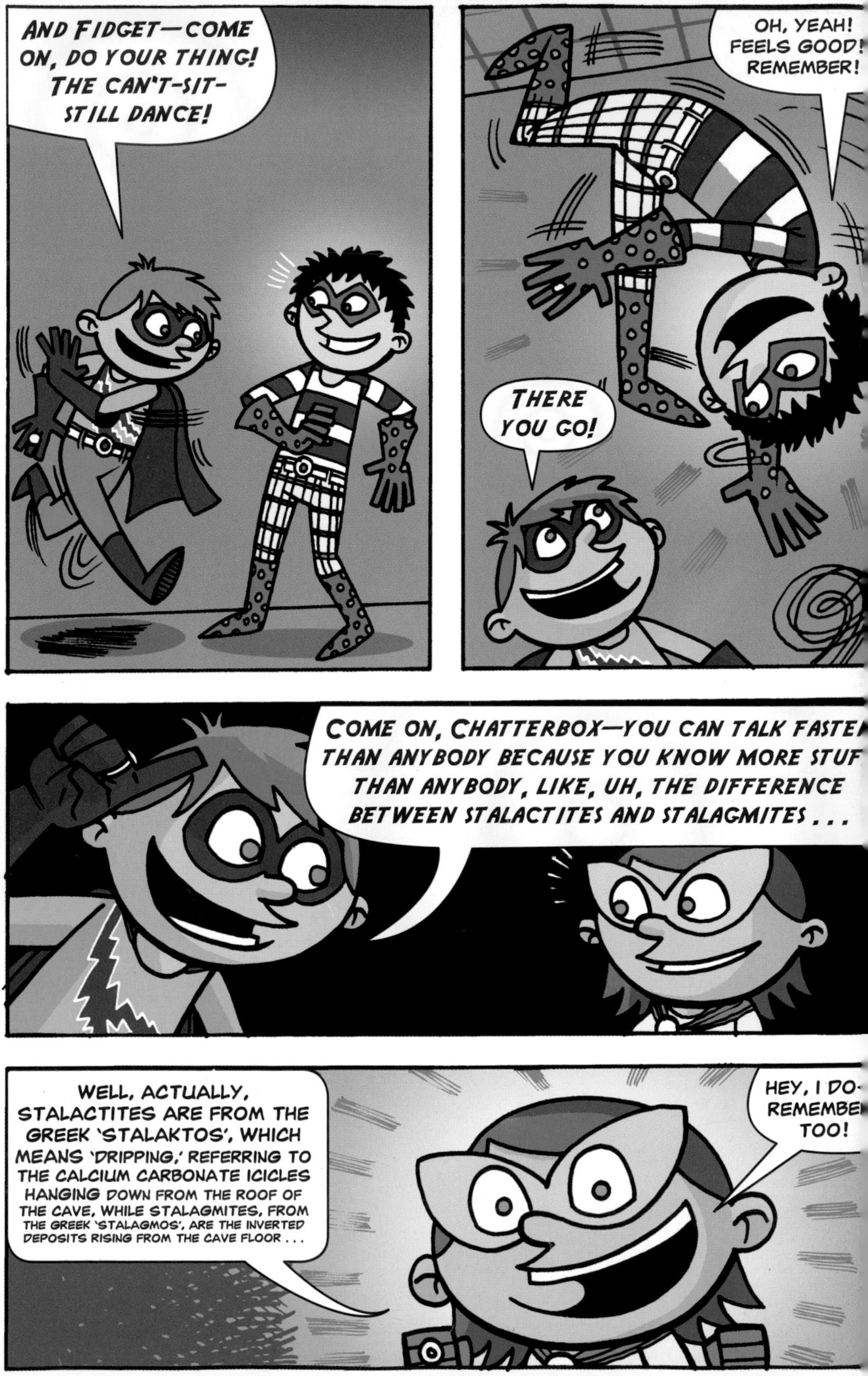
AND FIDGET—COME ON, DO YOUR THING! THE CAN'T-SIT-STILL DANCE!
OH, YEAH! FEELS GOOD! REMEMBER!
THERE YOU GO!
COME ON, CHATTERBOX—YOU CAN TALK FASTE THAN ANYBODY BECAUSE YOU KNOW MORE STUF THAN ANYBODY, LIKE, UH, THE DIFFERENCE BETWEEN STALACTITES AND STALAGMITES . . .
WELL, ACTUALLY, STALACTITES ARE FROM THE GREEK 'STALAKTOS', WHICH MEANS 'DRIPPING,' REFERRING TO THE CALCIUM CARBONATE ICICLES HANGING DOWN FROM THE ROOF OF THE CAVE, WHILE STALAGMITES, FROM THE GREEK 'STALAGMOS', ARE THE INVERTED DEPOSITS RISING FROM THE CAVE FLOOR . . .
HEY, I DO-REMEMBE TOO!

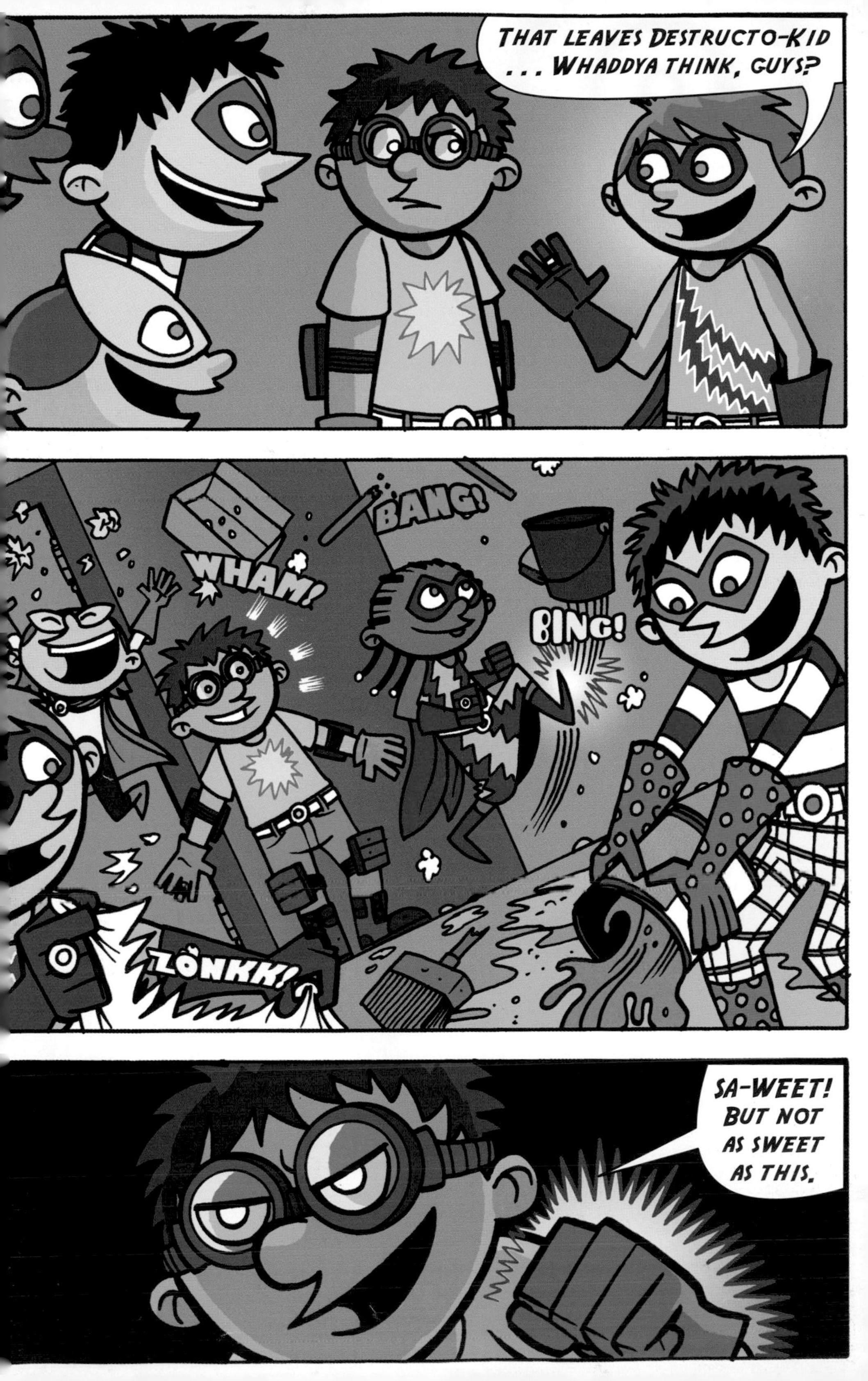
THAT LEAVES DESTRUCTO-KID . . . WHADDYA THINK, GUYS?
WHAM!
BANG!
BING!
ZONKK!
SA-WEET! BUT NOT AS SWEET AS THIS.

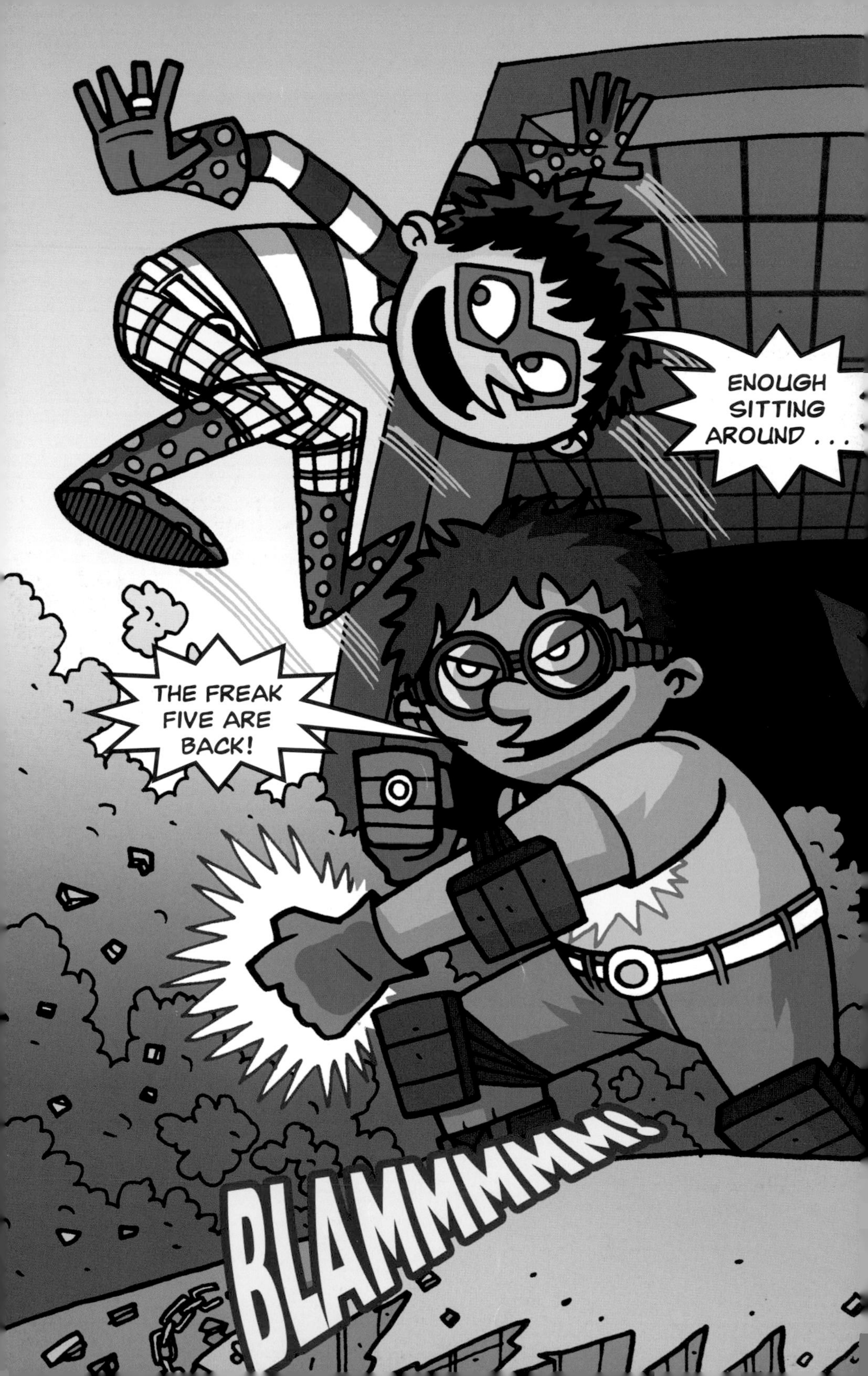
ENOUGH SITTING AROUND . . .
THE FREAK FIVE ARE BACK!
BLAMMMMMM!

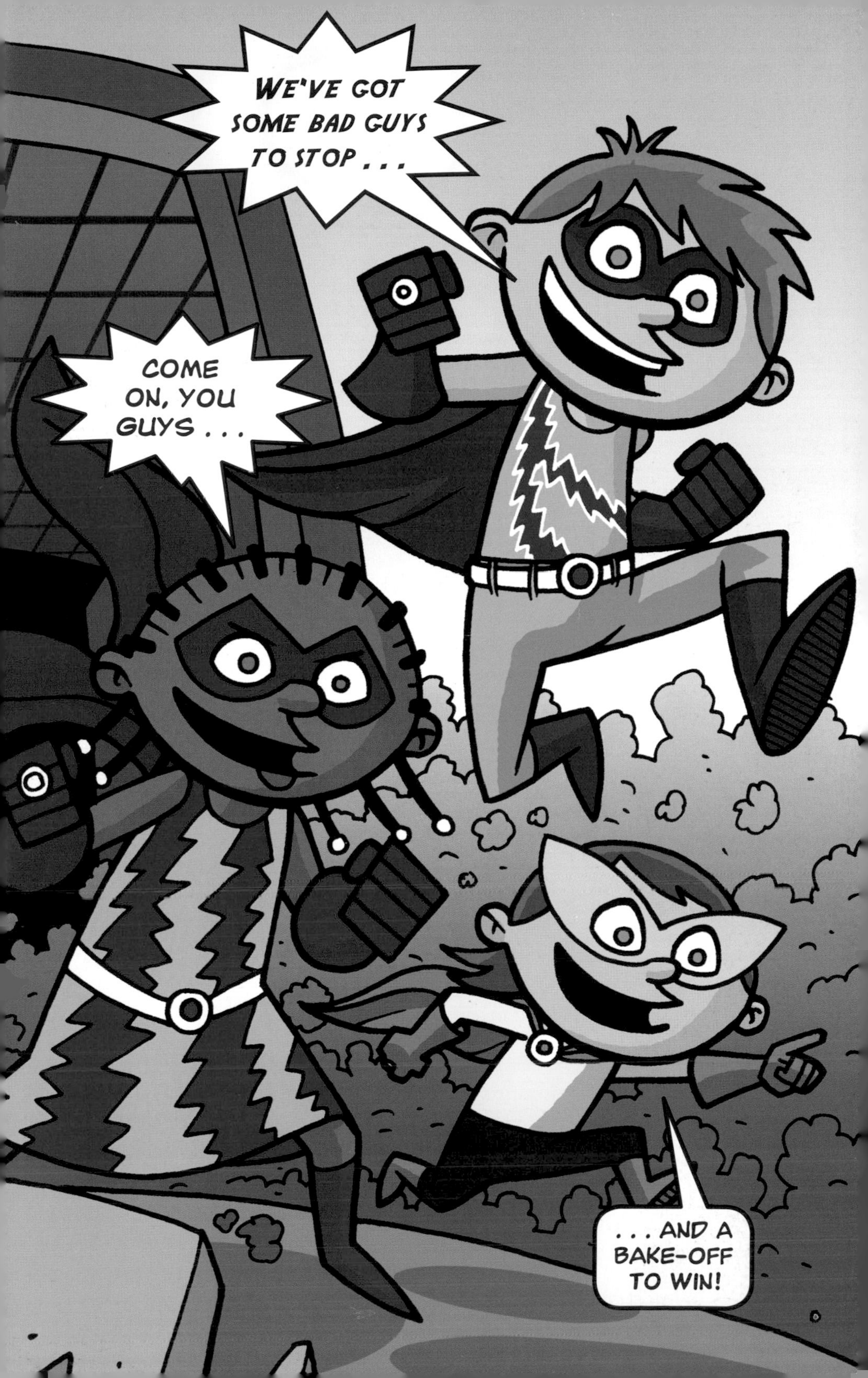
WE'VE GOT SOME BAD GUYS TO STOP . . .
COME ON, YOU GUYS . . .
. . . AND A BAKE-OFF TO WIN!

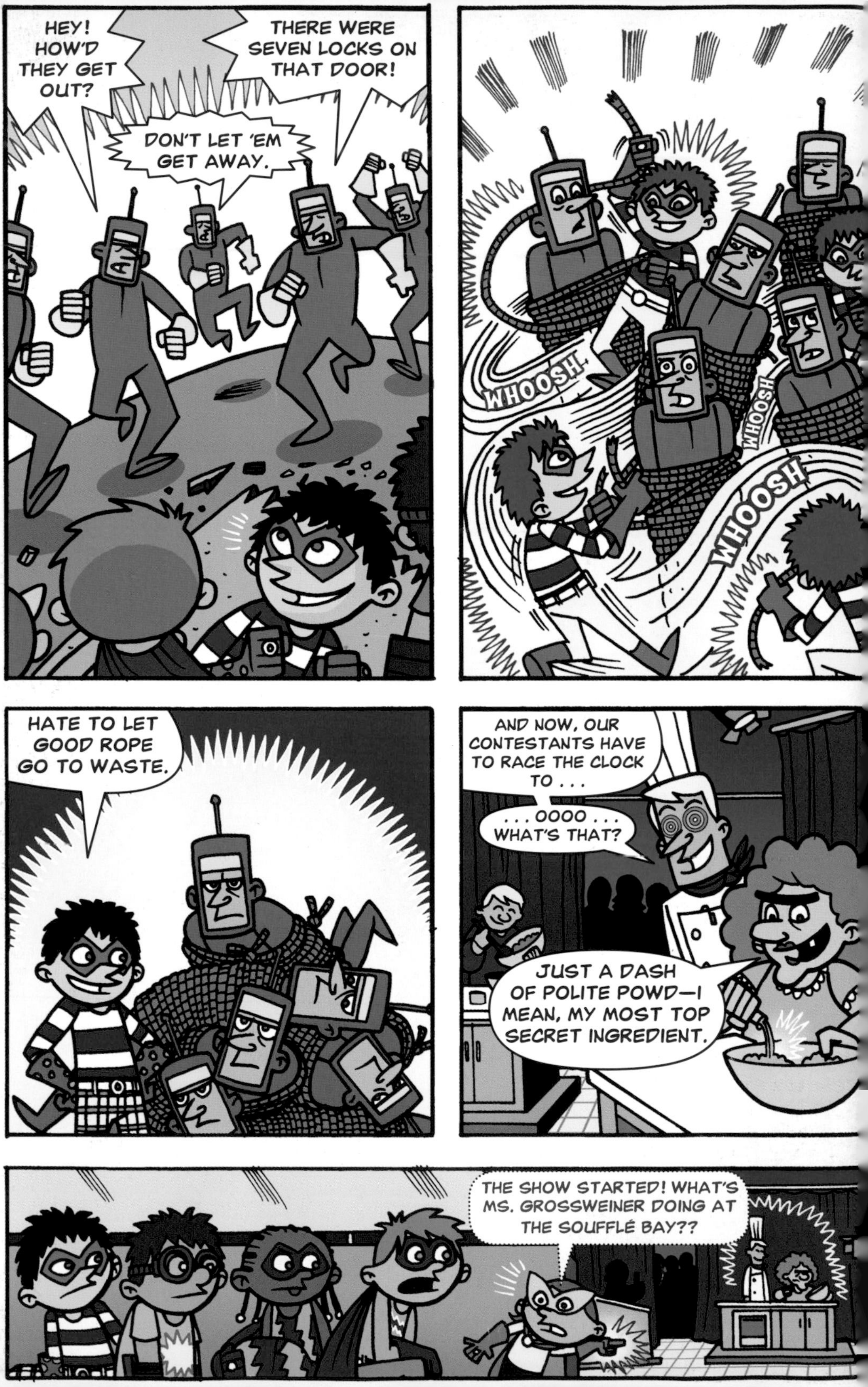
HEY! HOW'D THEY GET OUT?
THERE WERE SEVEN LOCKS ON THAT DOOR!
DON'T LET 'EM GET AWAY.
WHOOSH
WHOOSH
WHOOSH
WHOOSH
HATE TO LET GOOD ROPE GO TO WASTE.
AND NOW, OUR CONTESTANTS HAVE TO RACE THE CLOCK TO . . .
. . . OOOO . . . WHAT'S THAT?
JUST A DASH OF POLITE POWD—I MEAN, MY MOST TOP SECRET INGREDIENT.
THE SHOW STARTED! WHAT'S MS. GROSSWEINER DOING AT THE SOUFFLÉ BAY??

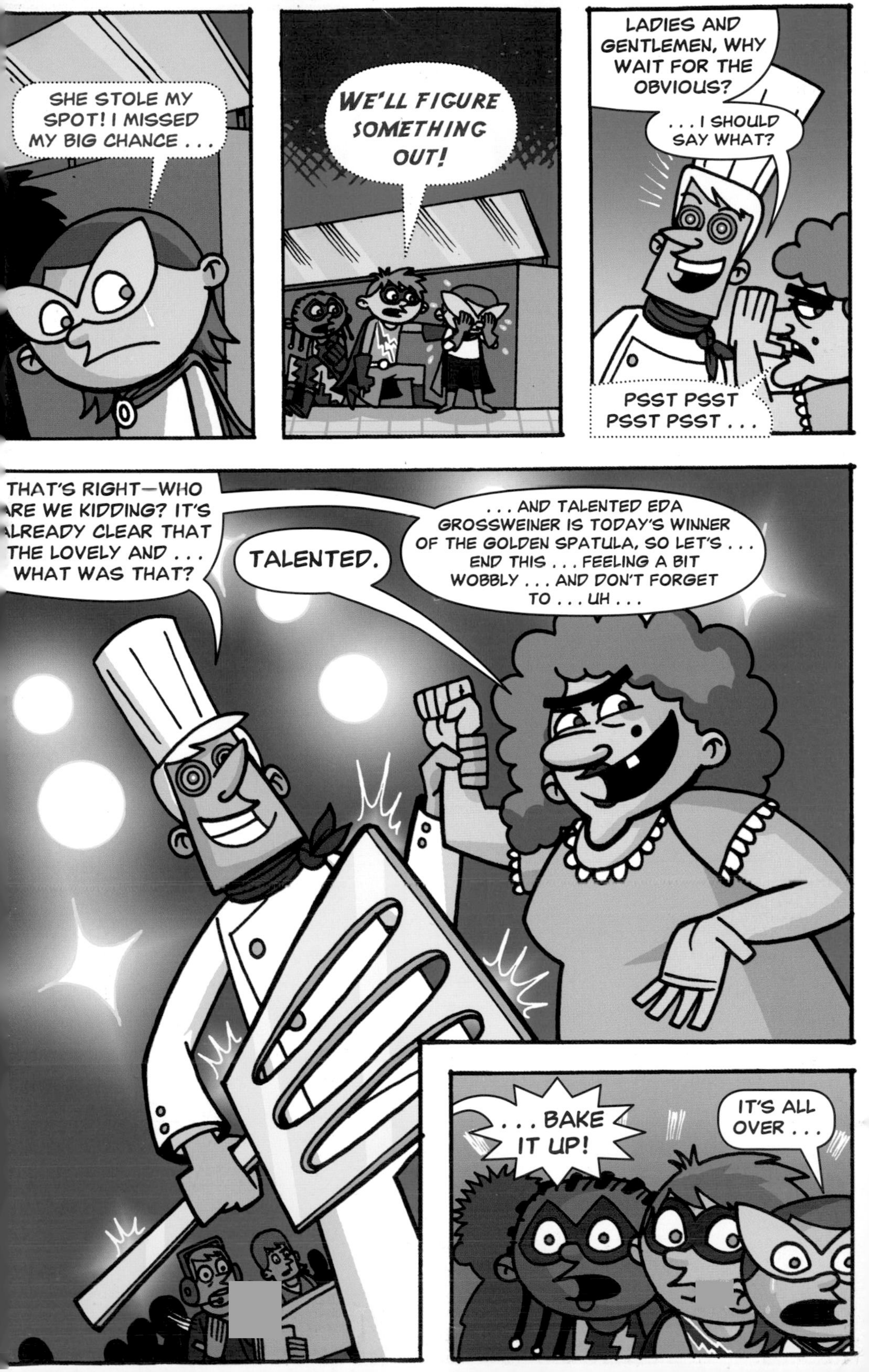
SHE STOLE MY SPOT! I MISSED MY BIG CHANCE . . .
WE'LL FIGURE SOMETHING OUT!
LADIES AND GENTLEMEN, WHY WAIT FOR THE OBVIOUS?
. . . I SHOULD SAY WHAT?
PSST PSST PSST PSST . . .
THAT'S RIGHT—WHO ARE WE KIDDING? IT'S ALREADY CLEAR THAT THE LOVELY AND . . . WHAT WAS THAT?
TALENTED.
. . . AND TALENTED EDA GROSSWEINER IS TODAY'S WINNER OF THE GOLDEN SPATULA, SO LET'S . . . END THIS . . . FEELING A BIT WOBBLY . . . AND DON'T FORGET TO . . . UH . . .
. . . BAKE IT UP!
IT'S ALL OVER . . .

SINCE THERE'S TIME LEFT, I MUST LET THE WORLD KNOW THAT MY AWARD-WINNING MAC-AND-CHEESE SOUFFLÉ IS NOW AVAILABLE IN YOUR VERY OWN HOME . . .

THAT'S RIGHT. GROSSWEINER'S GOURMET MAC-AND-CHEESE SOUFFLÉ, COMING TO A GROCERY STORE NEAR YOU!

YOUR BRATS— ER—KIDS'LL LOVE IT, BECAUSE IT'S MAC AND CHEESE.

GROSSWEINER'S GOURMET MAC & CHEESE SOUFFLÉ

AND PARENTS'L BUY IT BECAUS IT'S SOUFFLÉ. S WHAT ARE YO WAITING FOR .

. . . GO FOR THE GROSSWEINER'S!

OH NO.

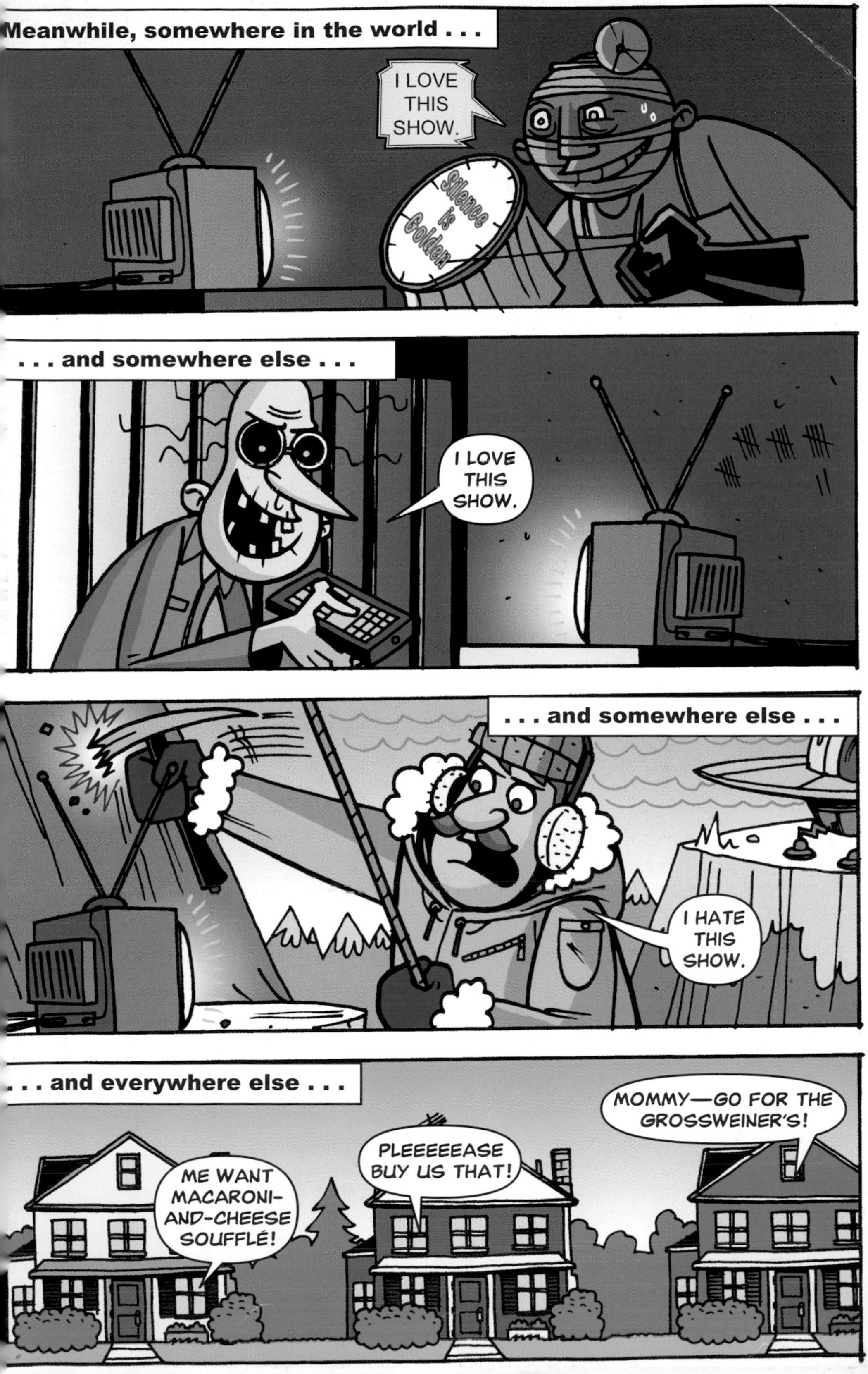
Meanwhile, somewhere in the world . . .
I LOVE THIS SHOW.
Silence is Golden
. . . and somewhere else . . .
I LOVE THIS SHOW.
. . . and somewhere else . . .
I HATE THIS SHOW.
. . . and everywhere else . . .
MOMMY—GO FOR THE GROSSWEINER'S!
PLEEEEEASE BUY US THAT!
ME WANT MACARONI-AND-CHEESE SOUFFLÉ!

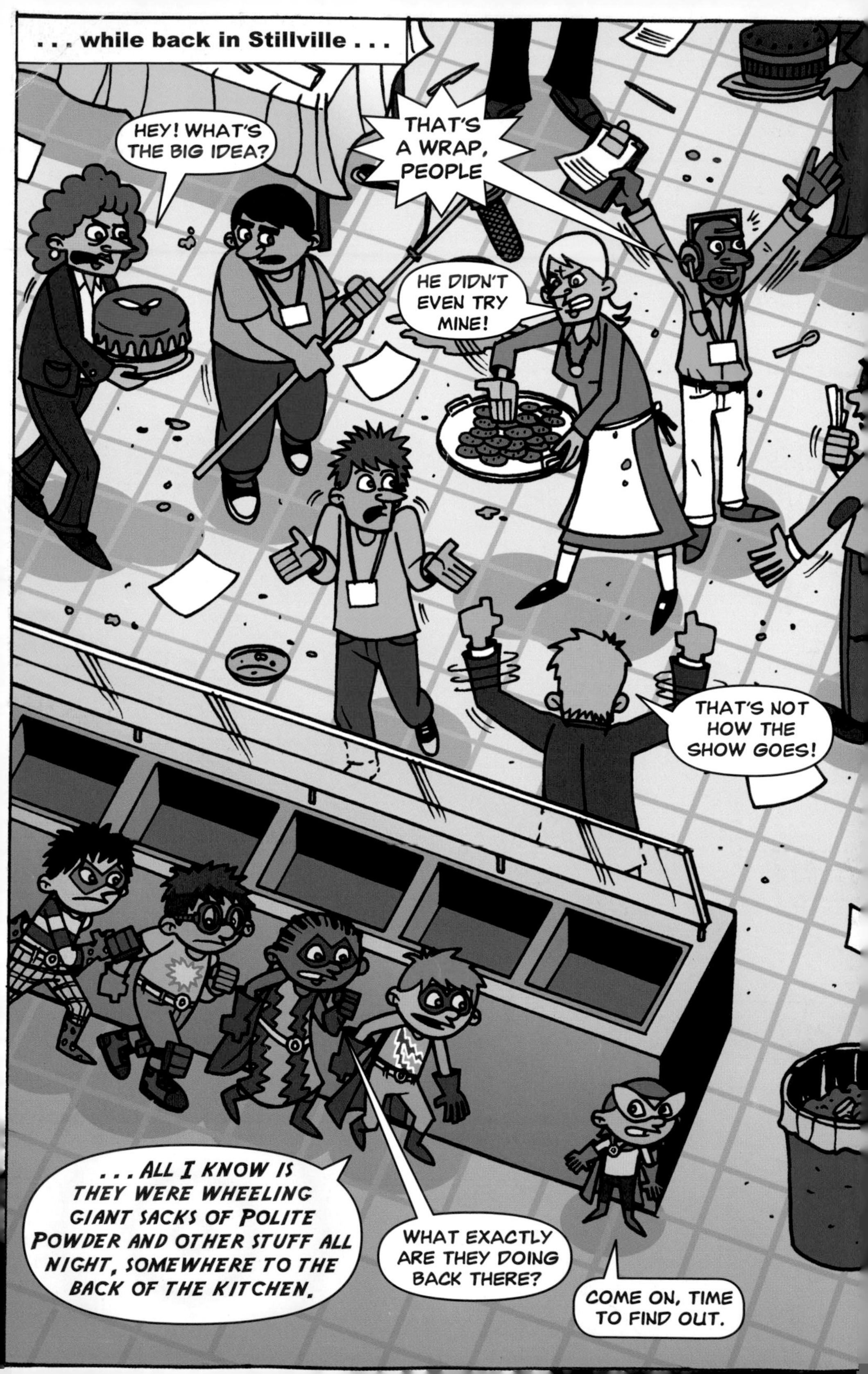

. . . while back in Stillville . . .
HEY! WHAT'S THE BIG IDEA?
THAT'S A WRAP, PEOPLE
HE DIDN'T EVEN TRY MINE!
THAT'S NOT HOW THE SHOW GOES!
. . . ALL I KNOW IS THEY WERE WHEELING GIANT SACKS OF POLITE POWDER AND OTHER STUFF ALL NIGHT, SOMEWHERE TO THE BACK OF THE KITCHEN.
WHAT EXACTLY ARE THEY DOING BACK THERE?
COME ON, TIME TO FIND OUT.

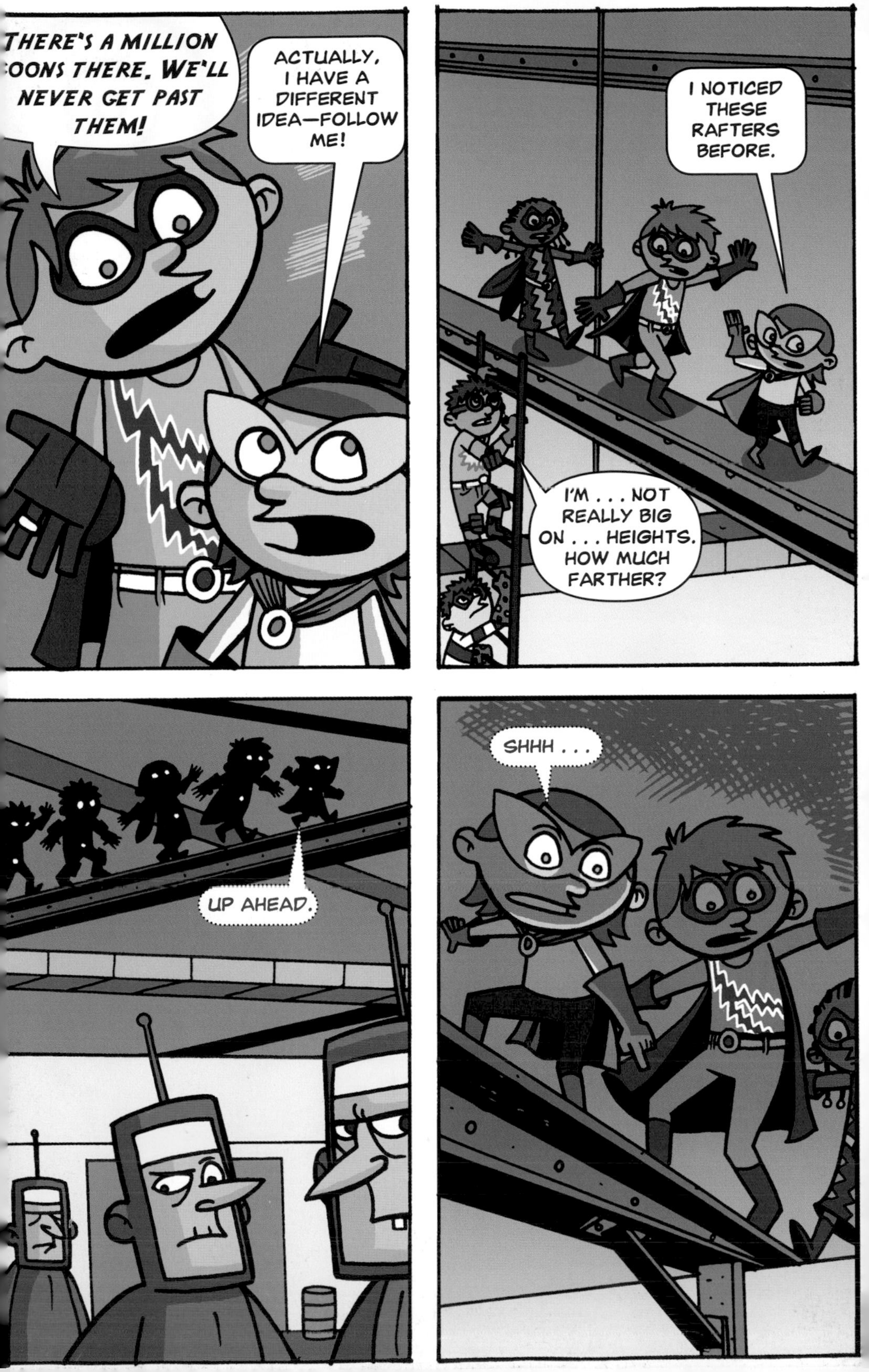
THERE'S A MILLION
OONS THERE. WE'LL NEVER GET PAST THEM!
ACTUALLY, I HAVE A DIFFERENT IDEA—FOLLOW ME!
I NOTICED THESE RAFTERS BEFORE.
I'M . . . NOT REALLY BIG ON . . . HEIGHTS. HOW MUCH FARTHER?
UP AHEAD.
SHHH . . .

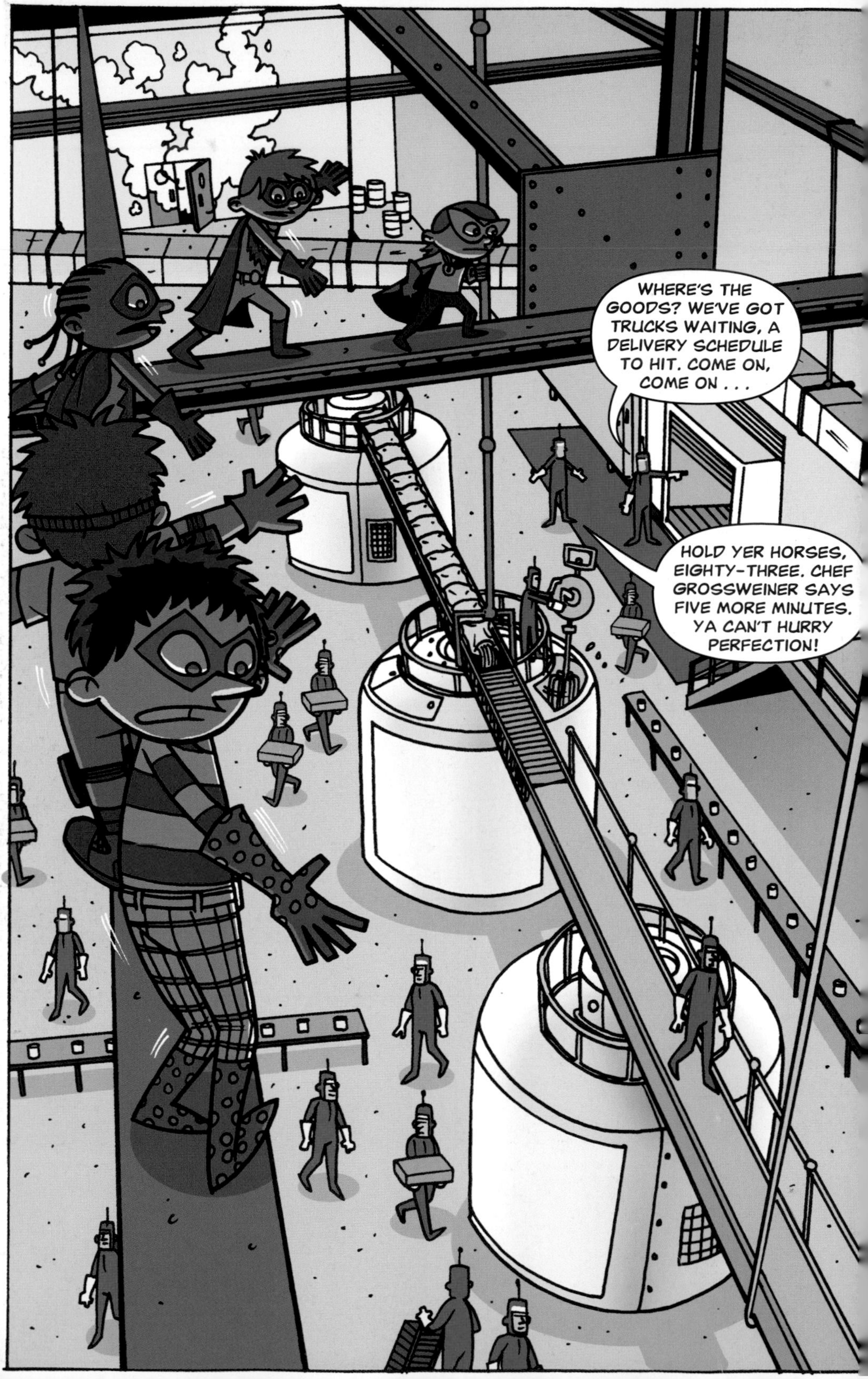
WHERE'S THE GOODS? WE'VE GOT TRUCKS WAITING, A DELIVERY SCHEDULE TO HIT. COME ON, COME ON . . .
HOLD YER HORSES, EIGHTY-THREE. CHEF GROSSWEINER SAYS FIVE MORE MINUTES. YA CAN'T HURRY PERFECTION!

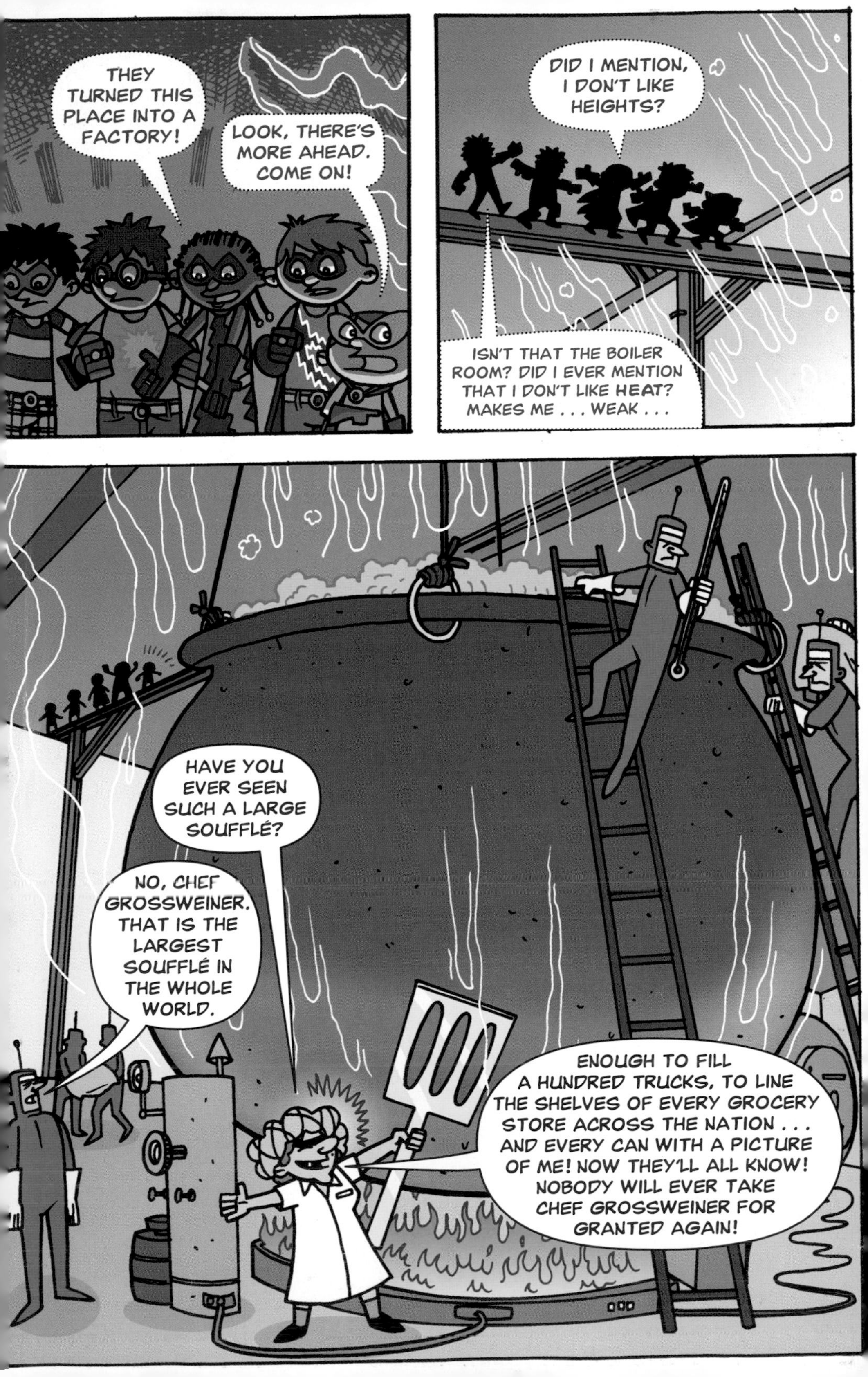
THEY TURNED THIS PLACE INTO A FACTORY!
LOOK, THERE'S MORE AHEAD. COME ON!
DID I MENTION, I DON'T LIKE HEIGHTS?
ISN'T THAT THE BOILER ROOM? DID I EVER MENTION THAT I DON'T LIKE HEAT? MAKES ME . . . WEAK . . .
HAVE YOU EVER SEEN SUCH A LARGE SOUFFLÉ?
NO, CHEF GROSSWEINER. THAT IS THE LARGEST SOUFFLÉ IN THE WHOLE WORLD.
ENOUGH TO FILL A HUNDRED TRUCKS, TO LINE THE SHELVES OF EVERY GROCERY STORE ACROSS THE NATION . . . AND EVERY CAN WITH A PICTURE OF ME! NOW THEY'LL ALL KNOW! NOBODY WILL EVER TAKE CHEF GROSSWEINER FOR GRANTED AGAIN!

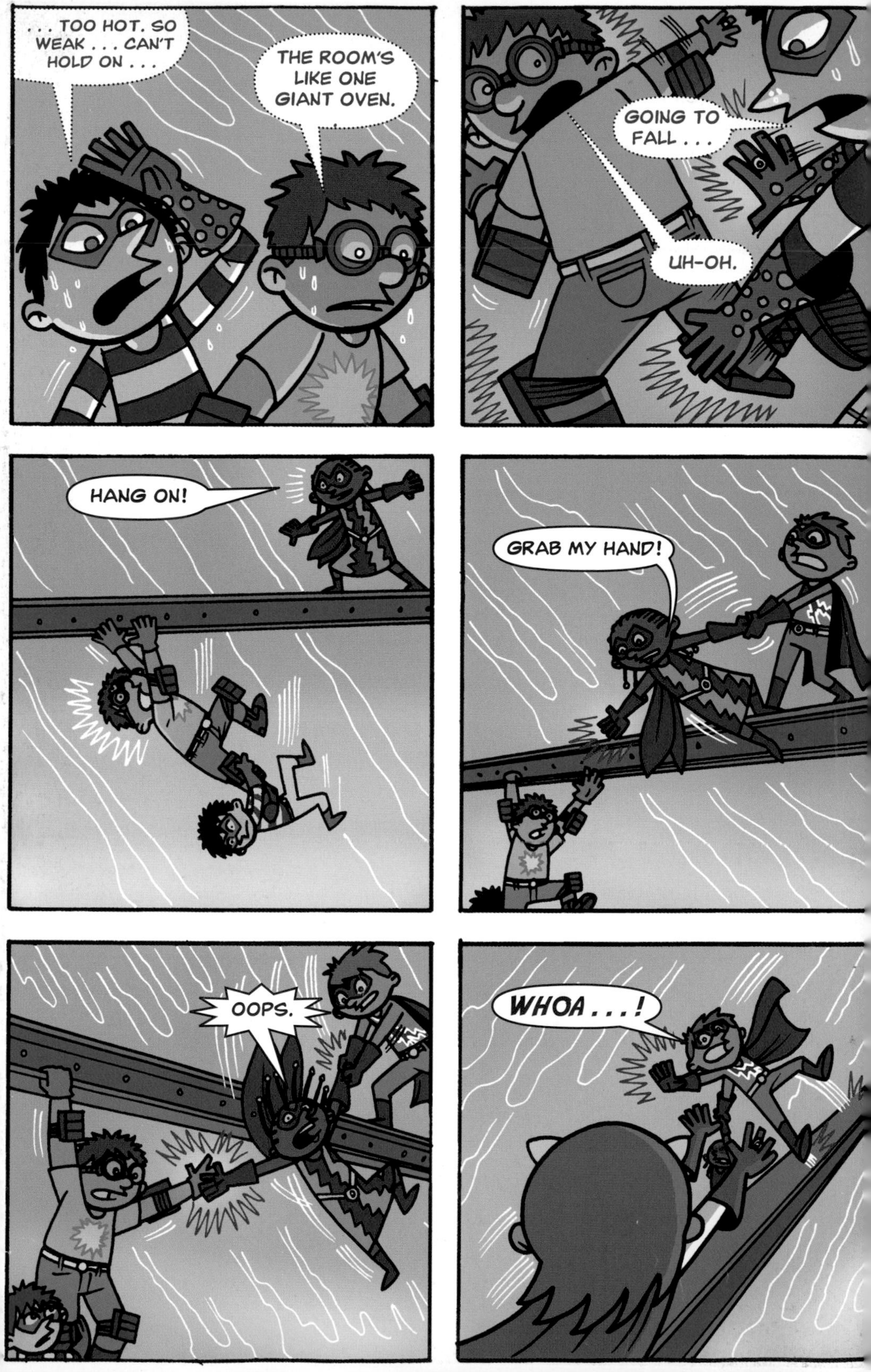
. . . TOO HOT. SO WEAK . . . CAN'T HOLD ON . . .
THE ROOM'S LIKE ONE GIANT OVEN.
GOING TO FALL . . .
UH-OH.
HANG ON!
GRAB MY HAND!
OOPS.
WHOA . . . !

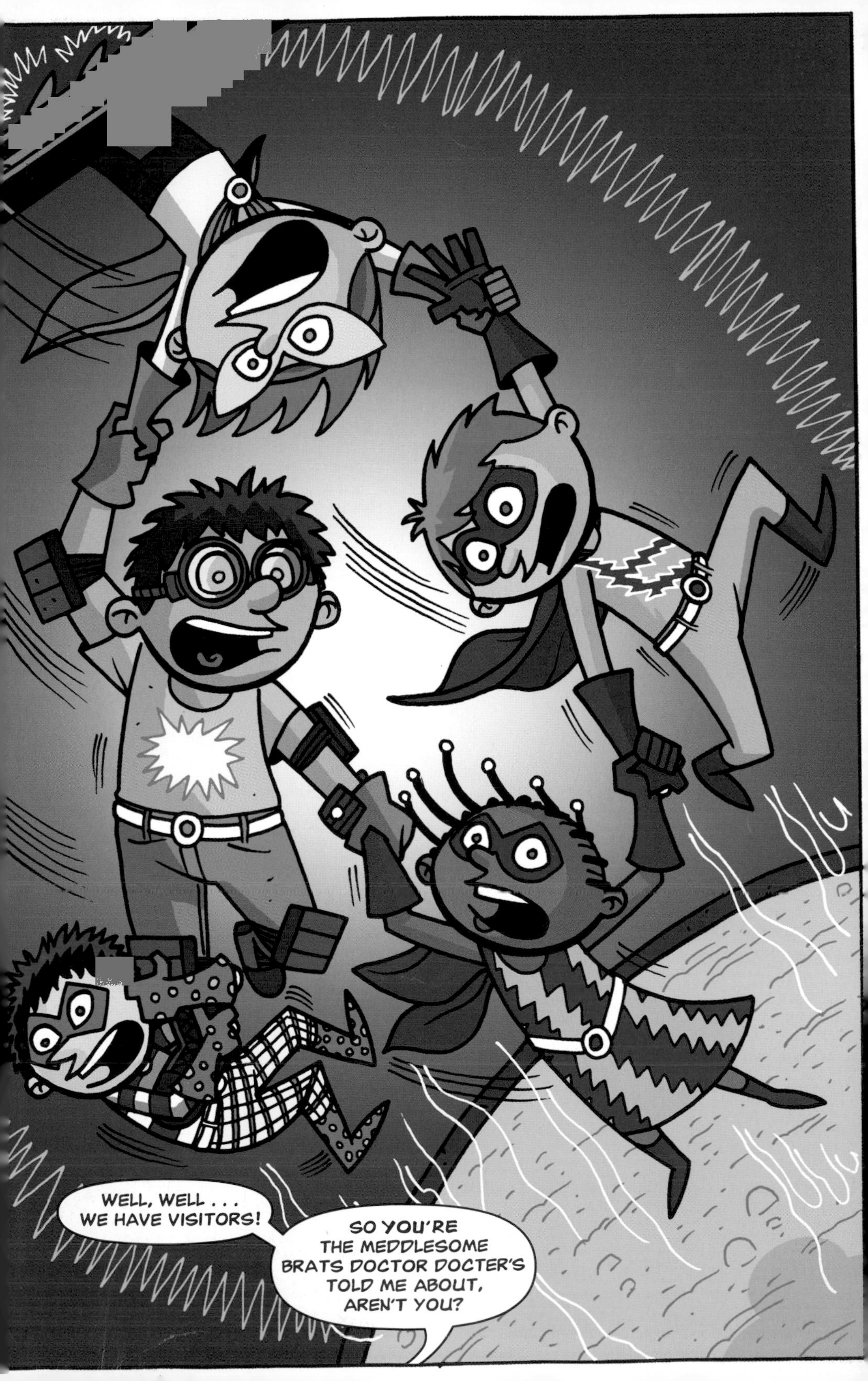
WELL, WELL . . .
WE HAVE VISITORS!
SO YOU'RE THE MEDDLESOME BRATS DOCTOR DOCTER'S TOLD ME ABOUT, AREN'T YOU?

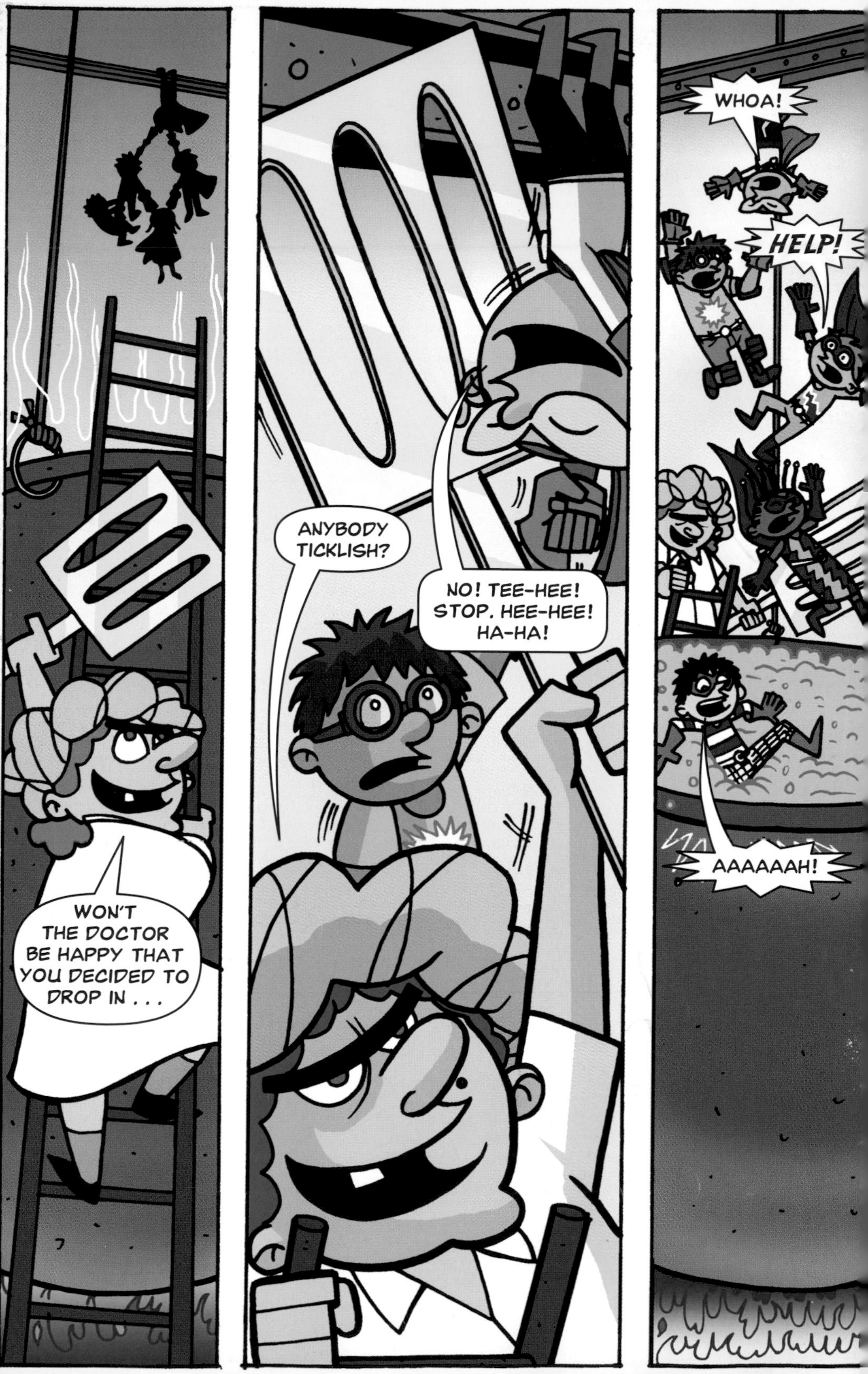
WON'T THE DOCTOR BE HAPPY THAT YOU DECIDED TO DROP IN . . .
ANYBODY TICKLISH?
NO! TEE-HEE! STOP. HEE-HEE! HA-HA!
WHOA!
HELP!
AAAAAAH!

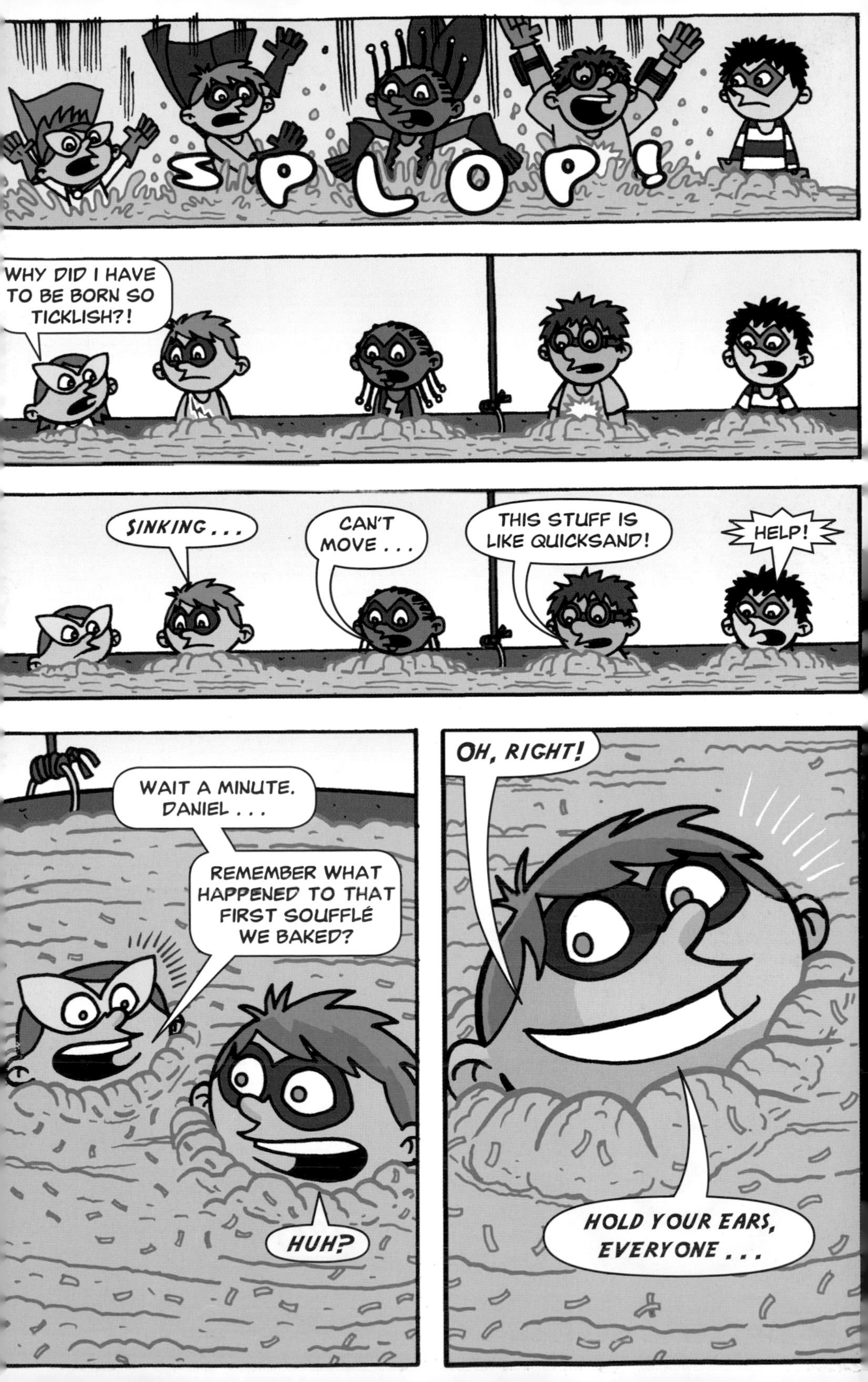
SPLOP!
WHY DID I HAVE TO BE BORN SO TICKLISH?!
SINKING . . .
CAN'T MOVE . . .
THIS STUFF IS LIKE QUICKSAND!
HELP!
WAIT A MINUTE. DANIEL . . .
REMEMBER WHAT HAPPENED TO THAT FIRST SOUFFLÉ WE BAKED?
HUH?
OH, RIGHT!
HOLD YOUR EARS, EVERYONE . . .

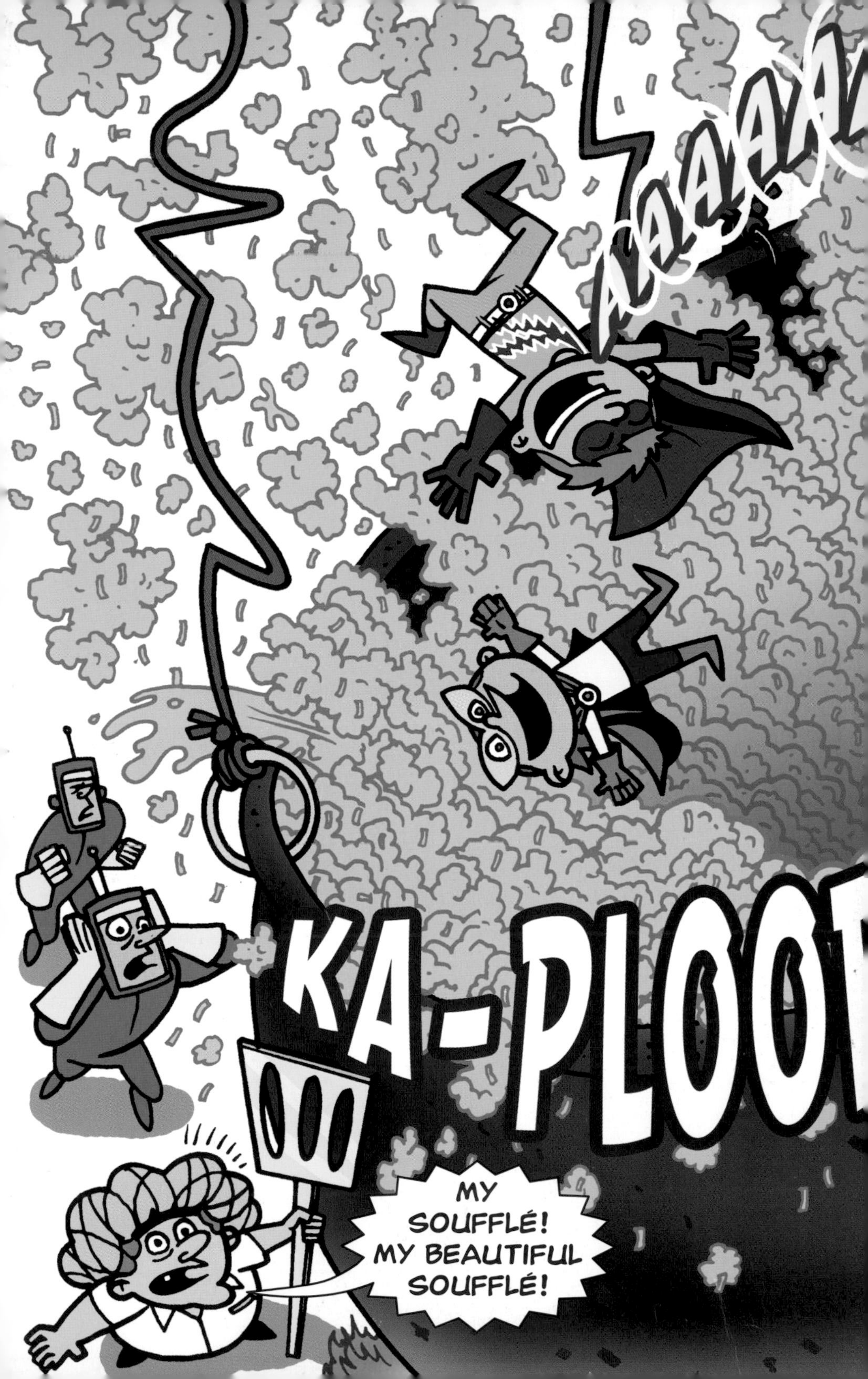

AAAAAA
KA-PLOO
MY SOUFFLÉ! MY BEAUTIFUL SOUFFLÉ!

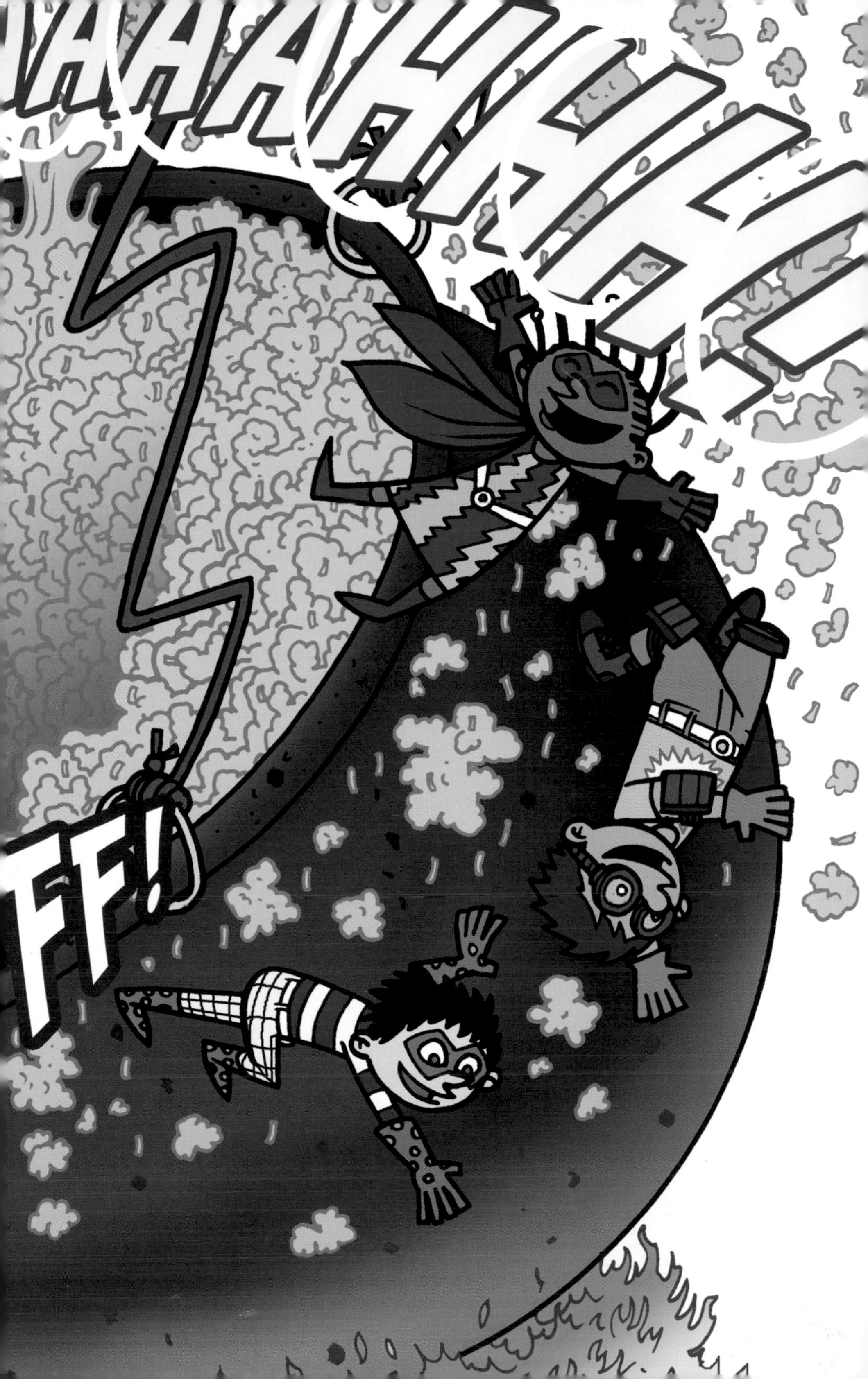
FF!

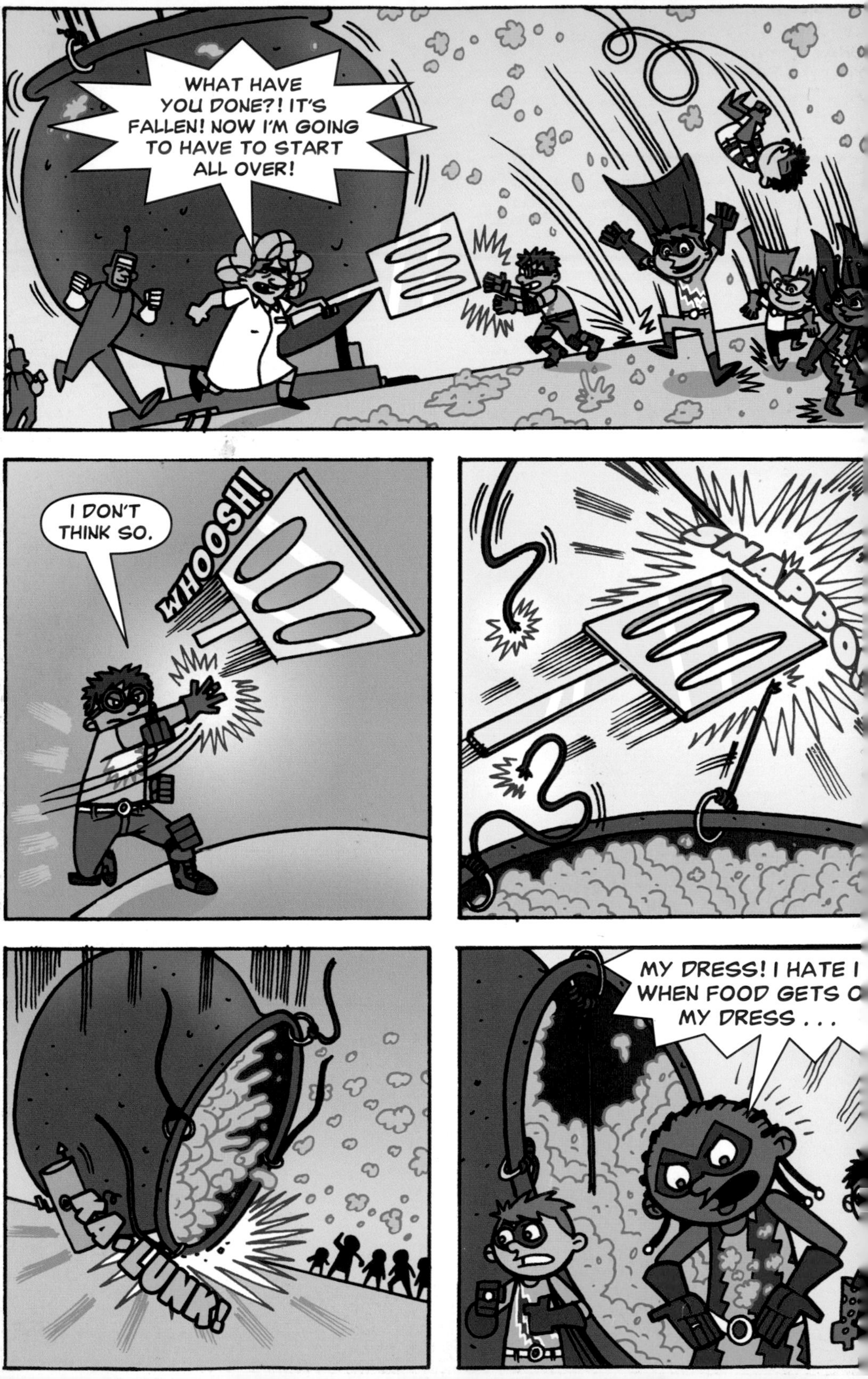
WHAT HAVE YOU DONE?! IT'S FALLEN! NOW I'M GOING TO HAVE TO START ALL OVER!
I DON'T THINK SO.
WHOOSH!
SNAPPO!
KA-LUNK!
MY DRESS! I HATE I
WHEN FOOD GETS O
MY DRESS . . .

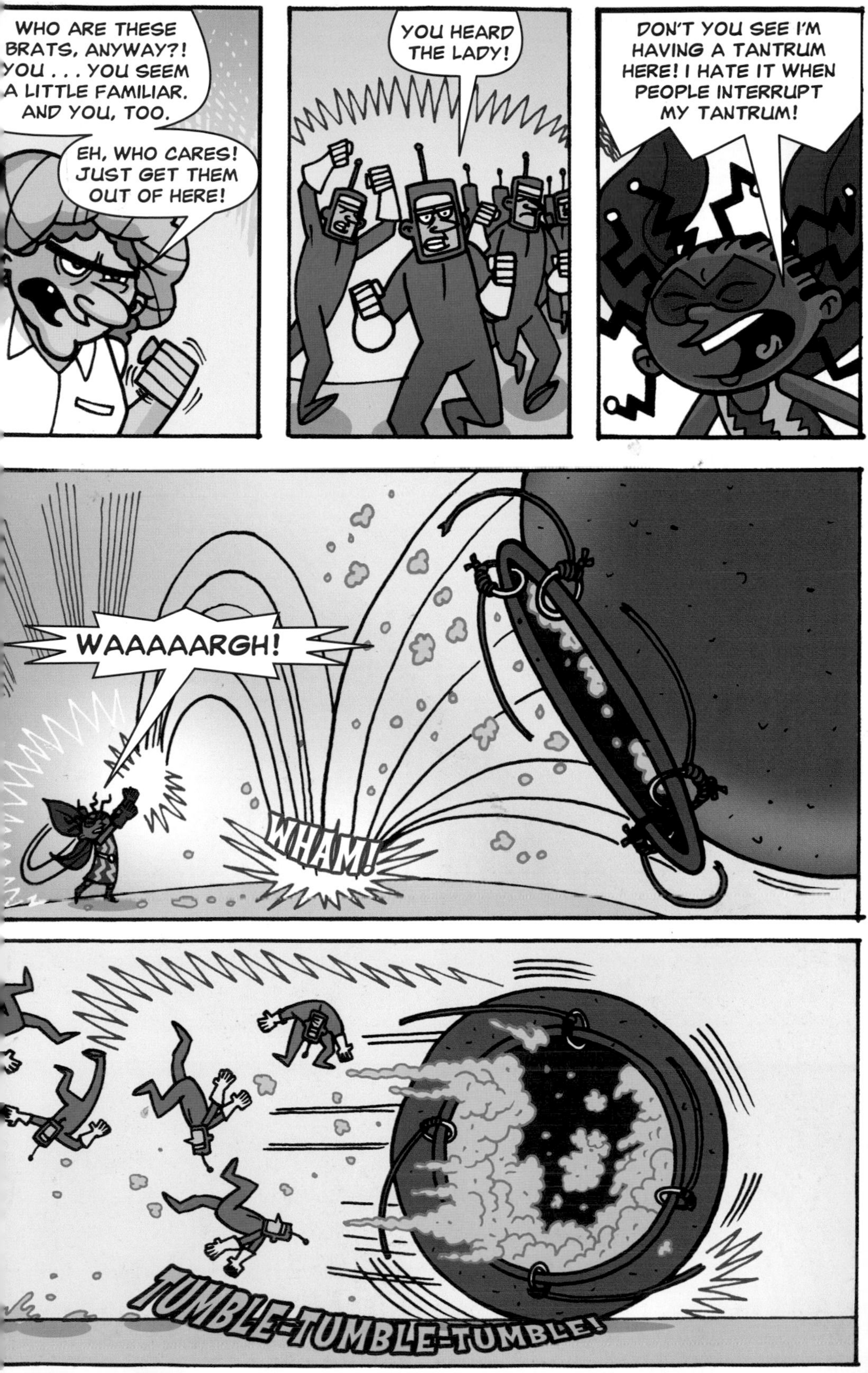
WHO ARE THESE BRATS, ANYWAY?! YOU . . . YOU SEEM A LITTLE FAMILIAR. AND YOU, TOO.
EH, WHO CARES! JUST GET THEM OUT OF HERE!
YOU HEARD THE LADY!
DON'T YOU SEE I'M HAVING A TANTRUM HERE! I HATE IT WHEN PEOPLE INTERRUPT MY TANTRUM!
WAAAAARGH!
WHAM!
TUMBLE-TUMBLE-TUMBLE!

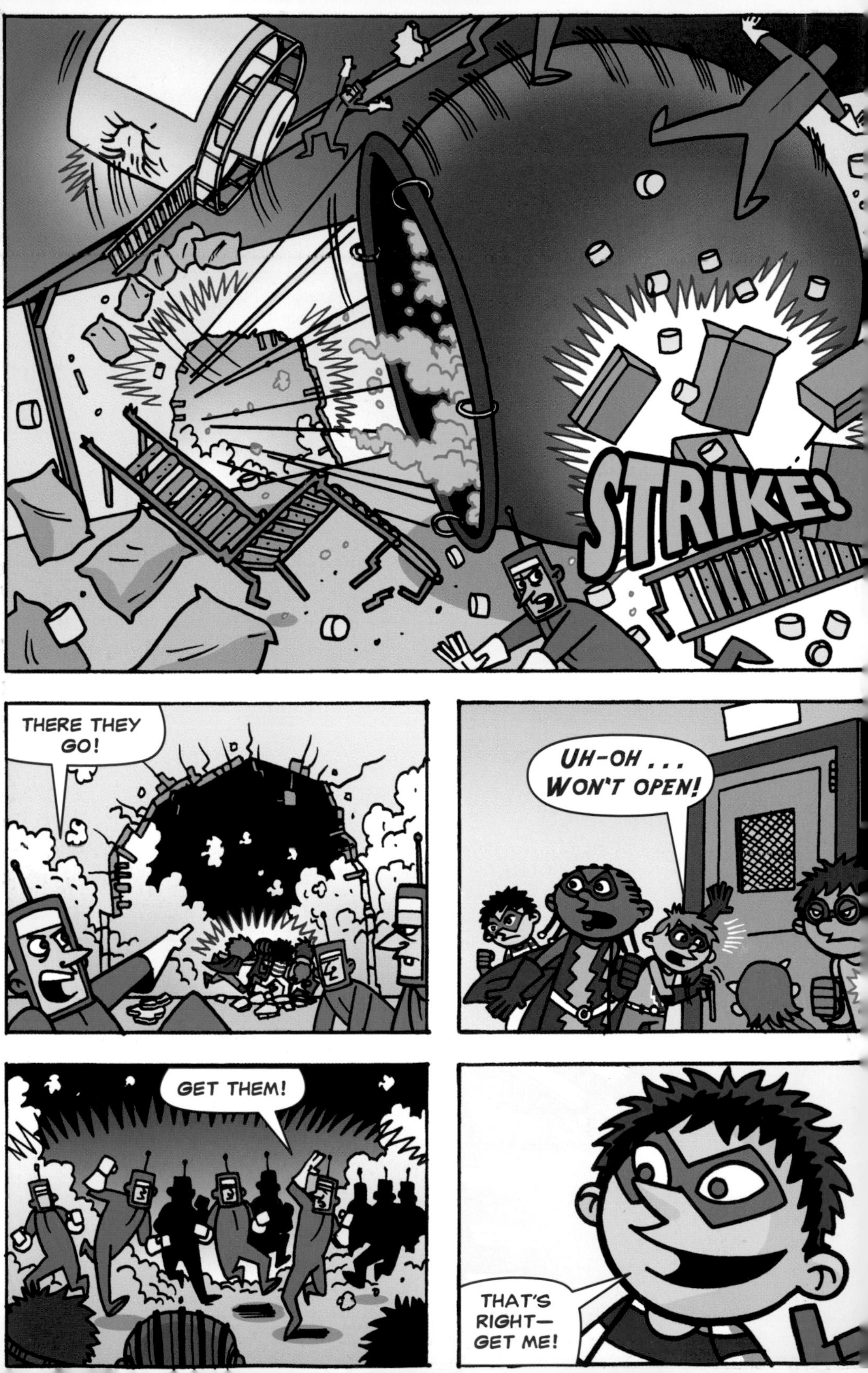
STRIKE!
THERE THEY GO!
UH-OH . . . WON'T OPEN!
GET THEM!
THAT'S RIGHT— GET ME!

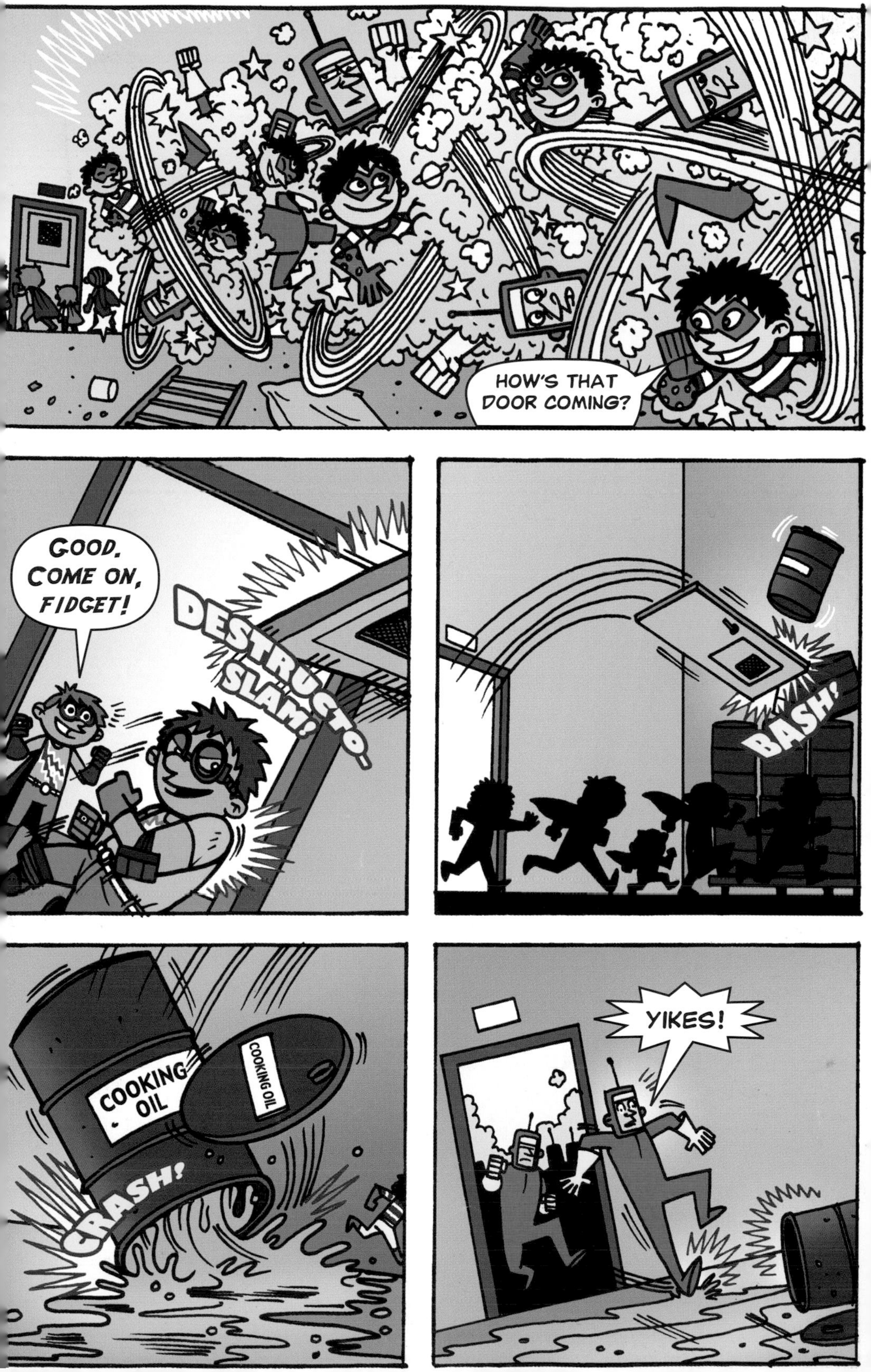
HOW'S THAT DOOR COMING?
GOOD. COME ON, FIDGET!
DESTRUCTO-SLAM!
BASH!
COOKING OIL
COOKING OIL
CRASH!
YIKES!

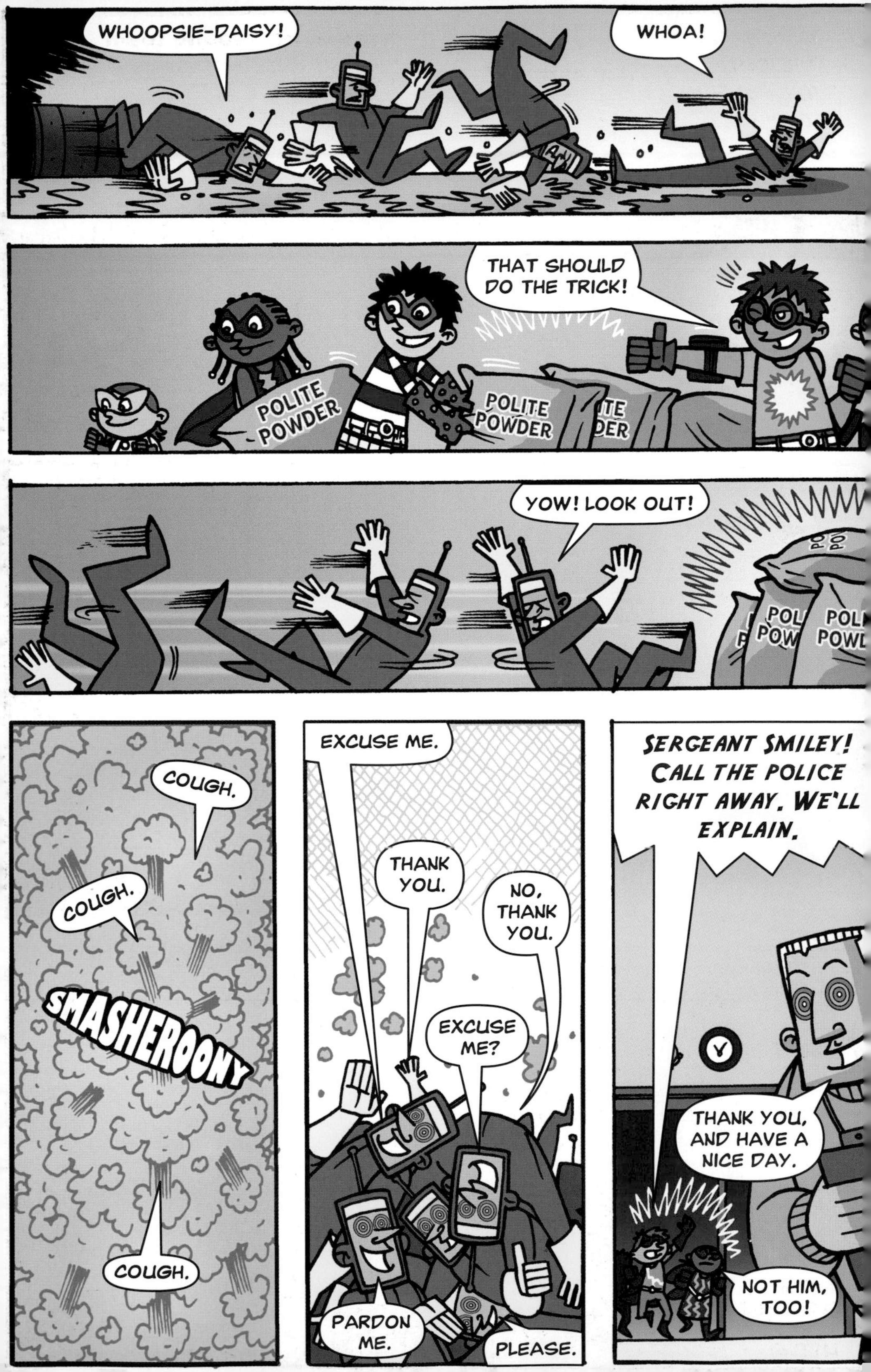
WHOOPSIE-DAISY!
WHOA!
THAT SHOULD DO THE TRICK!
POLITE POWDER
POLITE POWDER
YOW! LOOK OUT!
COUGH.
COUGH.
SMASHEROONY
COUGH.
EXCUSE ME.
THANK YOU.
NO, THANK YOU.
EXCUSE ME?
PARDON ME.
PLEASE.
SERGEANT SMILEY! CALL THE POLICE RIGHT AWAY. WE'LL EXPLAIN.
THANK YOU, AND HAVE A NICE DAY.
NOT HIM, TOO!

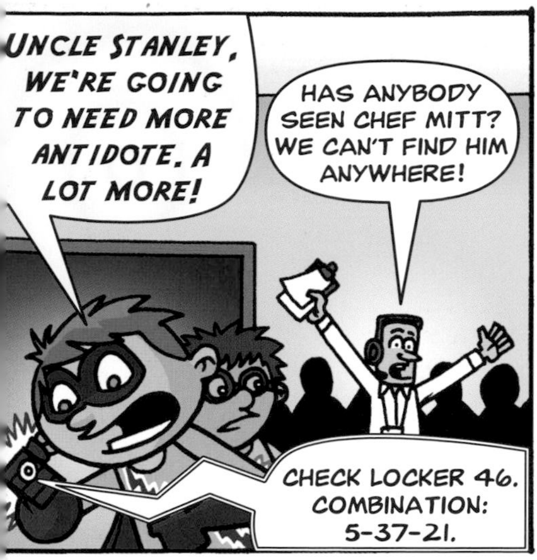
UNCLE STANLEY, WE'RE GOING TO NEED MORE ANTIDOTE. A LOT MORE!
HAS ANYBODY SEEN CHEF MITT? WE CAN'T FIND HIM ANYWHERE!
CHECK LOCKER 46. COMBINATION: 5-37-21.

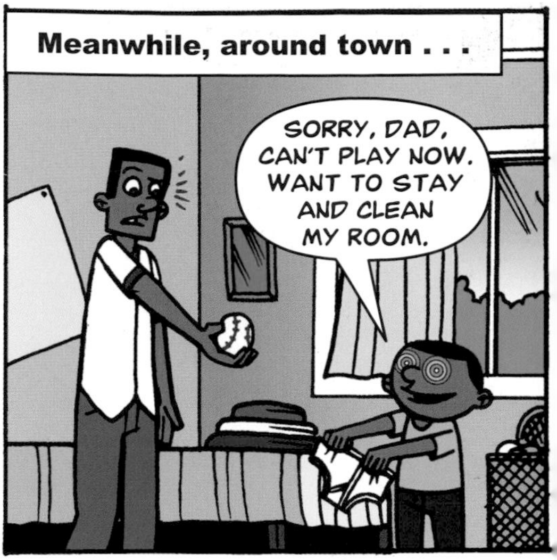
Meanwhile, around town . . .
SORRY, DAD, CAN'T PLAY NOW. WANT TO STAY AND CLEAN MY ROOM.

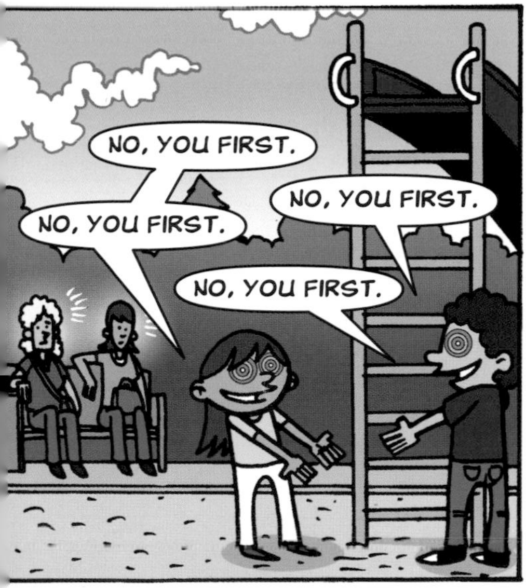
NO, YOU FIRST.
NO, YOU FIRST.
NO, YOU FIRST.
NO, YOU FIRST.

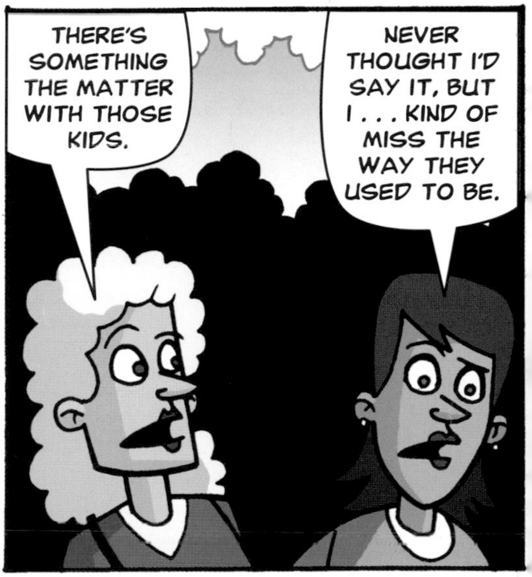
THERE'S SOMETHING THE MATTER WITH THOSE KIDS.
NEVER THOUGHT I'D SAY IT, BUT I . . . KIND OF MISS THE WAY THEY USED TO BE.

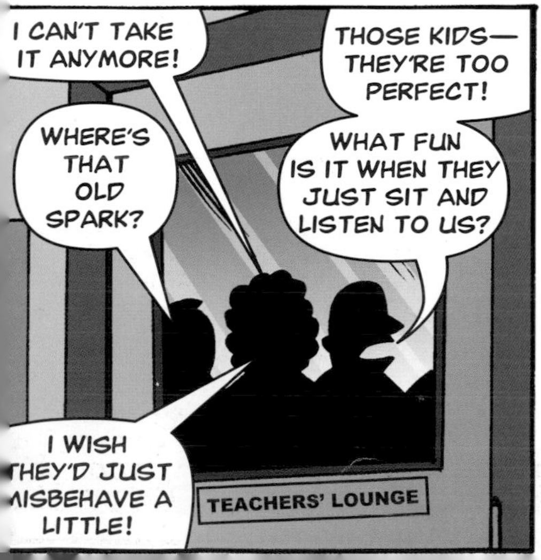
I CAN'T TAKE IT ANYMORE!
THOSE KIDS—THEY'RE TOO PERFECT!
WHERE'S THAT OLD SPARK?
WHAT FUN IS IT WHEN THEY JUST SIT AND LISTEN TO US?
I WISH THEY'D JUST MISBEHAVE A LITTLE!
TEACHERS' LOUNGE

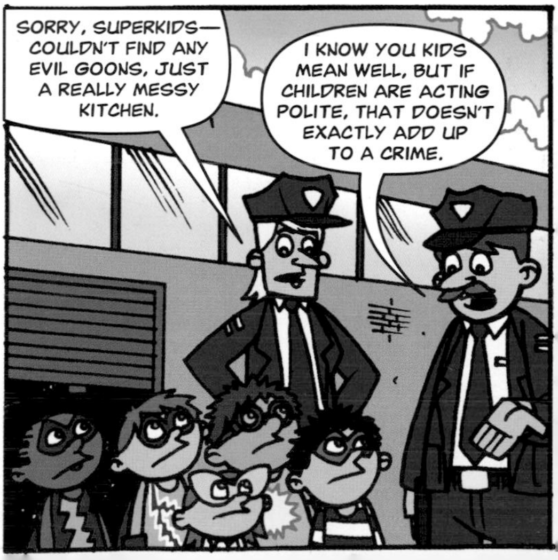
SORRY, SUPERKIDS—COULDN'T FIND ANY EVIL GOONS, JUST A REALLY MESSY KITCHEN.
I KNOW YOU KIDS MEAN WELL, BUT IF CHILDREN ARE ACTING POLITE, THAT DOESN'T EXACTLY ADD UP TO A CRIME.

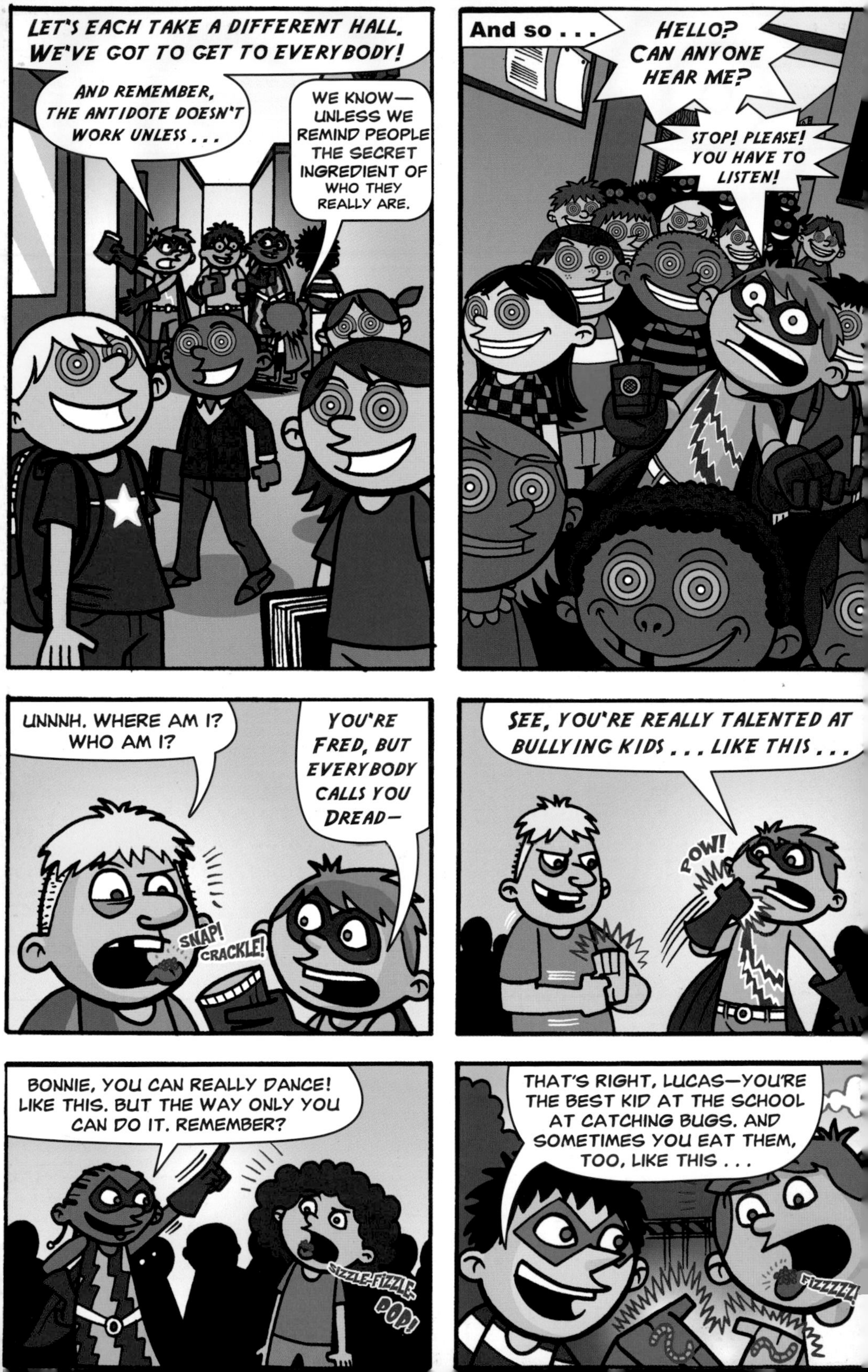
LET'S EACH TAKE A DIFFERENT HALL. WE'VE GOT TO GET TO EVERYBODY!
AND REMEMBER, THE ANTIDOTE DOESN'T WORK UNLESS . . .
WE KNOW— UNLESS WE REMIND PEOPLE THE SECRET INGREDIENT OF WHO THEY REALLY ARE.
And so . . .
HELLO? CAN ANYONE HEAR ME?
STOP! PLEASE! YOU HAVE TO LISTEN!
UNNNH. WHERE AM I? WHO AM I?
YOU'RE FRED, BUT EVERYBODY CALLS YOU DREAD—
SNAP!
CRACKLE!
SEE, YOU'RE REALLY TALENTED AT BULLYING KIDS . . . LIKE THIS . . .
POW!
BONNIE, YOU CAN REALLY DANCE! LIKE THIS. BUT THE WAY ONLY YOU CAN DO IT. REMEMBER?
SIZZLE-FIZZLE-POP!
THAT'S RIGHT, LUCAS—YOU'RE THE BEST KID AT THE SCHOOL AT CATCHING BUGS. AND SOMETIMES YOU EAT THEM, TOO, LIKE THIS . . .
FIZZZZZ!

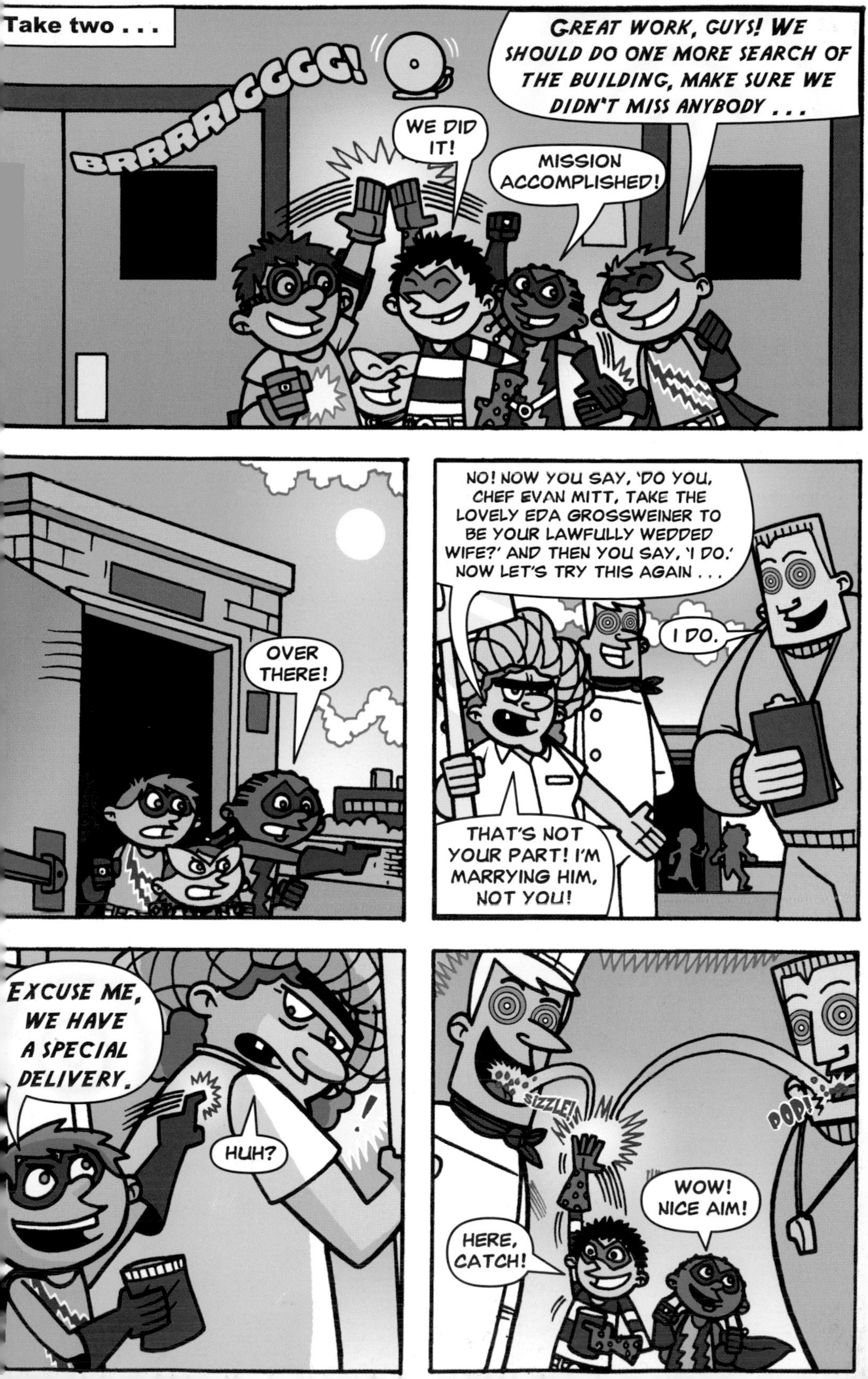
Take two . . .
BRRRRIGGGG!
GREAT WORK, GUYS! WE SHOULD DO ONE MORE SEARCH OF THE BUILDING, MAKE SURE WE DIDN'T MISS ANYBODY . . .
WE DID IT!
MISSION ACCOMPLISHED!
OVER THERE!
NO! NOW YOU SAY, 'DO YOU, CHEF EVAN MITT, TAKE THE LOVELY EDA GROSSWEINER TO BE YOUR LAWFULLY WEDDED WIFE?' AND THEN YOU SAY, 'I DO.' NOW LET'S TRY THIS AGAIN . . .
I DO.
THAT'S NOT YOUR PART! I'M MARRYING HIM, NOT YOU!
EXCUSE ME, WE HAVE A SPECIAL DELIVERY.
HUH?
SIZZLE!
POP!
WOW! NICE AIM!
HERE, CATCH!

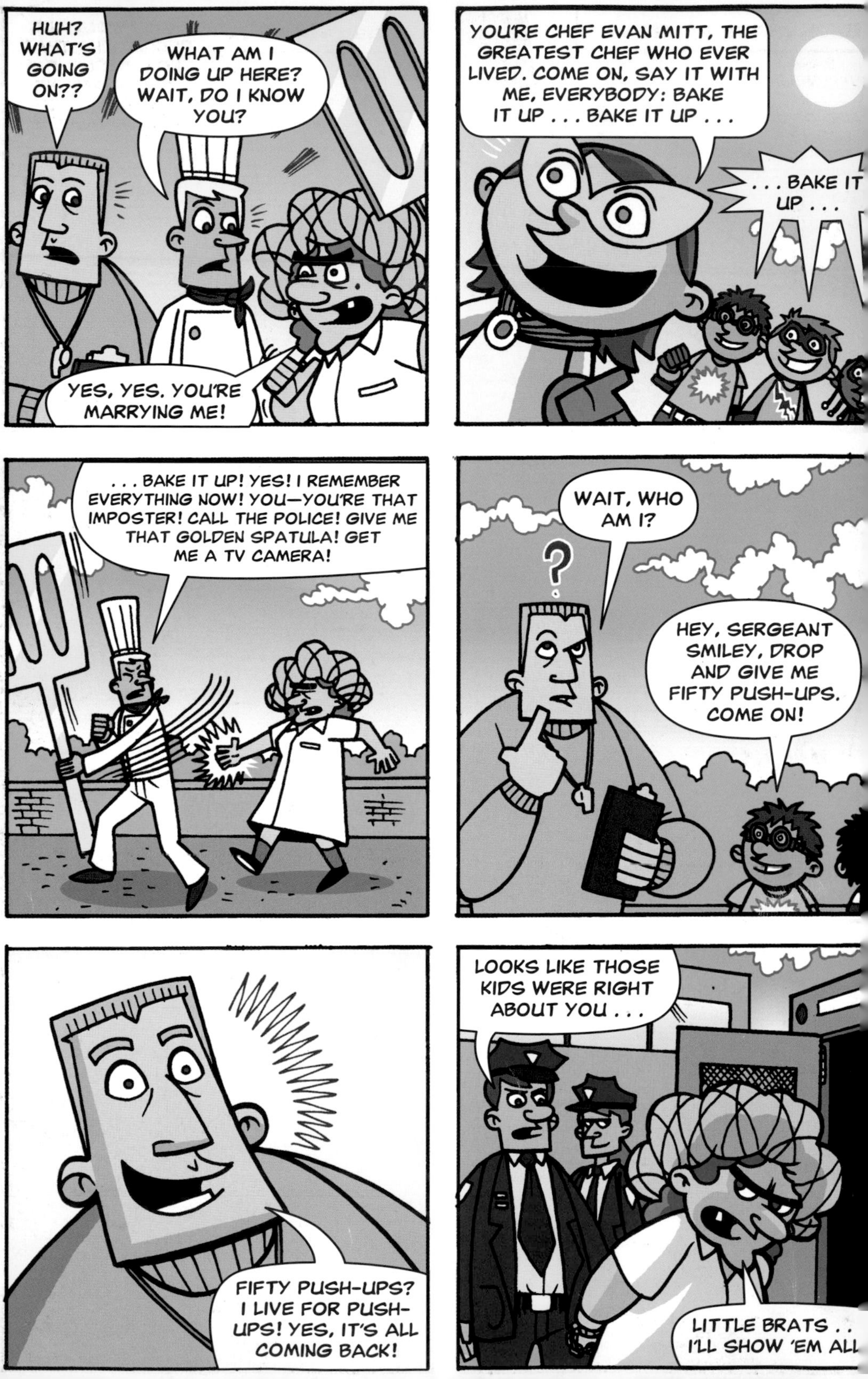
HUH? WHAT'S GOING ON??
WHAT AM I DOING UP HERE? WAIT, DO I KNOW YOU?
YES, YES. YOU'RE MARRYING ME!
YOU'RE CHEF EVAN MITT, THE GREATEST CHEF WHO EVER LIVED. COME ON, SAY IT WITH ME, EVERYBODY: BAKE IT UP . . . BAKE IT UP . . .
. . . BAKE IT UP . . .
. . . BAKE IT UP! YES! I REMEMBER EVERYTHING NOW! YOU—YOU'RE THAT IMPOSTER! CALL THE POLICE! GIVE ME THAT GOLDEN SPATULA! GET ME A TV CAMERA!
WAIT, WHO AM I?
?
HEY, SERGEANT SMILEY, DROP AND GIVE ME FIFTY PUSH-UPS. COME ON!
FIFTY PUSH-UPS? I LIVE FOR PUSH-UPS! YES, IT'S ALL COMING BACK!
LOOKS LIKE THOSE KIDS WERE RIGHT ABOUT YOU . . .
LITTLE BRATS . . I'LL SHOW 'EM ALL

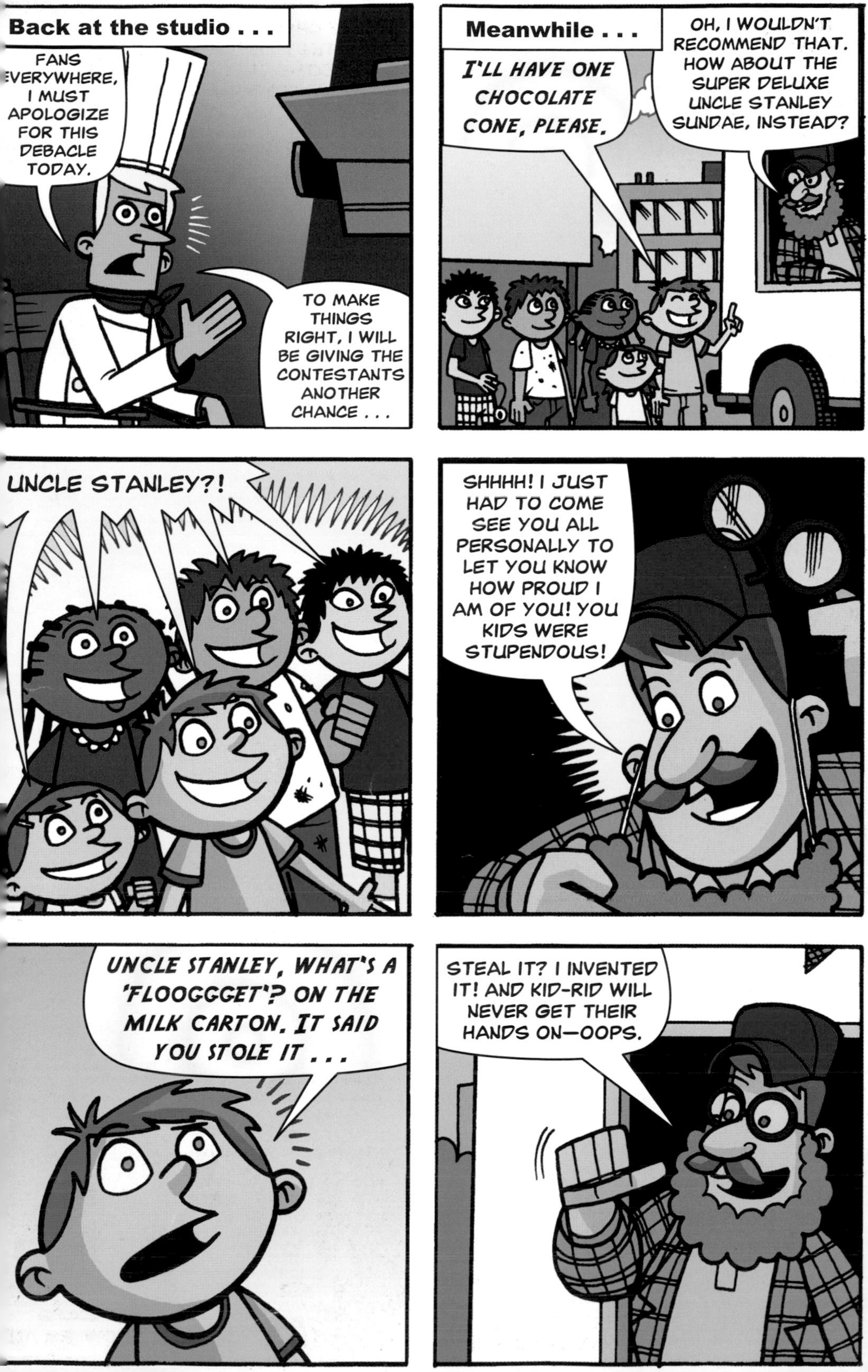
Back at the studio . . .
FANS EVERYWHERE, I MUST APOLOGIZE FOR THIS DEBACLE TODAY.
TO MAKE THINGS RIGHT, I WILL BE GIVING THE CONTESTANTS ANOTHER CHANCE . . .
Meanwhile . . .
I'LL HAVE ONE CHOCOLATE CONE, PLEASE.
OH, I WOULDN'T RECOMMEND THAT. HOW ABOUT THE SUPER DELUXE UNCLE STANLEY SUNDAE, INSTEAD?
UNCLE STANLEY?!
SHHHH! I JUST HAD TO COME SEE YOU ALL PERSONALLY TO LET YOU KNOW HOW PROUD I AM OF YOU! YOU KIDS WERE STUPENDOUS!
UNCLE STANLEY, WHAT'S A 'FLOOGGGET'? ON THE MILK CARTON. IT SAID YOU STOLE IT . . .
STEAL IT? I INVENTED IT! AND KID-RID WILL NEVER GET THEIR HANDS ON—OOPS.

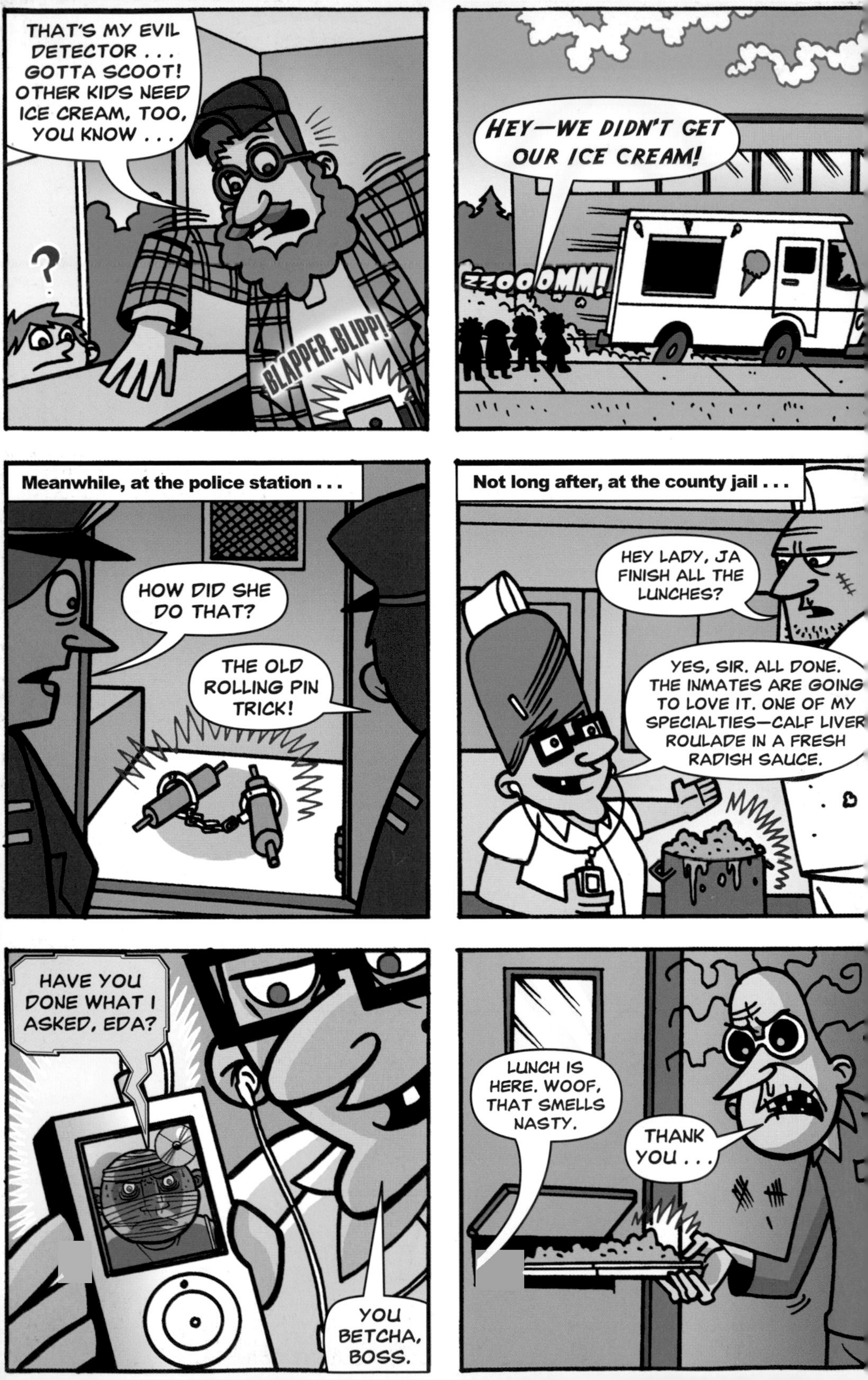
THAT'S MY EVIL DETECTOR . . . GOTTA SCOOT! OTHER KIDS NEED ICE CREAM, TOO, YOU KNOW . . .
?
BLAPPER-BLIPP!
HEY—WE DIDN'T GET OUR ICE CREAM!
ZZOOOMM!
Meanwhile, at the police station . . .
HOW DID SHE DO THAT?
THE OLD ROLLING PIN TRICK!
Not long after, at the county jail . . .
HEY LADY, JA FINISH ALL THE LUNCHES?
YES, SIR. ALL DONE. THE INMATES ARE GOING TO LOVE IT. ONE OF MY SPECIALTIES—CALF LIVER ROULADE IN A FRESH RADISH SAUCE.
HAVE YOU DONE WHAT I ASKED, EDA?
YOU BETCHA, BOSS.
LUNCH IS HERE. WOOF, THAT SMELLS NASTY.
THANK YOU . . .

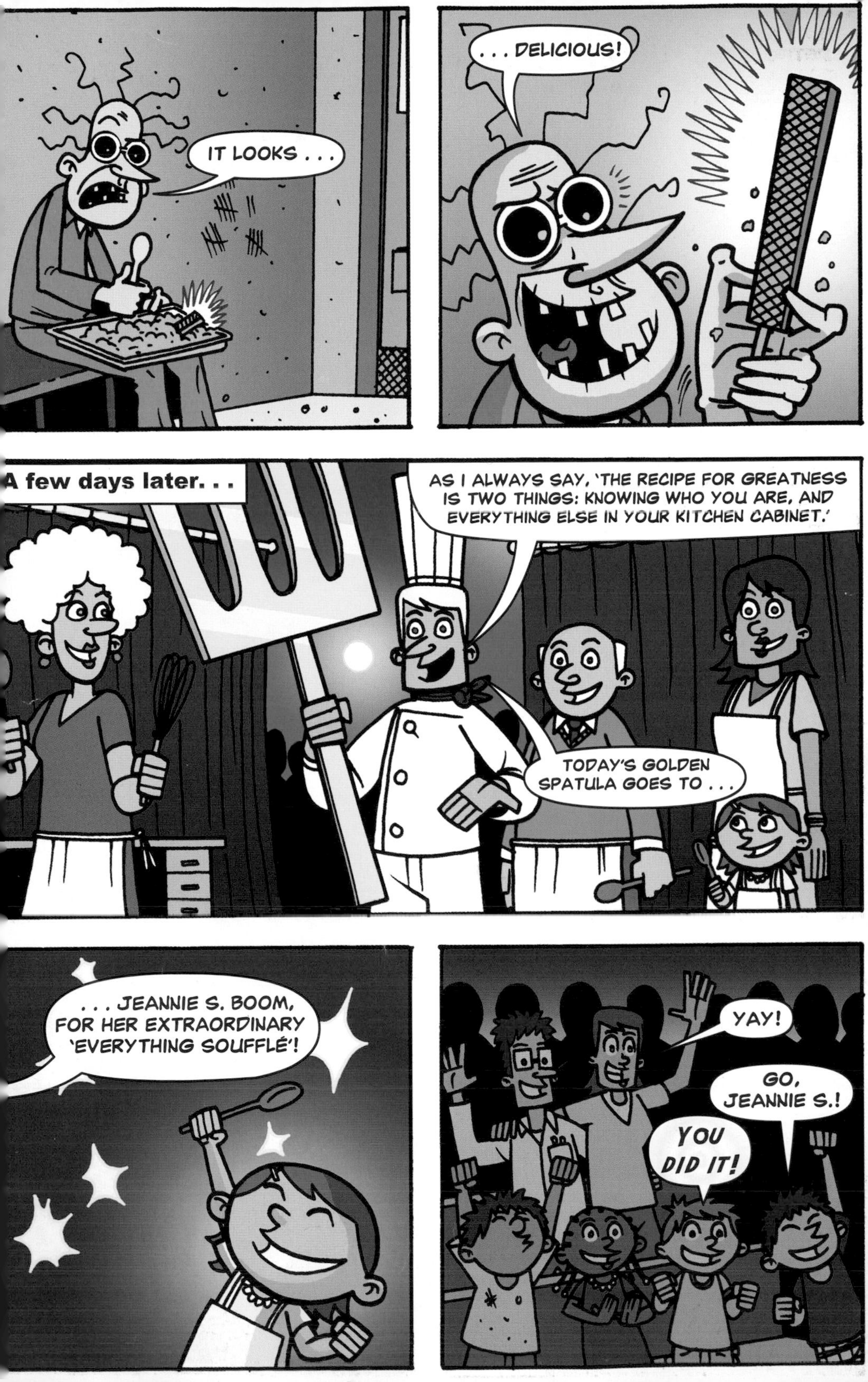
IT LOOKS . . .
. . . DELICIOUS!
A few days later. . .
AS I ALWAYS SAY, 'THE RECIPE FOR GREATNESS IS TWO THINGS: KNOWING WHO YOU ARE, AND EVERYTHING ELSE IN YOUR KITCHEN CABINET.'
TODAY'S GOLDEN SPATULA GOES TO . . .
. . . JEANNIE S. BOOM, FOR HER EXTRAORDINARY 'EVERYTHING SOUFFLÉ'!
YAY!
GO, JEANNIE S.!
YOU DID IT!

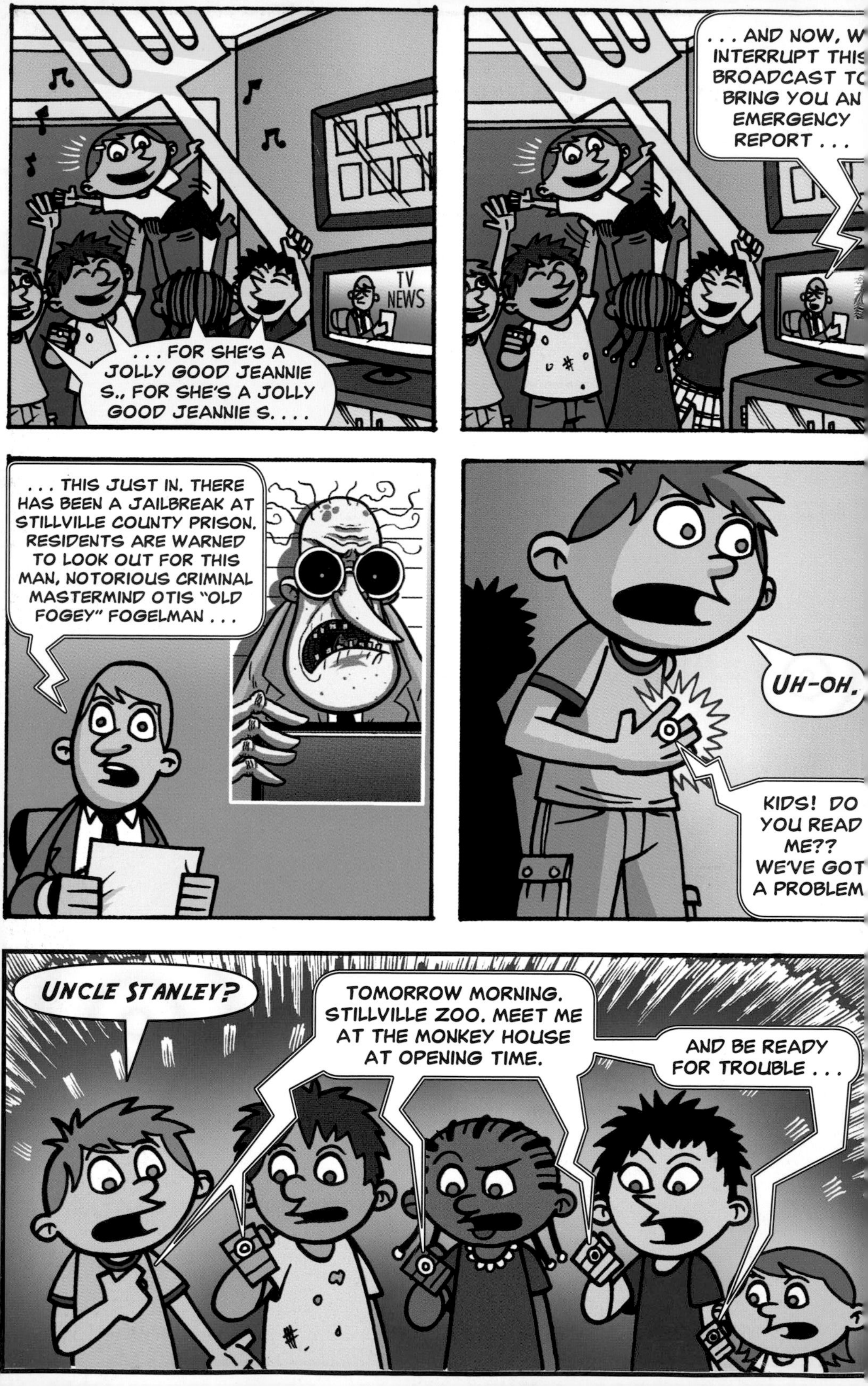
TV NEWS
. . . FOR SHE'S A JOLLY GOOD JEANNIE S., FOR SHE'S A JOLLY GOOD JEANNIE S. . . .
. . . AND NOW, W INTERRUPT THIS BROADCAST TO BRING YOU AN EMERGENCY REPORT . . .
. . . THIS JUST IN. THERE HAS BEEN A JAILBREAK AT STILLVILLE COUNTY PRISON. RESIDENTS ARE WARNED TO LOOK OUT FOR THIS MAN, NOTORIOUS CRIMINAL MASTERMIND OTIS "OLD FOGEY" FOGELMAN . . .
UH-OH.
KIDS! DO YOU READ ME?? WE'VE GOT A PROBLEM
UNCLE STANLEY?
TOMORROW MORNING. STILLVILLE ZOO. MEET ME AT THE MONKEY HOUSE AT OPENING TIME.
AND BE READY FOR TROUBLE . . .

. . . And there you have it—the whole story of how Loud Boy, Tantrum Girl, Destructo-Kid, Fidget, and Chatterbox narrowly saved the children of the world from a fate of eternal politeness. And just like Chef Mitt says, they discovered that the recipe for greatness is two things: a happy ending, and staying tuned for the next exciting adventure . . .

**—TO BE CONTINUED—**

Greetings from
THE STILLVILLE ZOO

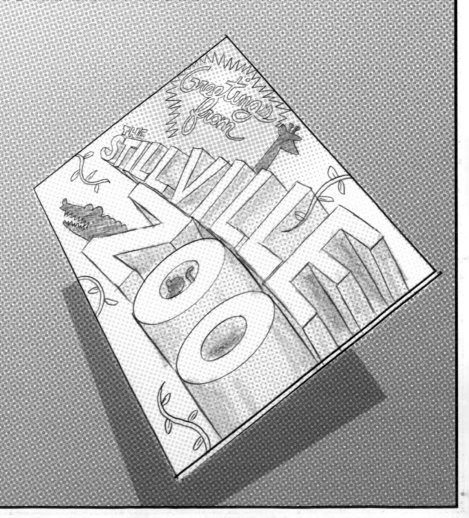

# THE ADVENTURES OF
# DANIEL BOOM
## A.K.A LOUD BOY

### #3
### Game On!

Is Loud Boy trapped inside the cyber-world of his favorite video game? Are his sister and friends held captive by an evil robot? How could any of this take place in the sleepy little town of Stillville?

Trouble heats up for our heroes when *Pig Planet*, the latest video game sensation, sweeps into town and Daniel Boom gets hopelessly hooked. Try as they might, Jeannie S., Sid, Rex, and Violet cannot break him of his addiction. Little do they know that the cranky old scientists at Kid-Rid are behind this heinous plot. Now, the Freak Five must unravel the truth and stop Kid-Rid from sucking children all over the world into the pixilated universe of their game consoles. But are they too late? Come join Loud Boy and the gang as they play for their lives in the next exciting episode of mystery, mayhem, and more loud adventure . . . GAME ON!

To Daniel, Micah, and Noah—the original Loud Boys!
—D. J. Steinberg

GROSSET & DUNLAP
Published by the Penguin Group
Penguin Group (USA) Inc., 375 Hudson Street, New York, New York 10014, USA
Penguin Group (Canada), 90 Eglinton Avenue East, Suite 700, Toronto, Ontario
M4P 2Y3, Canada (a division of Pearson Penguin Canada Inc.)
Penguin Books Ltd., 80 Strand, London WC2R ORL, England
Penguin Group Ireland, 25 St. Stephen's Green, Dublin 2, Ireland
(a division of Penguin Books Ltd.)
Penguin Group (Australia), 250 Camberwell Road, Camberwell, Victoria 3124,
Australia (a division of Pearson Australia Group Pty. Ltd.)
Penguin Books India Pvt. Ltd., 11 Community Centre,
Panchsheel Park, New Delhi—110 017, India
Penguin Group (NZ), 67 Apollo Drive, Rosedale, North Shore 0632,
New Zealand (a division of Pearson New Zealand Ltd.)
Penguin Books (South Africa) (Pty.) Ltd., 24 Sturdee Avenue,
Rosebank, Johannesburg 2196, South Africa

Penguin Books Ltd., Registered Offices: 80 Strand, London WC2R ORL, England

Library of Congress Cataloging-in-Publication Data is available.

ISBN 978-0-448-44699-8                    10 9 8 7 6 5 4 3 2 1